LEAVE ME

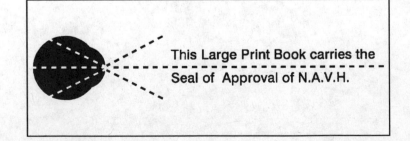

This Large Print Book carries the
Seal of Approval of N.A.V.H.

LEAVE ME

GAYLE FORMAN

THORNDIKE PRESS

A part of Gale, Cengage Learning

DISCARD

GALE
CENGAGE Learning·

Farmington Hills, Mich • San Francisco • New York • Waterville, Maine
Meriden, Conn • Mason, Ohio • Chicago

GALE
CENGAGE Learning®

Thorndike Press® Large Print Core.
The text of this Large Print edition is unabridged.
Other aspects of the book may vary from the original edition.
Set in 16 pt. Plantin.

LIBRARY OF CONGRESS CATALOGING-IN-PUBLICATION DATA

Names: Forman, Gayle, author.
Title: Leave me / Gayle Forman.
Description: Large print edition. | Waterville, Maine : Thorndike Press Large Print, 2016. | Series: Thorndike Press large print core
Identifiers: LCCN 2016027730 | ISBN 9781410491619 (hardback) | ISBN 1410491617 (hardcover)
Subjects: LCSH: Working mothers—Fiction. | Home—Psychological aspects—Fiction. | Self-realization in women—Fiction. | Self-actualization (Psychology)—Fiction. | Large type books. | BISAC: FICTION / Contemporary Women.
Classification: LCC PS3606.O74773 L43 2016b | DDC 813/.6—dc23
LC record available at https://lccn.loc.gov/2016027730

Published in 2016 by arrangement with Algonquin Books of Chapel Hill, a division of Workman Publishing

Printed in the United States of America
1 2 3 4 5 6 7 20 19 18 17 16

For Willa and Denbele

■ ■ ■ ■

NEW YORK CITY

■ ■ ■ ■

1

Maribeth Klein was working late, waiting to sign off on the final page proofs of the December issue, when she had a heart attack.

Those first twinges in her chest, however, were more a heaviness than a pain, and she did not immediately think *heart*. She thought indigestion, brought on by the plate of greasy Chinese food she'd eaten at her desk the hour before. She thought anxiety, brought on by the length of tomorrow's to-do list. She thought irritation, brought on by the conversation with her husband, Jason, who when she'd called earlier was having a dance party with Oscar and Liv, even though their downstairs neighbor Earl Jablonski would complain and even though keeping the twins up past eight upped the odds that one of them would wake in the night (and wake her up, too).

But not her heart. She was forty-four years

old. Overtaxed and overtired, but show her a working mother who wasn't. Besides, Maribeth Klein was the sort of woman who when she heard hoof beats did not think horses, let alone zebras. She thought someone had left the TV on too loud.

So when her heart began seizing, Maribeth merely excavated a bottle of Tums from her desk and sucked on them while willing Elizabeth's office door to open. But the door remained shut while Elizabeth and Jacqueline, *Frap*'s creative director, debated whether or not to tweak the cover now that sex tapes of the famous young actress gracing it had emerged on the Internet.

An hour later, the decision was made and the last of the proofs were signed off on and shipped to the printer. Before leaving, Maribeth stopped by Elizabeth's office to say good-bye, which she immediately regretted. Not just because Elizabeth, noting the hour, remarked how tired Maribeth looked and offered her a car-service voucher home — a kindness that embarrassed Maribeth, though not enough to decline it — but because Elizabeth and Jacqueline had been deep in conversation about dinner plans and had stopped talking as soon as Maribeth entered the room, as if they'd been post-gaming a party to which she hadn't been invited.

At home, she fell into a fitful sleep, waking up with Oscar sprawled on the bed next to her and Jason already gone. And even though she felt worse than she had the night before — exhausted and nauseous, from the poor night's sleep and the Chinese food, she assumed, but with her jaw aching, too, for reasons she did not understand, though she would later learn that these were all actually signs of her ongoing heart attack — she dragged herself out of bed and somehow got Liv and Oscar dressed and walked the ten blocks to BrightStart Preschool, where she maneuvered the gauntlet of the other mothers, who regarded her with a cool condescension because, she suspected, she only did drop-offs on Fridays. Jason handled the other mornings (something the Bright-Start mothers positively lionized him for) so that Maribeth could get to her desk early enough to leave by four-thirty.

"A short workday," Elizabeth had promised. "Fridays off." This was two years ago, after Elizabeth had been anointed editor-in-chief of *Frap,* a new (and well-funded) celebrity lifestyle magazine, and those were the bright, shiny apples she'd used to lure Maribeth back to full-time work. Well, those and the ample salary, which she and Jason needed to pay for the twins' upcoming preschool, the cost of which, Jason had joked, was "exorbitant squared." At the time, Maribeth was freelancing from home but not earning anything like a full-time salary. As for Jason's job at a nonprofit music archive, well, the tuition would've eaten half of his annual take. There was an inheritance from Maribeth's father, but generous as it had been, it would've covered only one year, and what if they didn't get a spot at the public pre-K (the odds of which, people claimed, were worse than getting into Harvard)? They really needed the money.

Though the truth was, even if preschool had been free, like it was in France, apparently, Maribeth suspected she would've taken the job just for the chance to finally work side by side with Elizabeth.

The short work day turned out to be eight hours, and much longer during the closes. Those Fridays off turned out to be her busiest day of the week. As for working side by side with Elizabeth, well, that hadn't quite worked out as expected either. Nothing had, really, except perhaps for preschool. That was just as expensive as they'd anticipated.

At circle time, Maribeth opened the book Liv had carefully selected for today's reading, *Lilly's Purple Plastic Purse,* and blinked as the words danced across the page. Earlier that morning, after she'd retched bile into the toilet, she had suggested to her daughter that perhaps she should postpone the reading until the following Friday, prompting Liv to throw a fit: "But you never come to school," her daughter had wailed. "You can't break a promise!"

She managed to get through the whole book, though she could tell by Liv's scowl that her performance was lackluster. After circle time, she said good-bye to the twins and took a bus the ten blocks back home, where, instead of going to bed, as she so desperately wanted, she checked her e-mail. At the top of the queue was a message, sent to her personal and work accounts, from Elizabeth's assistant, Finoula, asking if Maribeth could do a crash edit on the attached article. Next up in her inbox was the to-do list she had e-mailed herself from work last night. It contained twelve items, thirteen if you included the article Finoula had just sent. Though she generally avoided putting anything off — when she did, her lists only metastasized — she mentally shuffled the day, prioritizing what could not be delayed (ob-gyn, CPA, meet Andrea), what could be (call with Oscar's speech therapist, dry cleaners, post office, car inspection), and what might be passed off to Jason, whom she called at work.

"Hey, it's me," she said. "Do you think you can figure out dinner tonight?"

"If you don't feel like cooking, let's order in."

"We can't. It's the twins parenting potluck. We're hosting," she reminded him. Because even though it was on the calendar, and even though she'd told him about it earlier in the week, and even though the potlucks had been happening every other month for more than four years now, they still caught him by surprise. "And I'm not feeling great," she added.

"So cancel," he said.

She knew he'd say that. Jason was very fond of the easy way out. But the only time anyone had canceled a potluck was two years ago, right after Hurricane Sandy. And, yes, she knew this wasn't Jason's thing. But she'd joined this group when the twins were six weeks old and she'd been body-bruised from the exhaustion of it all and so unbelievably lonely from being home all day with just them. And, yes, maybe some of the parents were annoying (like Adrienne, with her changing dietary demands for Clementine and Mo based on whichever nutritional

study she'd just read about in the *Times* —
no dairy, no gluten, now it was paleo). But
these had been her first parenting friends.
Even if she didn't exactly like them all, they
were her comrades in arms.

"I'm just worn out," she told Jason. "And
it's too late to cancel."

"It's just I've got a crazy day," Jason said.
"We have tens of thousands of files to
migrate before the database upgrade."

Maribeth imagined a world in which a
crazy day excused her from having to deal
with dinner. Excused her from anything.
She would like to live in such a world.
"Can't you just cook something? Please."
Don't tell me to order pizza, Maribeth
thought, her chest clenching, though not
from stress, as she thought, but from the
blood bottlenecking through her narrowed
coronary artery. *Please don't tell me to order
pizza.*

Jason sighed. "Fine. I'll make the chicken
with olives. Everyone likes that."

"Thank you." She felt almost tearfully
grateful to be off the hook, and residually
angry because she was always on the hook.

It took her fifteen minutes to walk the
three blocks to the café where she'd arranged to meet Andrea Davis, a former colleague of hers from the *Rule*. She would've

15

liked to cancel that appointment, but Andrea, who was divorced and had two teenage children, was out of a job now that the shopping magazine where she'd been working had folded. Just like the *Rule* had folded. Just like so many of the magazines they'd worked at had folded.

"You're so lucky to be at *Frap,* with Elizabeth," Andrea told her over coffee, the smell of which was making Maribeth want to gag. "It's brutal out there."

Yes, Maribeth knew this. It was brutal. She was lucky.

"We're a long way from the *Rule,*" Andrea said. "Remember after 9/11 when we tore up the entire issue and remade it from scratch? Those late nights, all of us working together, the smell of burning plastic in the air. Sometimes I think those were the best days of my life. Isn't that sick?"

Maribeth wanted to say that sometimes she felt that way, too, but at the moment she'd grown so breathless she could hardly speak.

"Are you okay?" Andrea asked.

"I'm feeling off," Maribeth admitted. She didn't know Andrea all that well, which made it easier to tell the truth. "Strange symptoms. Like pains. In my chest. I'm worried it might be my . . ." She couldn't finish.

"Your heart?" Andrea asked.

Maribeth nodded, as the implicated organ clenched again.

"I go to the ER at least once a year, convinced I'm having a heart attack. I get the pain in my arm and everything." Andrea shook her head. "Anyhow, it's nothing. Okay, not nothing, it's reflux. With me anyhow."

"Reflux?"

Andrea nodded. "Acid reflux. A byproduct of this thing called stress. Perhaps you've heard of it?"

Of course, stress. That made more sense. But *Frap* had just done a profile on a twenty-seven-year-old sitcom star who'd been diagnosed with MS. "You just never know," the actress had said in the article. And then two weeks ago Maribeth's mother had called and mentioned that her friend Ellen Berman's thirty-six-year-old daughter had been diagnosed with stage-four breast cancer. Although Maribeth had never met Ellen Berman or her daughter, she felt terrible for her and freaked out enough to schedule an ob-gyn appointment (and she really did need to schedule a mammogram, too; she'd only had one since the twins were

17

born.) Because that actress was right: You never knew.

And in fact, Maribeth did not know that at that point, her heart tissue had begun to die from lack of oxygen. So she carried on with her day. Promised Andrea she'd ask Elizabeth about any openings or leads and then took a cab to the CPA's office to drop off the year's receipts so their tax returns — already on extension since April — could be prepared in time for the deadline next week. Then she hailed a cab uptown to Dr. Cray's office because even though she was dizzy now and wanted nothing more than to go home and crash, she was already six months late for her annual ob-gyn exam and she didn't want to wind up like Ellen Berman's daughter.

And because she did not know that the exhaustion she was feeling was a result of the decreased oxygenated blood now flowing through her, she told Dr. Cray's nurse she was feeling fine, even as the nurse took her vitals and noted that her blood pressure seemed abnormally low and asked her if she might be dehydrated. Maybe she was. Maybe that was it. So she accepted a cup of water.

She did not think heart. And perhaps she never would have, had it not been for Dr.

Cray asking Maribeth if she was okay.

The question itself was pro forma. But Dr. Cray — who had delivered Oscar and Liv and had seen Maribeth through so much — happened to ask it right as she was doing the breast exam, right as her fingers were gently probing the flesh of Maribeth's left breast, just above her heart, which no longer hurt, but felt tight, drumlike, a sensation that called to mind her pregnant belly, leaving Maribeth no choice but to reply, "Well, actually . . ."

2

Two hours later, Maribeth was starting to panic.

After reassuring her that it was probably nothing, Dr. Cray had put Maribeth in a car service to the nearest ER and called ahead to let them know she was coming. "Just to get checked out, just to be on the safe side," she'd said. Upon arrival, Maribeth had been tagged with a wristband, taped up with monitors, and shunted into a cardiac observation unit, where she'd been observed, primarily by an unending series of doctors, none of whom looked old enough to legally drink, let alone practice medicine.

In the car over to the hospital, she'd called Jason at work and gotten his voicemail. Remembering that he said he would be off-site for part of the day, she'd called his cell and had gotten voicemail again. Typical. He was allergic to talking on the phone. She hadn't bothered leaving a message. After all, she was in a car service, similar to the one that had ferried her home from work last night. It hadn't seemed unreasonable that this would all be over in an hour or two.

Instead, she'd texted Robbie, who had started babysitting the twins when they were a year old and Maribeth had started getting enough freelance work to justify hiring someone. Back then, Robbie had been a sweet, creative NYU theater major. Now she was a graduate, a bona-fide actress with an erratic schedule. So Maribeth wasn't entirely surprised when she'd texted back: *Can't. Got a call back!!!!!!!* with a series of emoticons to underscore her excitement. And then she added a *Sorry,* with a few sad-face emojis to telegraph her regret.

Now it was getting close to two-thirty and the twins would be getting out of school soon with no one to pick them up. She tried Jason again. And got voicemail again. This time, there really was no point leaving a message. He wouldn't be able to get to BrightStart in time. And Jason had unre-trieved messages on his cell phone dating back to the last presidential election.

She called the school. The receptionist, a model-pretty but grossly incompetent young woman who regularly lost forms and checks, answered. Maribeth asked if it might be okay for Oscar and Liv to stay a little late that afternoon.

"I'm sorry but we don't offer aftercare," the receptionist said, as if Maribeth were some random stranger inquiring, not a parent who'd been with the school for more than a year now.

"I know that but I'm in, well . . . I've been unavoidably detained."

"BrightStart's policy clearly states pickup is no later than three-thirty," she said, the connection hissing. The reception in here was terrible.

"I'm aware of the policy but this is an . . ." She hesitated. Emergency? It was looking less like her heart than like a colossal waste of time. "An unavoidable situation. I won't be able to get there by three-thirty, nor will my husband or babysitter. I know the teachers stay later. Can't Oscar and Liv just play in a corner? I can't imagine I'm the only parent this has ever happened to." Though, who knew? Maybe she was. The Tribeca neighborhood where the school was, and where Maribeth had lived in a rent-stabilized loft for more than two decades, had become one of the wealthiest zip codes in the country. Sometimes it seemed as if even the nannies had nannies.

The receptionist made an unpleasant sound and put Maribeth on hold. A few minutes later she returned, saying that one of the other parents had offered to take the twins.

"Oh, okay. Who?"

"Niff Spenser."

Niff Spenser wasn't technically a Bright-Start parent. She had two BrightStart graduates, both now ensconced in a K-12 prep school, and a third child who would be starting next year. She volunteered in the "gap year," as she called it, to "stay in the loop," as if preschool had a steep learning curve you couldn't afford to loosen your grip on. Maribeth couldn't stand her.

But Jason wasn't answering and Robbie was busy. For a flash, she thought of Elizabeth, but it felt inappropriate, less like calling a friend than a boss.

She got Niff's number from the receptionist and texted her Jason's information, promising he'd collect the twins before dinner. She texted Niff's info to Jason and told him that she'd been held up and to coordinate a pickup with Niff. *Please confirm you have received the text,* she wrote.

Got it, he texted back.

And just like that, a decision seemed to

have made itself. She would not tell Jason why she'd been held up until it was all over. And if it turned out to be nothing, maybe she wouldn't tell him at all. Odds were, he wouldn't ask.

Maribeth examined the monitor on her finger. A pulse ox. She recalled her father wearing one after his stroke. The monitors taped to her chest itched; she suspected it would take a good scrubbing tonight to get the glue off. "Excuse me," she called to one of the ER residents, a stylish young woman who wore expensive shoes and spoke with a Valley Girl lilt. "Do you know when I might get out of here?"

"I think they, like, ordered another blood draw," the doctor said.

"Another one. Why? I thought my EKG was normal."

"It's procedure."

More like covering their asses or padding the bill. Maribeth had once edited an exposé about profit-driven hospitals.

With that she remembered the piece Finoula had sent. She might as well cross something off her list. She pulled it up on her phone. It was an interesting premise — about celebrities who were harnessing social media for philanthropic purposes; Maribeth vaguely recalled suggesting it in a pitch meeting — but it was terribly executed. Usually, Maribeth could read an article and immediately see the problems in structure or logic or voice and know how to fix them. But she read the piece a second time, then a third, and couldn't see the forest for the trees, couldn't see how to make it right.

It was the hospital. Hardly a conducive workplace. She needed to get home. It was almost dinnertime. Jason would probably be back with the kids by now. He might even start to, if not worry, then wonder. She closed the article and saw several missed calls from the landline. She called and Jason answered almost right away. "Maribeth," he said. "Where are you?"

The sound of Jason's steady, sonorous voice shook something loose in her. Maybe because his phone voice resembled his radio voice, it still had the power to ricochet her back twenty-five years in time, to those nights when Maribeth and her friends would listen to his Demo-Gogue show from their dorm and muse over who he really was (his on-air name was Jinx) and what he was really like. "I'll bet he's ugly as sin," her roommate Courtney had said. "Hot voice, hideous face." Maribeth, who worked for the college newspaper, had no opinions as to his looks, but she was certain that he would be an unbearable snob, like all the film and music writers on staff were. "You should interview him and find out," Courtney had dared.

"Where are you?" Jason repeated. Now she heard the irritation in his voice. And then she heard why. In the background was the clatter of adults and children. Many, many children.

The potluck. Tonight. Shit!

"I thought you wanted me to make the chicken, but we don't have any in the house and now people are here," Jason said. "Are you getting food?"

"No. I'm sorry. I forgot."

"You *forgot*?" Now Jason sounded pissed. Which she supposed she understood, but it still made her chest clench again. Because, really: How many times had Jason spaced something leaving her to mop up the mess?

"Yes, I forgot," she said, her voice snappish. "I had other things on my mind, what with being stuck in the ER all afternoon."

"Wait? What? Why?"

"I was having chest pains so Dr. Cray sent me just to get checked out," she explained.

"What the fuck?" Now Jason sounded angry, truly angry, but in a different way from before. Like he was sticking up for her against a bully.

26

"It's probably nothing, just stress," she said, feeling foolish for having told him, and more foolish for having told him out of spite. "They've had me under observation for hours."

"Why didn't you call me?"

"I tried, but you didn't answer, and anyway, I thought I'd be out of here by now."

"Where are you?"

"Roosevelt."

"Should I come up?"

"Not with everyone in the house. Just tell them I had to work late and then order some pizza. They're letting me out soon." She pounded her chest with her fist, hoping that might make the resurgent pain go away.

"Shouldn't I be with you?"

"By the time you got up here, I'd be discharged. It was just an overblown case of heartburn." In the background, she heard Oscar begin to cry. "What's going on?"

"Looks like Mo took Creepy Lovey."

Creepy Lovey was a defaced teddy bear that Oscar couldn't sleep without. "Better get it back," she told Jason. "And can I talk to him? Or Liv?"

As Jason tried to corral the children, her phone made that mournful tone sound, down to its last 10 percent, and then, a few seconds later, made another sad sound, and died.

"I'll be home soon," she called. But they could no longer hear her.

Later a grandfatherly doctor wearing a polka-dot bow tie showed up. He introduced himself as Dr. Sterling and told Maribeth he was the on-call cardiologist. "There was an abnormality on one of your EKGs so we ordered that second blood test and this one showed elevated levels of troponin," he explained.

"But the earlier EKG was normal."

"That's not atypical," he replied. "My guess is that you've had what we sometimes call a stuttering infarct."

"A what?" Maribeth asked.

"Ischemia, probably ongoing for the past twenty-four hours or so, which is why you've had intermittent pain, and now your blood work suggests complete occlusion of one of the arteries."

"Oh," Maribeth said, struggling to take it in. "I see."

"So, we're going to send you to the cardiac cath lab to look for any underlying blockages in your coronary arteries, and if we determine a blockage, we'll place a stent right then and there."

"When is all this happening?"

"Lickety-split. As soon as we can get you upstairs."

"Now?" She looked at the clock. It was past seven. "It's Friday night."

"You have plans to go out dancing?" He was amused by his joke.

"No. I just wondered if we could do this, this stent thing next week?"

"Oh, no. We need to get in there before any more damage is done."

Damage. She didn't like the sound of that. "Okay. How long does it take? I mean, when can I expect to get out of here?"

"My, my, are you always in such a hurry?" he asked. He chuckled again, but this time there was the slap to it, as if the underlying message was *I see how you got yourself here.*

But at this very moment twelve four-year-olds were rampaging around her apartment. Someone was going to have to clean up after them, to find the Goldfish crackers that Mo always stashed away in the closet, or the soiled diapers that Tashi always left in the kitchen garbage (because Ellery still would only crap in Pampers). Someone was going to have to make sure the pantry was stocked with all the ingredients for Saturday-morning chocolate chip pancakes.

And that was just tonight. In the coming

days, someone had to get the kids to their ballet classes, their soccer clinics, their speech therapy sessions, their playdates, their birthday parties. To take them shopping for their Halloween costumes, to the pediatrician for their flu shots, to the dentist for their cleanings. Someone had to plan the meals, pay the bills, balance the checkbook. Someone had to get it all done, while still getting all the work-work done.

Maribeth sighed. "It's just I have a house full of four-year-olds and a very busy weekend."

He stared at her for a long moment, frowning. Maribeth looked back, disliking him already, and that was before he said, "You do realize you've had a heart attack?"

Using the phone at the nurse's station, she called Jason and got the voicemail again. As calmly as possible, she told him what was happening: the tests, her being admitted overnight, probably for the weekend. She never said the words *heart attack*. She couldn't make herself do it. Nor did she say that she was scared. "Please get here as soon as you can," she told his voicemail.

As she waited, she filled out the admission paperwork. It was calming in its way, perhaps because it was familiar. She'd done this before her C-section, before Oscar's ear-tubes surgery. Name, address, insurance number, social security. Repeat. There was something Zen about it. Until she got to the family history.

She never knew how to fill these out. She'd learned that she was adopted when she was eight, but back then, it had just been another piece of identifying information: She lived on Maple Street. She rode a blue Schwinn. She was the best speller in third grade. She was adopted. It had never occupied much mental real estate until she'd tried to get pregnant herself, and then there were so many unanswerable questions: Was anyone in her family Portuguese? Jewish? Cajun? Was there a history of Down syndrome? Cleft palate? Huntington's disease? A family history of infertility? Well, that last one she could reliably answer, at least with regard to her birth mother, but everything else was a mystery.

And then her children were born and the mystery only increased. Oscar was a carbon copy of his father, the same hazel eyes, the same weak chin, but by sixteen months Liv had long blond hair, almond-shaped green eyes, and a fierce, sometimes dictatorial manner that Jason joked heralded a future leader, a Sheryl Sandberg, or a Hillary Clinton even. "You sure you didn't get inseminated with the wrong egg," more than one person had quipped.

The joke was stinging. Because Maribeth didn't know where Liv got that princess hair from, or those apple eyes, let alone their intense gaze. Looking at the little genetic puzzle that was her daughter had opened up if not quite sadness in Maribeth, then a sonar ping of sorrow. But she didn't have time to dwell on it. Because, twins.

She left the forms blank.

Jason burst in just before ten. "Oh, Lois," he said, reviving an old nickname he hadn't used in years, which was Maribeth's first clue that he was scared, too. They had known each other half their lives, and even with the ten-year break in there, they could find each other's tender spots in the dark. Besides, Maribeth knew that Jason became unhinged when she was hospitalized. He'd been that way before her C-section, too, though he'd later admitted to her it was less the surgery than the nightmares he'd been having in which she died during the delivery.

"Hey Jase," she said softly. She wanted to say *I love you,* or *Thank you for coming,* but if she did, she thought she might cry. So she asked where the kids were.

"With Earl."

In the rock, paper, scissors of emotions, irritation killed sentimentality. "Jablonski? Are you kidding me?"

"It was late."

"So you left them with our misanthropic, possibly alcoholic, downstairs neighbor? Did you attach signs that read, 'Molest Me'?"

"Come on. Earl's grumpy, but he's not a bad guy."

"Jesus, Jason. Why didn't you send them home with the Wilsons?" The Wilsons were one of the families in the parenting group who lived in the neighborhood.

"It didn't occur to me," he said. "They were tired so I asked Earl to come up. I can try the Wilsons now but they're probably asleep."

"Forget it."

He sat down on the edge of her bed. "How you feeling?"

"Fine. I just want to get this over with." She paused. "Maybe you should ask the Wilsons to take them tomorrow. Liv and Tess have ballet together."

"Right. Ballet."

"And Oscar has soccer."

"We'll figure it out."

"How? We can't tag team it. You'll need someone to step in."

"Okay, I'll call the Wilsons." He reached for his phone.

"Not now. It's late. Just text or e-mail or call in the morning."

He nodded. "What about Sunday?"

They had a birthday party on Sunday. And afterward Liv had a playdate and Oscar speech therapy. She didn't want to have to think about all this now. "I don't know, Jason."

"We could send them to Lauren's for the weekend." Lauren was Jason's little sister, who lived near Boston with her husband and four children.

"How are they going to get there? And back?"

"I could ask Lauren to pick them up. She knows what's up."

"You told her?"

"Well, yeah. I called her in the cab. She was with my dad when he had his heart attack." Jason's father, Elliott, had a heart attack when he was in his seventies, when you were supposed to have such things. "So what do you think? Lauren?"

She put her head in her hands. The logistics of their weekends generally made her feel like an air traffic controller, but right now, she just couldn't keep the planes in the air. "I don't know. Can you just leave me out of it? Until this is over?"

He mimed a force field around her. "You're in a bubble."

An orderly and a nurse arrived with a gurney. "Would you like a mild sedative?" the nurse asked.

"I'd prefer a strong one," Maribeth deadpanned.

As they prepped her for the transfer, Jason squeezed her hand, saying not to worry, that everything would be fine. Which was what he always said. Maribeth never really believed this, though she used to appreciate the sentiment's low-key optimism; it balanced her propensity for, as Jason put it, always waiting for the other shoe to drop.

She wanted to believe it now. So much. But when Jason leaned over and kissed her on the forehead, she could feel he was trembling, and she had to wonder if even *he* believed it.

But then the sedative took effect and everything went so nice and soft. She heard Jason say, "I love you." She said she loved him, too. Or she thought she did. She might've just imagined it.

In the cath lab, the mood felt light, festive,

befitting eleven on a Friday night. The radiologists and nurses bantered and Maribeth observed it through a narcotic fog. She could feel pressure when the catheter was inserted but couldn't feel it being threaded up to her heart. When the dye was released, there was a warm sensation, strange, but not entirely unpleasant.

"Can you cough for me, Maribeth?" someone asked.

She coughed.

"Excellent."

She felt something then, which was strange, because hadn't they told her she wasn't meant to feel anything at this point?

"What just happened?" she heard someone ask.

"Her BP's dropping!" came the reply.

The mood changed as suddenly as a cloud blocking the summer sun. Everything happened fast after that. There was a chorus of alarms, a jerking of movement. A mask over her face. In that final moment before everything went dark, Maribeth thought — less in fear than a sort of awe — how easily it could all leave you.

3

She opened her eyes. She couldn't breathe. Except she was breathing. But it *felt* like she couldn't breathe.

A bright light shone in her face. She blinked. She tried to speak but she couldn't.

Was she dreaming?

It didn't feel like she was dreaming. She was freezing. Had someone left the AC on? Why was the AC on? She didn't think it was summer.

She woke up again. The bright light was still there.

She still couldn't speak.

Was she dead?

She hoped she wasn't dead because she felt dreadful.

Maybe this was hell.

She didn't think she believed in hell.

Her cheek itched. Her jaw ached. She became vaguely aware of a throbbing pain in her leg. Left. No, right. She was confused. She was cold.

There was something in her throat. As soon as she recognized the foreign object, she gagged on it.

A woman peered over her. Brown skin, alert eyes. She rubbed Maribeth's forehead. "That's the ventilator; it's breathing for you. Relax and try not to fight it."

A ventilator? Had she been in some kind of accident? Where were the twins? Panic rose up in her. She tried to breathe but she couldn't. She gagged again. And then it went dark.

Someone was calling her name. She knew the voice. Jason. It was Jason.

Relief.

She tried to say his name.

She couldn't.

"Nurse! She's awake."

Jason. Relief.

"She's choking. Can you give her something to calm her down?" he asked.

No! Don't give me something to calm down, Maribeth thought. She was already so foggy. She needed to stay here. She didn't want to get left behind.

"A little something," the nurse said. "We want her to stay awake so we can get her off the ventilator. She'll be more comfortable once her breathing tube is out. So Maribeth, if you bear with us, your surgeon will be here soon."

Surgeon? What was going on? She looked to Jason but he didn't get it. She tried the nurse.

"You had emergency bypass surgery," the nurse told her.

The words penetrated but their meaning did not.

"The angioplasty went wrong," Jason explained. "It punctured your artery so they had to rush you into emergency surgery."

"Can you tell me your pain level?" the nurse asked, showing her a chart going from one to ten, one being a happy face and ten being a very sad face.

The pain was unlike anything she'd experienced before, all encompassing, and yet, also removed. She couldn't rate it.

"Let's call it a five," the nurse said.

She felt something warm prickle into her hand. After that, she felt nothing at all.

She woke up again, an unfamiliar doctor hovering over her. "Good morning, we are going to take your tube out now," he said.

Her bed was tilted up and before she knew what was happening she was being ordered to exhale sharply. She tried to but it was as if she'd forgotten how to breathe.

"On three," the doctor said. "One, two . . ."

The sensation was like throwing up in slow motion. When the tube came out, she simultaneously gulped in air and retched. She cupped her hands around her mouth, to catch the vomit that didn't come.

"Nothing in your stomach, thanks to this," the doctor said. He fingered another tube, one going down her nose.

Maribeth slumped back. Nurses were bustling about. One gave her a sip of water through a straw while the doctor read her charts.

"Where's? My? Doctor?" Maribeth croaked.

"I am your doctor. Dr. Gupta," he answered. He went on to explain that he was her thoracic surgeon. He had been called in to perform her emergency bypass after the angioplasty punctured her artery. "It is very rare. Only the second case I've ever seen, and the other lady was much older than you. You are quite exceptional," he said, as if this were a good thing.

"My husband?" she gasped.

"No idea." He carried on, telling her about the surgery, a double bypass. "In addition to the punctured vessel, you had a second artery with a significant lesion so as long as we were inside, we grafted that, too. It's a better long-term fix in the end than the stent so you came out well."

Huzzah.

He went on to explain what to expect — some discomfort from the leg where they'd harvested an artery and from the sternum, which they'd sawed through to reach her heart. Also some cognitive symptoms, so-called pump head, from the heart-lung bypass machine.

"The what?"

"The bypass machine. What we routed your blood through to oxygenate it and pump it while your heart was stopped."

He said it so casually. *While your heart was stopped.* And suddenly, she was yanked from the fog.

She placed her wired-up hand across her taped-up chest. She felt her heart beating there, as it had been since she was a baby, no a fetus even, nestled inside the womb of a mother she had never known. But it had stopped beating. She wasn't sure why, but this felt like a threshold she had crossed, leaving everyone and everything she had ever known on the other side.

4

A week later, Maribeth was discharged. She didn't feel remotely ready. It had been that way the last time she'd gotten out of a hospital, but back then, at least it had felt like she and Jason were in cahoots. "They're leaving us alone with them," Jason had joked about the twins. "I had more practice with my dad's Skylark." Now she was all alone.

"I have something to tell you," Jason said as Maribeth sat in a wheelchair, waiting for a cab. There was something to his tone. If she wasn't getting out of the hospital after open-heart surgery, Maribeth might've thought he was about to cop to an affair.

"What?" Maribeth asked warily.

"You know how I promised to keep you in the bubble when you were in the hospital, so you didn't have to worry about anything?"

"Yes."

"So, I did some things. While you were in the bubble."

It took a moment for Maribeth to understand what he meant. She was pretty sure she'd have preferred the affair. She shook her head. "No."

"I kept her out of the hospital," Jason said. "I even kept you from knowing about it."

"You took the easy way out. Again."

"Easy way out? I asked for help."

"How is my mother help?"

"She's another set of hands. And the twins love her."

"Great. The twins get quality time with Grandma and I get a third person to take care of." A fourth person, she wanted to say, but didn't.

As the cab sped downtown, Maribeth wanted to turn around, go back to the hospital. On a good day, it took all of her mental reserves to deal with her mother. And this was not a good day.

Jason tentatively touched her on the shoulder. "You okay?"

"You know how you always ask why I'm waiting for the other shoe to drop?" she asked.

He nodded.

"This is why."

43

■ ■ ■ ■

Welcome home Mommy! Get well soon! read the butcher-paper sign taped to the front door.

She was about to see her children. She had not seen them in a week except for the proof-of-life videos Jason made on his phone to show her each day. She missed them, in an aching, primal, animal way. But standing in front of the door now, she felt paralyzed by dread. Maybe she shouldn't have asked Jason to keep them home from school today.

Jason opened the door.

On the entry table was a vase of lilies next to a huge stack of mail. The dread deepened.

"Maribeth, is that you?" she heard her mother call.

And deepened again.

"It's me," she said.

"Liv, Oscar, did you hear that? Mommy's home!"

Her mother appeared, dressed up in Chico's autumnal Palette for Women of a Certain Age. She gingerly embraced Maribeth, then stood back to look at her, her hand over her own heart. "My poor girl."

Just then Oscar came running. He leaped

44

toward her, yelling, "Mommy!"

She didn't mean to wince. But her chest was so very tender and Oscar so very puppylike. Keeping him only a little bit at bay, she buried her face in his hair, inhaling that boyish sweaty scent that never fully went away, even after a bath.

"Hello, Mommy." As Liv approached, taking tentative balletic steps, every ounce of her controlled, ladylike, Maribeth caught a glimpse of the woman her four-year-old daughter would someday become. It made her feel inexplicably sad.

Maribeth braced herself for another hug, but Liv just kissed her lightly on the cheek and stepped away. Last year when Maribeth had a stomach bug, Liv had treated her coolly until she was back to normal.

"It's okay, baby," she said. "I'm still me."

Liv wrinkled her nose, as if she didn't fully buy that. Maribeth wasn't sure she did, either.

5

The discharge from the hospital, the ride downtown, the arrival home, all exhausted Maribeth, so she excused herself for a nap. When she woke up, it was unusually quiet for the loft, which didn't have real walls to mute the clamor of family life.

She called to Jason, who was working at home for the next week.

"Hey." He smiled. "It's good to see you home, Lois."

"It's good to be home. Where is everyone?"

"Your mom and Robbie took the kids to the playground. Do you want anything?"

Maribeth looked at the clock. "I think the nurse is coming at three. Maybe some lunch?"

"Sure. We ordered pizza before. Brick oven. There's a few slices left."

"Not pizza."

"Right, special diet. We've been mostly doing take out. I'll organize a grocery delivery. Do you want to give me a shopping list? We can do FreshDirect."

"Yeah, okay," she said. "For now, maybe some soup."

"Is canned okay?"

"It's really high in sodium. Supposed to avoid that."

"I can run to the deli."

"It's okay. I'll go forage in the fridge."

"We've been keeping it together here with rubber bands and bubble gum," Jason said. "We'll get back on track soon."

Maribeth was finishing up her lunch of yogurt and an apple with peanut butter when the visiting nurse arrived. Luca was pleasantly plump and wore the crooked smile of an accomplice.

She checked the dressing on her chest and the one on her leg. "Healing nicely," she said.

"Yes, I'm so looking forward to the scars," Maribeth said.

"Some women see their scars as a badge. I've worked with breast cancer survivors who go for tattoos instead of reconstructions. You could get a really nice one along your leg, like this." She lifted her pant leg and showed a daisy chain circling her ankle.

"Funny. My husband used to say that scars were like tattoos but with better stories."

"I can see that, too. As for the chest." She tapped her own ample cleavage, "it fades so much it looks like décolletage. It's very sexy."

"Now you know why I finagled myself a bypass surgery," Maribeth said.

Luca laughed. "A sense of humor will go a long way."

"That and some real food and I'll be set." And as if on cue, her stomach gave a good loud gurgle.

Luca looked at the yogurt container, the apple core. "What else have you eaten today?"

"Cereal at the hospital."

"It's almost four o'clock."

"Is it?"

Luca stopped typing notes. "You need to take care of yourself."

"I'll get some groceries delivered tomorrow."

Luca frowned. "Take care of yourself by asking for help."

"I'm trying."

Luca hooked Maribeth up to a portable blood pressure cuff and then a portable EKG machine. All the data went straight to her iPad. "Looks good," she said. "Get some rest. Eat. You'll feel much better soon."

At just that moment the front door opened and the kids bounded in with her mother.

· "Is Mommy here?" Liv shouted.

"She's in her room," Jason said.

"Mommy?" Oscar yelled. "I want Mommy."

And just like that, the quiet apartment was filled with noise. Within seconds, Oscar was jumping on the bed, coming perilously close to Maribeth's bad leg.

Luca arched an eyebrow as she packed up the rest of her things.

"Will you do bedtime tonight?" Oscar asked. "Grandma doesn't do voices and Daddy doesn't know how to catch Liv's bad dreams."

"I'm supposed to be taking it easy," Maribeth said, looking to Luca for confirmation. But she had quietly slipped out.

"You haven't done stories forever," Liv said. "And Grandma promised you would."

"I said maybe she would," her mother said.

"What if I tuck you in and Daddy reads?"

She looked to Jason for backup, but he was just standing there, smiling. When she'd learned they were having twins — not a huge surprise in the world of IVF — she'd thought they could handle it, no problem. *Two of them, two of us.* But the math never seemed to work out so neatly. It was like fifth-grade division; there was always a remainder.

She tried again, widening her eyes at Jason in a silent SOS.

"Can't blame them for missing you," Jason said. "We all have."

All she wanted was for someone to tuck her in, read her a story with a happy ending. But they all just stood there watching her: her mother, Jason, Oscar, Liv. She told the twins she would do bedtime tonight.

6

They started coming right away, the visitors. People she really didn't want to see, like Niff Spenser and Adrienne and the Wilsons, bearing food she either could not eat (like rich casseroles) or didn't want to (what exactly was the appeal of those edible arrangements?). Her mother treated each visitor like a dignitary, offering elaborate coffee and tea service and then leaving the mess in the sink. Maribeth found the visits painful and exhausting. Every time someone came, she felt obliged to entertain when she just wanted to stay in bed. But when she suggested that Jason discourage people from coming, he told her she needed to learn to accept help.

And then, Elizabeth came. One evening her first week home, carrying a tasteful but clearly expensive flower arrangement that Maribeth recognized as coming from the florist they used for visiting celebrities.

"Elizabeth!" Maribeth's mother exclaimed. "How wonderful of you to come. And those flowers. Are those peonies? In October? They must have cost a fortune."

"Hello, Mrs. Klein."

"It's Evelyn," Maribeth's mother corrected, as she had done for more than twenty years now. "You look gorgeous! That coat is beautiful. Is it wool? Maribeth, Elizabeth is here."

"I see that," Maribeth said.

Elizabeth slipped off her boots, a habit also decades old. Before he had complained about the noise of Maribeth's children, Earl Jablonski had complained about the sound of her and Elizabeth's heels clicking across the wood floors. "How is Earl?" she asked.

"Frustrated as ever."

"And how are you?"

She was tired. The twins were getting angry at her for not healing fast enough, for not doing bedtime often enough, for not walking them to school. She could feel Jason's impatience, too, in every which way. He'd been spooning her tight in the mornings, so she could feel his hard-on pressed right into the small of her back. It reminded her of after her C-section, when he'd been so full of pent-up desire it had felt like a threat.

Jason was out with the children now, taking them shopping for Halloween costumes, a task he seemed daunted by. Liv, meanwhile, had pitched a fit when Maribeth said she wouldn't be going. "You promised!" she'd cried. She had not promised, or if she had, it was before all this. Maribeth had been tempted to rip open her pajama top, to point at the scar on her chest. To tell Liv (and Jason, too) that her heart had stopped. Did they understand what that meant?

But she hadn't. She wasn't a crazy person. And besides, she'd gone to great pains to shield her children from her illness, not rub their faces in it.

"I'm doing great," she told Elizabeth.

"Would you like some coffee or tea?" her mother asked. "Or we could have wine. It's almost six o'clock."

"I'm fine. I don't need anything." She put the flowers down on the dining room table and made her way toward the living room area.

"New couches?" Elizabeth asked, pointing to the leather sofas they'd bought after Oscar had scribbled in Sharpie all over the upholstered ones.

"Not that new. We got them about two years ago." Had it been that long since Elizabeth had been over?

"From IKEA, can you believe it?" her mother chimed in. "Guess how much they cost? Less than a thousand dollars a piece."

Why did her mother have to announce that? To Elizabeth? Who had a five-thousand-dollar leather Barcelona sofa in her office at work. It wasn't that Maribeth cared about high design furniture, but the disparity just seemed to emphasize how far they'd drifted for reasons that Maribeth didn't fully understand.

And then to highlight it even further, Elizabeth asked: "Remember our trip to IKEA? When the bus broke down?"

It was not long after they'd moved into the loft, which Elizabeth had found because she had a nose for things like that — whispered-about sample sales, ten-table restaurants about to get their first Michelin star, rent-stabilized eighteen-hundred-square-foot lofts in Tribeca.

The space was pretty raw back then, no walls, barely a kitchen. Right after they'd signed the lease, they'd taken the bus to the IKEA in New Jersey to buy more kitchen cabinets. It had felt a little like being newlyweds, the two of them zooming down the aisles, bouncing on the display beds, pretending to drink coffees in the kitchens as they fantasized about the life they were embarking on together. It was the same way that they would sometimes meet after work for happy-hour cosmos and burgers and imagine a life of running friendly competing magazines, *Newsweek* and *Time, Vogue* and *Harper's Bazaar.* (That was back in the days before magazines started dropping like flies, taking with them any notion of sporting competition.) The lives they were conjuring may have been fantasy, but the joy they got from this shared daydream, that was real. Giddily, palpably real.

On the way back into the city, the bus had stalled on the New Jersey turnpike. People were complaining, barking at the beleaguered driver. But she and Elizabeth had remained under their halo, munching on cinnamon buns, painting their Technicolor future.

Suddenly Maribeth was embarrassed by the IKEA couches. Elizabeth now was an editor-in-chief. She lived in an Upper East Side brownstone with Tom Bishop, her hedge-fund-manager husband, and, when they were home from boarding school, his teenage children. Maribeth still rented the loft she and Elizabeth had first lived in twenty years ago. She wanted to move, to buy a house somewhere in Brooklyn, but New York real estate was a runaway train she had long since missed. She wished she'd had more foresight, like Elizabeth, who when Maribeth decided to move in with Jason, had offered to move out, buying a dirt-cheap condo in the Meatpacking District, which had quadrupled in value by the time she sold it to move in with Tom.

"Mommy! Wait till you see my costume."

Liv and Oscar burst into the loft, trailed by a defeated-looking Jason. When they saw Elizabeth, they stopped, recognizing her from computer slideshows more than anything else.

"What are you going to be?" Elizabeth asked Liv.

"A pretty witch," Liv replied.

"What's a pretty witch?" Maribeth asked.

"Wait. I'll show you." Liv raced back toward her room.

"Me, too," Oscar said, following his sister.

Elizabeth stood. "Jason," she said, greeting him with a cordial kiss on the cheek.

"Elizabeth, so good to see you," he replied.

Jason went to check his e-mail. Liv returned in her costume, which was less a pretty witch than a slutty one. It was also about five sizes too big so it would need to be altered. Well done, Jason.

"She looks like one of those awful child beauty queens," Maribeth whispered as Liv admired herself in the mirror.

"I was thinking more dwarf prostitute," Elizabeth said.

"Oh, god. You're right."

For a second, they laughed, easily, like before.

"Mommy had a operation and she said it hurts to laugh," Oscar said. He was dressed as a policeman, which made his protectiveness even sweeter.

"It's okay, Oskie. It's Elizabeth. You remember her?" Maribeth said.

"She's Mommy's best friend and now she runs the magazine where Mommy works," Maribeth's mother explained, returning with wine. She turned to Elizabeth. "It was so generous of you to give her that job."

"I had to snap her up before someone else did," she said. "She's the best in the business."

Maribeth admired, as she always had, how well Elizabeth handled her mother. Like now, Maribeth's mother was placing a wineglass in front of Elizabeth and Elizabeth was covering the rim with her fingers until the moment her mother looked about to pour right through her hand and then she accepted the wine as if she'd asked for it all along.

"Do you think you could get us some

mineral water, Mom?" Maribeth asked.

"Of course!" her mother chirped.

"Speaking of work, I'll probably be able to start back next week," Maribeth said, though that seemed optimistic. Taking a shower was still an enormous exertion. "Working from home maybe."

"Don't worry about it."

"I know you must be scrambling. But I think I'll be able to dig out of the hole."

"Don't give it another thought. Take as much time as you need." Elizabeth waved her hand, a perfect expression of noblesse oblige.

When Elizabeth said things like that, Maribeth felt, not for the first time, that she didn't know her at all anymore. Elizabeth had once been as broke and hungry as Maribeth, but now she seemed to regard jobs as something one did not for necessity but for fulfillment, like a hobby. Though maybe that wasn't fair. Elizabeth probably took her hobby more seriously than Maribeth took her job.

"Next week," Maribeth repeated. "I have some ideas about who to farm the work out to. And I think I can probably do big-picture edits now even."

"It's taken care of." Elizabeth's tone was not sharp, exactly, but definitely authorita-

58

tive, bosslike, and Maribeth felt put into place.

Elizabeth grimaced. "I only mean the important thing is for you to get better," she added in a softer tone.

"I appreciate that but I still have to pay my bills, Elizabeth."

She hated herself for saying that. It made her sound petty and jealous of Elizabeth's life, of her money, of the job. When if she was jealous of anyone, it was of her old self, the one who could rightfully call Elizabeth her best friend. The one who still had ambition and focus and wasn't so harried all the time. The one who had a heart that worked properly.

Elizabeth looked so mortified that for a second Maribeth feared she might do something hideous, like try to loan her money. But she only whispered, "Please don't worry."

Liv reappeared, changed back into her clothes, carrying a set of paper dolls. "Want to play?" she asked Elizabeth.

In the early days, Elizabeth had been, if not a constant presence in the twins' life, a regular one. In the past few years, however, as Oscar and Liv slowly animated into actual humans, Elizabeth had receded. So Maribeth wasn't entirely surprised when she

59

stood up and told Liv that she'd love to but she had to get back to work.

After she was gone, Maribeth offered to play paper dolls. Liv looked at her as if she were the consolation prize, which was basically how Maribeth felt about every friend she'd made since Elizabeth. But Liv said okay.

7

A week after she got home, Maribeth had her follow-up with Dr. Sterling. Her mother offered to take her, but the thought of the tag-team assault of Mom and Dr. Grandpa was more than she could bear. Still, she knew she shouldn't go alone. Couldn't go alone, really. What if she couldn't get a cab home? What if the elevators stopped working? Things that had never occurred to her before now kept her up at night.

"Do you think you could maybe take me?" she asked Jason the night before the appointment. He had been working from home, but long, frantic hours — he was still monitoring the migration of thousands of audio files in advance of that planned database upgrade. She heard her tone, like a supplicant's. It made her angry, though she wasn't sure at whom. "You can bring your laptop with you."

"Sure," Jason said.

She felt it then: the gratitude, the resentment, seemingly competing emotions that these days twined together like strands of DNA.

She was glad she'd suggested he bring his laptop because they waited nearly two hours for her appointment with Dr. Sterling. All the while Maribeth seethed. And worried about what the seething was doing to her heart, which made her seethe more. Shouldn't a cardiologist know better?

She had disliked Dr. Sterling from the moment she'd met him in the ER. His bedside manner had not improved during her week in the hospital, when he treated her with an obsequious condescension, always talking about getting "Mommy" back home to her babies. Jason said he was scared she was going to sue, but Dr. Sterling hadn't performed the angiogram, and he'd faulted Maribeth's own arteries for the rupture — they were tortuous, he said — and anyhow, everything else had turned out fine and she wasn't going to sue. But she did need to find herself a new doctor, one she would choose and not simply get assigned to.

When the nurse finally called her in, she looked at Jason, who was tapping away on his laptop. "Do you want me to come with?" he asked.

He'd always come in for their ob-gyn appointments. Sometimes, after the sonograms, he'd trace the letters of whatever the favored names of the day were in the goo before he toweled it off her.

"That's okay," she said. "You just keep working."

Twenty minutes later they were in a cab heading home. Dr. Sterling had pronounced her "healing beautifully" and sent her on her way with a sheaf of brochures. Though she had brought a list of questions, in the end she had not asked any, because she could feel him rushing (who was in the hurry now?) and also because in the hospital, every time she'd tried to bring up how she was truly feeling — untethered, as if in some ways her heart was not a part of her body anymore — he warned her against "ruminating."

Jason's phone rang. She could tell it was important because he picked up right away and spent several minutes speaking to one of his colleagues in the indecipherable jargon of his job. After he hung up, he turned to her. "So the doctor said everything is going all right?"

She had already given him a rundown of the checkup in the elevator. "Yep. All good."

Jason paused. "So you think it's okay if I go back to the office tomorrow? They're really in crunch mode now."

"I'm sorry my heart attack came at such an inconvenient time."

"No one said that." The cab lurched to a stop as a jaywalker, eyes glued to his phone, stepped into traffic. The pressure of the seatbelt sent a cascade of pain through Maribeth.

"I'm sorry. You're right," she said.

"So it's okay if I go back to the office?"

No. It wasn't okay. She hurt all over. She wasn't ready to be left alone with her mother, with the kids. She was scared.

"Of course it is," she said.

"Good." When he smiled, his eyes crinkled and he looked genuinely happy, and somehow this made everything worse. "But I think we should probably get your mom to stay another week, until you're completely better."

She deflated even more. "Another week?"

"She's helpful. In her way. Another pair of hands. And she's, you know, free."

She looked out the window. They were going home. She was doing fine. The doctor had just said so. Why, then, did she feel like weeping? Why did she want to burrow into Jason's neck, to beg him not to go?

Jason kissed her on the temple. "I told you everything would work out. Another week or two and we'll be back to normal."

8

Her mother was thrilled to stay on. "I'm having such fun with you all."

Maribeth forced a smile. Said thank you.

"And if I can keep you from spending any of your hard-earned money on babysitters, all the better. Even with insurance, I remember how the bills piled up with your father. And with you not working . . ."

"I'm still working, Mom," she said. "I'm on leave." The truth was, she wasn't sure what she was on. Leave? Disability? She should probably call someone in HR.

"Not really full-time," her mother said. "And Jason's salary . . ."

Jason worked as the head archivist for a music library. It was his dream job — he'd relocated from San Francisco for it — but the pay was awful, at least by Manhattan standards. One time Maribeth had complained to her mother how she didn't understand why a company would go through all the trouble to relocate someone only to pay him a barely livable salary. Ever since, her mother had acted as if she and Jason were a step away from welfare.

"You know," her mother barreled on, "that was why I made sure your father left some of his money to you in his will. Three months before the stroke, almost like I knew."

Maribeth kept smiling. It felt like her face was encased in plaster.

"I'd hoped you'd use that money to buy a nice house," her mother finished. "Maybe in the suburbs, like Ellen Berman's daughter."

"The one with breast cancer?"

"You can't blame that on the suburbs."

"We don't want to live in the suburbs, Mom."

"Maybe you can work less, somehow. I'm sure Elizabeth would find a way. She's always been so generous to you."

"Thanks for making me sound like a charity case."

"Oh, I don't mean it like that. I just want you to slow down." She paused, frowning. "I suppose I hoped you'd use all this as a wakeup call."

"A wakeup call?"

"Herb Zucker had a heart attack, lost

67

thirty pounds, and started meditating."

"I should lose thirty pounds and start meditating?"

"No, you've always been too thin. But you should take a look at your life. Your priorities."

Maribeth understood her mother was singing a version of her own sad song: the hamster wheel that was her life. But hearing the lament from her mother didn't make her feel supported, only accused.

"My priorities are just fine," she said.

"I just wouldn't want you to go through this again," her mother added.

"Me neither."

Her mother leaned in close, as if to divulge a juicy secret. "Jason told me that it might be genetic." She looked at Maribeth meaningfully. "So you can't blame me."

What a thing to say. It reminded Maribeth of when she and Jason had started the fertility treatments and her mother had been, oddly, almost gleeful. "It's like I passed something to you after all," she'd said. That this sentiment was both unwelcome and off base — the doctors never thought Maribeth had any medical issues related to her infertility aside from her "advanced maternal age" — never seemed to occur to her mother.

"Why would I blame you?" Maribeth asked.

Her mother looked away. Then she clapped her hands together, as if officially ending the discussion. "What would you like for dinner? I thought we might get that brisket from the Jewish deli."

"Brisket is kind of fatty," Maribeth said.

Her mother put her hands on her hips. "At my age, I'm done counting calories."

"I meant me. I'm supposed to eat lean meats."

"Oh, we can get you a nice barley soup. Or a turkey sandwich. Do you have a menu?"

"No. We order online."

"I don't do computers."

"Why don't you tell me exactly what you want and I'll take care of it."

"Perfect."

Jason was working late so Maribeth put both kids to bed that night. Oscar had already fallen asleep and Maribeth was finishing Liv's last book when out of nowhere her daughter asked, "If you die, will Grandma be our mommy?"

Maribeth was shaken. She had thought they'd successfully masked the gravity of what was going on. Mommy was sick but the doctors were making her better, that kind of thing. It was the first time the d-word had come up.

"I'm not going to die for a very long time, sweetie," she said.

"If you die, can Robbie be our mommy?"

"It doesn't work like that. And I'm not going to die."

Oscar roused. "I don't want you to die," he pleaded sleepily.

"I'm not going to die," she said. *Yet,* she thought. *Please don't let me die yet.* "Go night-night, sweetie."

A minute later, she heard Oscar's snores. Liv was wide awake, blinking those huge eyes of hers, twirling a seam on her nightgown. "If you die, tell Daddy to marry someone nice. I don't want a mean stepmommy, like Cinderella."

A tight feeling seized her chest, though Maribeth knew from previous conversations with Liv it wasn't her heart, just her daughter's uncanny ability to hit the tender spots. Because she had been thinking about this every day since she'd woken up from her bypass. What would happen to the twins if something happened to her?

She snapped off the light. "Go to sleep," she said.

9

Now that Jason was back in the office, he was working longer hours than ever. He blamed the database upgrade, but Maribeth suspected he was looking for reasons to stay out of the loft. If she could do the same, she would.

The place was a disaster. Her mother was not much of a housekeeper, and cleaning had never been Robbie's thing, so the mountains of laundry grew by the day, which was unpleasant, but it was the dirty dishes in the sink with the potential to draw out every cockroach within a five-block vicinity that worried Maribeth.

So, she started doing dishes. And laundry. And because she could not face another meal of takeout, she began to cook simple meals. These small tasks robbed her of whatever energy she was regaining. When he got home from work, Jason scolded her for doing too much, and yet he continued working late.

One morning during her second week home, Maribeth went to the kitchen to fix a cup of coffee and found some of last night's dinner dishes, along with all of the morning's breakfast mess. As if waiting for her.

*Screw thi*s, she thought. Going to the office would be easier than this. Remembering the promise she'd made to Elizabeth the week before — a promise she had half forgotten about as Elizabeth had urged her to — she fired up her laptop. As she waited for her work e-mail to download, dread knotted her stomach.

She recognized this as re-entry anxiety. Two summers ago, right after Maribeth had gone back to work at *Frap,* Elizabeth had invited her and the family up to Tom's place in the Berkshires (well, now it was her and Tom's place) for a long weekend. At the last minute Elizabeth had said she and Tom couldn't come, but she'd implored Maribeth to go with Jason and the kids. They'd expected something rustic but instead had found an enormous colonial house with a private pond. The only thing rustic about it was that it was remote, and intentionally dewired. No cable TV. No Internet. Just a landline. You had to drive into Lenox to get cell reception. But it had been nice. Maribeth had turned off her phone, spending carefree hours hunting four-leaf clovers and observing tadpoles with the twins. But on the drive home, her phone had started chiming with e-mails and texts, making her feel like she'd missed something essential and was about to pay a price for it. Which was exactly how she felt now.

But no, there was nothing essential. In fact, there was hardly any mail at all. Which was odd. In any given day, between the staff-wide production notices and meeting announcements, and back and forth between her and various editors and writers, she usually had at least a hundred new messages. She looked through the inbox and saw that it cut off, abruptly, a few weeks ago, right around the time of her surgery. And several messages that had come in before the e-mail had been cut off had been read. But not by her.

She switched over to the webmail version in case it was a computer malfunction but it was the same thing. She checked her personal account to see if her e-mail was behaving wonky but it was fine. Weird. She called Elizabeth's assistant, Finoula.

"Finoula, hi, it's Maribeth Klein."

"Maribeth, hi! How are you feeling?"

"I'm great. Well, not great, but better. All

things considered."

"Good, good. Tricky business, the heart," Finoula said. "My granny had bypass surgery. She's back hauling wheelbarrows through her garden now."

"Oh. That's reassuring. Along those lines, I'm trying to wade back into things, get caught up on my e-mail, but there's nothing there."

"Right."

"Right?"

"Elizabeth's orders."

"Elizabeth?"

"She had IT take you off the system."

"She did?"

"Yes."

"Oh, okay. But someone went through my e-mails."

"Probably Andrea Davis. We brought her in."

"When?"

"I'm not sure exactly, when you were in hospital," Finoula said. "I can look it up if you want."

"That's okay."

"She's great, Andrea is. Hit the ground running."

"Yeah, she's a real pro," Maribeth said.

There was silence on the line.

"We're about to jump into a planning

meeting. Do you want me to see if I can catch Elizabeth?"

"Oh, no thanks."

"Take care, Maribeth."

"You, too, Finoula."

Maribeth hung up the phone and closed her laptop. For the first time in years, there was no assignment hanging over her head, no looming deadline. She should feel relief, but what she felt was betrayal.

Don't think about it. That's what Elizabeth had said. And meanwhile, she had hired Andrea. Had *already* hired her when she'd come to visit. Had barely waited for Maribeth's chair to grow cool.

Don't worry about it.

This was what happened when she didn't worry about it.

She kicked her laptop to the edge of the bed and it fell to the floor with a thunk. She wasn't fired. She knew Elizabeth would never do that. And it probably wasn't even legal. But as for replacing her, the truth was, Elizabeth had already been doing it for years. This only completed the job.

Jason didn't get home that night until nine o'clock. The twins were still awake because Maribeth lacked the energy to put them to bed and her mother had fallen asleep early.

75

"How come the kids are up?" Jason asked.

"I guess the magical bedtime elf gave our place a miss tonight."

He put his bag down. "Everything okay?"

She couldn't even answer.

He checked the time again, glanced toward the twins' room.

"Don't you dare criticize me."

"I wasn't," he said, defensively. "The database —"

"Yeah, the database upgrade," she interrupted. "I know. All of Tribeca knows how busy you are with your database upgrade."

"What is the matter with you?"

"What's the matter? I'm here alone all day with my mother and the kids and I still feel like shit." She paused, waiting for Jason to respond but he didn't say anything. "You're never here. I can't tell if you're trying to avoid home, or if you think that a week in the hospital, a week of recovery, was enough luxury for old Maribeth."

"What are you talking about?"

"You promised me a bubble," she said, her voice cracking.

"I'm trying, Maribeth. But keeping you in the bubble and keeping the house running and keeping on top of my job is no easy feat."

"Welcome to every fucking day of my life."

His jaw twitched. "Look," he said in a measured tone. "I know you've been through an ordeal and you're in pain, but can you try not to lash out at the people who are in it with you?"

"If I ever meet those people, I'll be sure to keep that in mind."

"You know what, you're being really . . ."

Childish. That's what she thought he'd say. "Selfish."

Selfish! She was being selfish? All she did was take care of everyone else. For the first time in her life, she needed to be taken care of, and this was what she got? She felt tears of rage come to her eyes and then shame because damn him if she was going to cry.

Selfish?

Jason. Elizabeth. Her mother. They could all go to hell.

10

Maribeth woke up the next morning draggy, fatigued, and achy, like she'd been hit by a truck in the night. She had not felt this wretched since the hospital. She was supposed to walk but it was raining out. This had prevented her mother from taking the kids to school because she hadn't wanted to catch a chill, so Jason had had to take them, causing him to leave late for some big off-site meeting and making him surly.

She put in a call to Dr. Sterling's office. The nurse asked about her symptoms. Maribeth said that her chest hurt. And she was achy.

"During physical activity?" the nurse asked.

"No, when I'm resting."

"I'll have the doctor call you back."

Five minutes later, the phone rang. But it wasn't Dr. Sterling. It was her CPA's office, calling to confirm that she had received and filed their return. "We never got your confirmation notice back," the receptionist said.

"What return?" Maribeth asked.

"We overnighted the returns to you," the receptionist said. "FedEx confirms receipt on the thirteenth."

She'd been in the hospital then. She told the receptionist she'd call back and went to the hall table. She always dealt with the mail, sorted the junk mail, paid the bills, and since she'd been ignoring it, it appeared that it had just been piling up.

She quickly weeded out the catalogs and credit card offers and tossed them in recycling. She put aside all the get-well cards, bank statements, and bills in another pile. She saw nothing from the CPA.

Then she noticed a thick FedEx envelope shoved between the mail rack and the wall. It was marked URGENT! She tore it open. Inside was the tax return with a cover letter instructing her and Jason to sign and mail it by the fifteenth.

She double-checked the date on the envelope. October 12. The package had sat here for more than two weeks, in a FedEx overnight envelope, addressed to both of them, marked urgent, and Jason had not thought to open it.

She called the CPA back to ask what to

do, but he was in a meeting. She called Jason at work. He didn't answer. She remembered he was off-site so she e-mailed and texted him to call her ASAP. "Urgent!" she wrote.

Her phone rang. Dr. Sterling's Gomer Pyle voice was on the other end.

"What seems to be the problem?" he asked.

"Oh, hi. I woke up today feeling really bad."

"How so?"

"Exhausted, achy. My chest hurts."

"When you're active or resting?"

"Resting."

"Does it feel like it did before? During your heart attack?"

"No. It's more throbby."

"Any shortness of breath?"

"Not really."

"Dizziness?"

"I'm not dizzy, but I just feel . . . unsteady. And tired. Worse than I have since any of this began."

"I wouldn't worry about it. The chest sounds skeletal."

"What about the achiness? And the exhaustion. Also, I have a headache."

"That sounds viral."

"Isn't that dangerous? I mean, am I compromised? I live with a pair of four-year-olds."

"While an upper respiratory infection isn't ideal right now, it's not going to kill you."

"How reassuring."

"If your children are anything like mine were, they always have something."

"They're disease vectors."

"If you're really concerned, remove them for a few days. But it just sounds like you have a garden-variety touch of something and the chest pain is a normal part of healing."

"I really don't feel right," Maribeth pressed on. "Are you sure I shouldn't come in?"

"If you think it's urgent, go to the ER. Otherwise, I'll transfer you to reception. You can come in tomorrow."

"I'll call if I'm not better."

"Sounds like a plan, Maryann." He chuckled at the rhyme.

"Maribeth," she corrected. But he'd already hung up.

Her mother poked her head in the bedroom. "Did I hear you on the phone with your doctor?"

"Yeah. I'm not feeling that great."

"What did the doctor say?"

"He was no help."

Her mother pursed her lips and shook her head. "Doctors don't know anything. I'm going to call Herb Zucker. He had the same surgery."

"Please don't." She didn't see how Herb Zucker, seventy-eight years old and retired, could have anything relevant to say about Maribeth's life.

"Don't be silly. I'm here to help."

After her mother disappeared to make the call, Maribeth thought about whom she really wanted to talk to: Elizabeth. The old Elizabeth, the one who, when Maribeth had come down with chicken pox at the age of twenty-four, had rented her every Cary Grant movie and bought her a pair of cashmere mittens to keep Maribeth from scarring herself when she scratched. The Elizabeth who'd visited her last week felt about as relevant to her life as Herb Zucker did.

Then she thought of Nurse Luca. Insurance covered the nurse visits for a week but she could pay for a visit out of pocket.

She went to the pile of mail and fished out the bank statement. There was $52,000 in the savings account she'd set up after receiving the bequest from her father. Maybe it wasn't enough to cover a down payment and closing costs on a house (or let's face it, an apartment) in anywhere but the farthest reaches of Brooklyn, but it was certainly enough for a session or two with Nurse Luca.

She called the nurse service. They said they'd get someone out first thing tomorrow and put in a request for Luca.

Outside, it was pouring. Which meant the window in the kitchen would leak. She rooted around in the pantry for the bucket and put it under the leak. Her mother was sitting at the table with a cup of tea, chattering away on the phone, to Herb Zucker presumably. They didn't seem to be discussing cardiac care. At one point, she looked up. "The phone's beeping."

"Probably needs to be charged."

Then her cell phone rang. It was Jason.

"What's wrong?" he asked.

"We didn't pay the taxes," Maribeth said.

"What?"

"The taxes. The returns, the payment coupons, they're sitting on the hall table with all the other mail you didn't bother to open."

"Shit, Maribeth, you scared me. I thought something *bad* had happened."

"Something *bad* did happen. We didn't pay our taxes."

"Something bad and irreparable. You have to stop sweating the small stuff."

"Death and taxes. They're linked together for a reason," Maribeth said.

"What are you talking about?" Jason asked.

"It's not the small stuff!" Maribeth cried.

"Try to keep things in perspective," he said.

Perspective? Try this perspective. My fist smashing into your face.

"They're not going to haul us off to jail," he said. "We'll just pay a penalty or something. Everything will work out fine."

"*Everything will work out fine?* Have you looked around lately?"

"Yeah."

"Does it seem like it's working out?"

"Yeah, it does, actually."

"In case you haven't fucking noticed, I had *bypass* surgery."

He paused. "I noticed. And you're getting better."

"I'm not getting better." She was yelling into the phone now. "I'm getting worse!"

"The doctor said you're doing fine. You're just getting yourself into a state."

A state? She was dancing on a surfboard, juggling knives, while they all went about business as usual. But it wasn't business as usual. She'd had open-heart surgery. And in spite of what Jason and Dr. Sterling thought, she wasn't getting better. And if she didn't get better . . . How would they manage? When Jason couldn't even pay the goddamn taxes on time.

"I hate you!" she yelled. Then turned off the phone and threw it across the room, burying her head under the pillow and crying herself to sleep.

11

She was dreaming of water. She could hear it. The ebb and flow of the waves.

Plink. She felt it now. It was raining inside her dream. *Plink.* And inside her room.

And then the bed shook and Liv shrieked, "Wake up! We have lice! Wake up now!"

She forced her eyes open. Liv was standing above her, along with Oscar, and Niff Spenser. All three of them were dripping wet.

"There was a check at school," Niff explained. "We tried to call, but we kept getting voicemail, so I volunteered to bring them home."

The beeping. It was the call waiting.

"Where's Grandma?"

"Napping," Oscar said.

"The front door was open so I just let us in," Niff said.

Maribeth blinked and looked at the clock. 12:13.

"Lice?"

"Unfortunately, both Oscar and Liv have them." Niff lowered her voice. "Pretty bad, the teachers said."

"So what do I do?" she asked Niff. "Use that shampoo?"

"Oh, no, those chemicals are quite literally poison," Niff said.

Oscar had no grasp of hyperbole. He jutted out his lower lip, a sign of imminent tears.

"Nobody's poisoning anybody," Maribeth said, reaching out to pat his head and then swerving and going for his shoulder instead.

"You can hire nitpickers to do it, but I learned to do it myself," Niff said. "There are videos online. You have to be very thorough to get the nits. They'll be checked before they're admitted back into the classroom and there's a strict no hat or wig-sharing policy for tomorrow's Halloween party."

Shit. Halloween wasn't until Friday but for some reason the party was tomorrow.

"We can't miss the Halloween party," Oscar said, chin going full tilt now.

"You're ruining everything!" Liv yelled at Maribeth.

"Liv! Manners!" Niff looked aghast. She

turned to Maribeth. "I can help if you want."

"Thanks," Maribeth said. "We'll take it from here."

After Niff left, Maribeth looked up a couple of nitpickers online. No one could come today, and besides, they would cost four hundred dollars, for the twins, plus more to check the adults in the household.

Her mother, up from her nap, padded into the bedroom in socked feet. "Did I hear the twins?"

"They were sent home from school with lice," she said. "We have to get rid of them."

"I think you use kerosene."

"No, you don't use kerosene. We use Pantene and a special comb, like this one." She pointed to her screen. "Can you run out to the drugstore for me?"

Her mother's eyes flitted to the window. It was pelting down a nasty, gray fall rain. "In this weather? I don't think I should."

"Someone has to go."

"Ask Jason."

"He's working off-site today. He won't get home until late."

"Doesn't everything here deliver?"

"Rite Aid does not deliver."

"Can't you order on the computer?" Her

mother gestured to the screen.

"I could but it wouldn't get here in time. I have to comb them out before school tomorrow. They're not allowed back in until they're clean."

"Can't Jason get the comb tonight and you do it tomorrow?"

"Tomorrow's the Halloween party," Liv hollered from across the loft.

"We can't miss the party," Oscar bellowed.

Maribeth sighed. "I'll go get the comb."

"I don't think you should go out in this weather," her mother said. "It's not the end of the world if they miss one party."

Hearing this, the twins began to cry.

Maribeth reached for her coat.

As she slogged through the rain, Maribeth wondered a few times if perhaps she *was* dreaming. It was a comforting thought because then this wasn't really happening. She wasn't out here, in the rain, walking to the drug store. When her local Rite Aid didn't carry the type of comb she was after, she almost cried. The pharmacist took pity on her and called across the street to a competing chain, which did have the comb.

She lugged everything home. The errand, which in her healthy days would've taken fifteen minutes, had taken nearly an hour.

She was wet, cold to the bone, and depleted, like something essential was draining out of her.

Back at home, they negotiated a movie — *Enchanted* — and then the three of them sat down on the sofa. She did Oscar first, guessing, correctly, that he'd be more compliant. He bopped his head to the "Happy Working Song" while Maribeth pulled out the disgusting creatures, one after the other. A half hour later, she was still pulling out nits.

"When is my turn?" Liv asked.

"I'm tired of this," Oscar said.

"Why don't you switch for a while?" her mother suggested. She had joined them and was now watching, too, as if this were family movie night.

Maribeth went to rinse off the comb and empty out the bucket under the leaking window. She made a mental note to call the super to apply another coat of sealant that never fully worked.

She dampened Liv's hair and began to brush the tangles out. "Owww!" Liv screamed, bucking so hard she nearly headbutted Maribeth. "You're hurting me."

As gently as she could, she tried again. Liv whipped around. "I said, you're hurting me!"

"Let's try putting the conditioner on," Maribeth said wearily. She began to squirt it on Liv's head.

"It's cold!"

"It'll warm up."

She pulled the comb through her hair. "Oww!" Liv yelled.

"Calm down!" Maribeth snapped.

"You calm down," Liv yelled back nonsensically.

Maribeth sank back into the sofa. She remembered those TV commercials for bubble bath from her youth.

Calgon, take me away, she thought.

Anyone?

"Why are you stopping?" Liv shrieked.

Maribeth spread the conditioner through Liv's hair. Then she gathered a small bunch of hair and combed through it. Out came four fat bugs. She went through the same bunch of hair, more bugs. Once more, and yet still more bugs.

She was infested. She was patient zero. They probably all had it now.

Her own head started to itch.

She went through the clump again. More bugs, and the telltale egglike nits, too. Again and again. And still more crap came out. It was never ending.

"You're hurting me!" Liv yelled every time

Maribeth ran the comb through.

"I can't hear the movie," Oscar complained every time Liv yelled.

"Shut up," Liv yelled every time Oscar complained.

"Mom," Maribeth said after several rounds of this. "Can you maybe sit between them?"

"Oh, what a nice idea. Scootch for Grandma."

Liv's hair was full of tangles. When the teeth caught on a particularly extravagant knot, Liv screamed and spun around. "I hate you!" she yelled. Then she shoved Maribeth right in the chest.

It hurt. It knocked the wind out of her. But most of all, it shocked her. But what shocked her more was what she did. Which was to hit Liv back. Not hard enough to hurt, but hard enough to betray.

Liv's mouth curled into a stunned O as she absorbed what had just happened. It was only after Maribeth apologized that Liv started to bellow.

It was the part of the movie when the Susan Sarandon character went from animated to live action. Maribeth's mother thought Liv was crying because she was scared. "It's okay, honey," she said. "The witch dies in the end." As if death was a comforting notion for a four-year-old.

Liv kept on crying, and then Oscar started up, too. Her mother suggested that they put on a different movie.

Maribeth excused herself, went into her room, where she too started to cry.

12

The next morning, Joanne, the Wilsons' babysitter, arrived at seven to comb out the twins' hair. Apparently, she'd instructed them to sleep with some kind of oil and a shower cap, which seemed far too easy, but such was the Jason way. After yesterday's crying jag, Maribeth had called him with the news that the kids had lice. "You fucking deal with it," she'd fumed to his voicemail. And he'd called the Wilsons. Shocker.

Joanne had offered to walk the twins to school with Maribeth's mother. "Go kiss Mommy good-bye."

Liv pouted as she puckered her lips sourly and turned toward Maribeth. Part of Maribeth wanted to refuse the kiss. She understood that she was the mother and had to be the adult here, but for once, could someone cut her a break?

Apparently not. Jason had slept on a blow-up mattress in the twins' room last night. A lot of trouble to telegraph his contempt. Maribeth, meanwhile, had not slept at all.

Policeman Oscar shuffled over for a kiss and then the twins left, along with Joanne and Maribeth's mother. Jason, who should've left for work an hour ago, paused by the bookcase. "Are you going to get out of bed today?" he asked.

"If I want to," Maribeth replied, acidly.

"Do you really think you're helping yourself by getting so worked up?" he asked. Like he was the wronged party here.

"No," Maribeth said flatly.

"Then don't," he said.

At eleven, the buzzer rang. When Maribeth opened the front door and saw Luca there, she broke down in big, gusty tears.

"Oh, no! That's not good," Luca said, motioning Maribeth over to the living room. She sat down on the sofa. "What's going on?"

Maribeth recounted the days since coming home. The sense of backsliding. Her family's unrelenting dependence on her.

Luca listened patiently. "I wish I could say you're the first woman who's had this complaint," she said.

"I'm not?" Maribeth said, feeling both

heartened because it wasn't just her and disheartened because, really?

Luca smiled wryly. "Would it surprise you to learn that one of the top fantasies for women is a prolonged hospital stay?"

"That's absurd."

"Not if you think about it. The exhausted, multitasking woman. A trip to the hospital, it's like the ultimate vacation. A chance to be the nurtured one instead of the nurturer. Guilt free, no less."

"But I *have* been in the hospital, for something really serious, and it hasn't changed a thing."

This wasn't entirely true. It had changed everything, but not the way she needed it to.

"That's why it only works as a fantasy," Luca replied.

"I don't know what I'm supposed to do. I don't know how I'm ever going to heal this way. I feel like I'm healing backwards, the end result being . . ."

She couldn't say it. Didn't have to. Luca acknowledged it with a nod. Then she started to unpack her equipment. "Let's take a look at you."

Luca did the exam. "Your EKG looks great and your heart and lungs sound fine. Your pulse is a little weak and I wouldn't be surprised if you were anemic so when you get your next blood work done, have them test for iron. But you appear otherwise healthy. You're clearly run-down, but not in any imminent danger I can see."

"That's good, I guess," she said before she started to cry again.

"It *is* good, Maribeth." Luca squeezed her hand. "You can be happy about that."

But how could she be happy when every day that she supposedly grew stronger — healthier — she felt more and more terrified? The specter of death had seemed abstract before, even after the heart attack, even as she was watching the image of her heart on the screen in the cath lab. But now it was real. It was a presence as physical and demanding of her attention as her twins. Maybe that was why she wanted to stitch Oscar and Liv into her body, and at the same time, she wanted to jettison them far away from her.

"Is there anything else going on?" Luca asked. By now, she'd been there more than twice the allotted time.

"No," Maribeth answered. "I mean, I'm probably just run-down, like you said."

Luca packed up. Before she left, she embraced Maribeth. Then she held her at arm's length and looked at her as if deciding something.

"I believe you have a healthy heart," she said. "The doctors have done their part. But if you want to get better, really better, well, you're going to have to do that for yourself."

■ ■ ■ ■ ■

PITTSBURGH

■ ■ ■ ■ ■

13

It had been surprisingly easy.

Maribeth had walked downstairs and hailed a cab, carrying only a hastily packed duffel bag with a few changes of clothing and her medications. She'd left her cell phone, her computer — pretty much everything else — at home. None of that felt necessary anymore. She had e-mailed Jason. An apology? An explanation? She wasn't sure. By the time she was in the cab, the details of her note had already begun to fade.

"Penn Station," she told the driver. She had not known that would be her destination until the words came out of her mouth.

Twenty minutes later, she was at the train station. Across the street was a branch of her bank. Maribeth was about to pull cash out from the ATM but instead she wandered into the lobby and asked a teller how much she could withdraw.

Twenty-five thousand dollars turned out to be surprisingly portable. It fit snugly into her duffel bag.

Easy.

When she entered the mildewy cavern of Penn Station, she still hadn't known where she was going. She'd thought maybe some quaint coastal New England town. And then she saw the departure board.

She bought her ticket for the Pennsylvanian and went to one of the cell phone kiosks for a burner phone (testing out a vocabulary acquired during that one season she'd managed to watch *The Wire*). The clerk handed her a pay-as-you-go flip phone with a 646 number. She paid for one hundred minutes of talk time. She went into a Duane Reade and bought a bottle of water, a pack of gum, and some lice shampoo, just in case. Then she boarded the train.

Easy.

When the train emerged onto the wetlands of New Jersey, Manhattan glittering in the afternoon sun, Maribeth thought it looked like something from a movie. Which was how it had felt. Like something happening to some actor on a screen. She was not Maribeth Klein, mother, leaving her two young children. She was a woman in a movie going somewhere normal, perhaps a business trip.

On the train, exhaustion overcame her, a different flavor from the dragged-down lethargy that had plagued her back home. It was the floppy satisfying tiredness one gets after a long day of doing nothing in the sun. Using her duffel bag as a pillow, she went to sleep.

Easy.

When she woke up and went to the café car to get something to eat, she found a discarded *City Paper* on one of the tables. Inside was a tiny real estate section, with not much advertised, but there was a one-bedroom in a neighborhood called Bloomfield. She called from the train and spoke to the landlord, an elderly sounding man with a thick accent (Italian? Eastern European?) who told her the apartment was available, and not only that, it was furnished. The rent was eight hundred dollars a month. For an extra fifty bucks, she could move in a few days before the first of the month. She took it sight unseen.

Easy.

She spent her first night in Pittsburgh in a janky motel near the train station. The next morning, she took a taxi to her new apartment and gave the landlord, Mr. Giulio, first month's rent, one month's deposit, and signed a month-to-month lease. There was no FBI-level background check required of a New York City rental. No broker fee amounting to 15 percent of a year's rent. Just sixteen hundred dollars. When she paid in cash, Mr. Giulio did not bat an eye.

Easy.

As for leaving, leaving Jason, leaving her children, she kept hearing Luca's words: *You have to do that for yourself.*

A task assigned to others, falling back to her. In some ways it was comforting.

So leaving them was not exactly easy. But it was something she already knew how to do.

14

The last thing she wanted was more doctors. But Maribeth needed a cardiologist. Or a surgeon. She would be missing her scheduled follow-up appointment with Dr. Gupta, so before checking out of the motel, she'd found a Yellow Pages in the dresser, right next to the Bible, and had ripped out a sheaf of pages. She'd felt a pang of guilt for destroying the book, but, really, who didn't have a smart phone anymore? Well, who besides her?

She'd spent Halloween morning in her new apartment calling cardiology practices. There were several; Pittsburgh was a medical town. Her new neighborhood was sandwiched between two hulking hospitals, which Maribeth found equal parts comforting and alarming. Most of the doctors were booked out, but after a dozen calls, she found a practice that had just had a last-minute cancellation for Monday.

As she waited for the taxi to take her to the appointment she wished she'd thought to steal the entire Yellow Pages. She'd spent most of the weekend holed up, sleeping and watching TV, subsisting on minestrone soup and yogurt from the little Italian grocery on the corner. Now that she was feeling steadier, there were things to figure out. Where was a proper grocery store? A pharmacy? Where might she get a nicer set of sheets than the stained ones the apartment had come with? Without Google at her constant disposal, she didn't know how she would find anything.

A scrawny tabby cat sidled up to her, lost interest, and then sniffed at an artfully carved jack-o'-lantern that was starting to rot. The handiwork, she guessed, of her upstairs neighbors, a young couple who were the only other tenants in the small frame building. The top floor, she knew, was vacant. Mr. Giulio had offered to show her the studio apartment there, but she'd declined, saying she could handle the rent on the one bedroom. (What she could not handle were the two flights of stairs to the attic.)

The door opened and a young man with a swoop of platinum hair emerged. He bent down to try to pet the cat, which scurried away.

"Is that yours?" Maribeth asked.

"We aren't allowed pets in the building," he replied.

"Oh. I didn't know. I just moved in to the ground-floor apartment here." She pointed. "But luckily I don't have a pet." She heard herself babbling and stopped.

"Welcome to our beautiful neighborhood," he said drolly, gesturing to the bleak, treeless block.

"Thanks. Hey, look, you don't happen to have a Yellow Pages?"

"They still make those?"

Maribeth suddenly felt so very old next to this young man, as she waited for a taxi driver to ferry her to a doctor.

"Sunny," he called over his shoulder. "Do we have a Yellow Pages?"

A young South Asian woman, Sunny presumably, appeared. She had deep dimples, a ponytail, and was wearing leggings and an oversized sports jersey. "Didn't we use it as a doorstop last summer?"

And now Maribeth felt 482 years old. Mercifully, the taxi pulled up. "Maybe another time," she said.

She arrived at the doctor's ten minutes early, as instructed, to complete the paperwork. She sketchily filled out the health history and left the insurance forms blank. So far, she had managed to exist on an entirely cash economy. She hadn't planned it that way — she hadn't planned any of this — but after so many years of being constantly available to everyone, she wanted to keep it that way.

"Excuse me, ma'am," the receptionist said after Maribeth had handed in her paperwork. "We'll need your insurance card."

"That's all right," Maribeth said. "I'm paying cash."

"You're paying cash?" She looked at Maribeth as if she'd just announced she would be paying with Pokémon cards.

"Yes," Maribeth said.

"Don't you have insurance?"

"I'll be paying cash," Maribeth said.

"If you can't afford insurance," the receptionist replied, "we can help you apply for it. It's very reasonable if you qualify for Medicaid. And we also offer discounts for the indigent."

Indigent? She'd showered for this morning's appointment, even washed her hair, albeit with lice shampoo, which had dried it to straw. Also she'd forgotten to get conditioner so maybe she did look a bit finger-in-socket. But still, the grooming had taken some effort.

"I'm paying cash," Maribeth said for the third time.

The receptionist had looked at the forms. "You're coming for postoperative care and you're paying cash?"

"That's right."

"How did you pay for your surgery? In cash?"

Maribeth was beginning to get flustered. But then she remembered Elizabeth's advice in situations like these: Act like you own it.

She took a deep breath. "How I paid for my surgery is neither here nor there. I just need to see a doctor, and I can pay cash. Up front. You won't have to bill anyone." Her voice sounded haughty, completely unlike her.

It seemed to work. The receptionist went to get the office manager.

Maribeth sat down and waited, feeling like she was about to be busted. As if it wasn't the office manager who was going to come out but her high school principal. Or Jason.

"Ms. Goldman."

It took Maribeth a few seconds to realize she was the Ms. Goldman being addressed. M. B. Goldman was the name she'd listed on her forms. An old nickname, her mother's maiden name.

"Yes. That's me."

The office manager, an attractive overweight woman wearing a red power suit, smiled. "I understand that you'd like to pay cash for your visits."

"Yes," Maribeth said.

"The thing is," the office manager said, "it's against our practice's policy."

"I don't see why this is such a problem." Maribeth knew from her C-section and Oscar's ear tube surgery the paperwork jungle of insurance companies. Oughtn't they be thanking her for saving them the trouble?

"The doctors might want to order tests. And with the Affordable Care Act, everyone should be insured. Particularly a cardiac patient."

"Shouldn't that be my concern?"

"I'm just trying to explain our policy." She paused. "Perhaps you should visit the ER?"

"I don't need an ER," she said. "I have money. I can leave a deposit."

The office manager looked genuinely apologetic. But she still shook her head.

"Can you at least refer me to a cardiologist who might see me?" She no longer sounded like someone who owned the world. She sounded like someone who was asking to borrow a teaspoon of it.

"What about Dr. Grant?" the receptionist asked.

The office manager frowned.

"Is Dr. Grant a thoracic surgeon?" Maribeth asked.

"A cardiologist. One of the founders of this practice," the receptionist said at the same time that the office manager was saying, "No, no. Not Dr. Grant."

"Why not? Will he take cash?" Maribeth asked.

"I bet he might," the receptionist started to say.

"I'm just not sure he's taking new patients," the office manager interrupted. She shot a warning look at the receptionist.

"So you can't refer me to anyone?" Maribeth asked.

"Not anyone who won't require insurance," the office manager said.

Maribeth looked at the receptionist who was now looking at the floor.

Well, so much for easy. She'd had a good run, she supposed.

Defeated, she gathered her things to leave. She was almost out the door when the receptionist tapped her back. "Stephen Grant," she whispered. "Give him a call."

15

When she got home, she pulled out her purloined section of the Yellow Pages. Many of the doctors and practices took out ads. Dr. Stephen Grant did not. He had a one-line listing. As the phone rang, she remembered the queer look on the office manager's face, a look of warning almost. A reception-ist picked up. She said they had an opening for the next day. Maribeth hesitated. It was one appointment. How bad could he be?

Dr. Stephen Grant's office was in a neigh-borhood called Friendship, not so very far from Maribeth's new apartment. In her old life, it would've been walking distance. In her new life, she could walk three blocks.

As she rode the bus, she stared out the window at the elegant brick homes that Pittsburgh seemed to have in blithe abun-dance, like an overripe tree dropping apples to the ground. A few days ago, in the taxi from the train station, Maribeth had been similarly amazed at how pretty it was here — she'd assumed Pittsburgh would be a, well, pit. But it wasn't. All the graceful sweeping trees dappled in fall colors, all the handsome houses with their stained glass windows, elaborate brickwork, tidy gardens. When the taxi had dropped her in front of her building, drab and with vinyl siding, she'd been disappointed, but mostly relieved. To run away was bad enough, but to land somewhere she might *enjoy* living, that felt obscene.

Though Dr. Grant's office was right next to one of the large hospitals, his practice was not in one of the adjacent modern buildings, as the first practice she'd tried had been, but attached to one of those large brick houses she'd admired. She walked past it twice — it was easy to miss, only a small plaque on the front door announcing the practice — and when she pushed open the front door, she felt as if she was about to barge into someone's living room.

Instead she found herself in a tiny waiting room with two chairs and a desk manned by an older black woman, her hair done up in an elaborate tower of braids. She gave Maribeth the same stack of paperwork to fill out that the other practice had, and

Maribeth handed it back, with both her family history and the insurance forms blank.

When the receptionist asked for her insurance card, Maribeth replied: "I'm paying cash," steeling herself for an argument that never came.

"Payment due at time of service," she said. "Hundred and fifty dollars."

A hundred and fifty dollars? Maribeth had expected it to be at least three hundred dollars, maybe more for tests. To be safe, she'd taken five hundred from her stash (or stashes; she had secreted bills throughout the apartment, hoping that if someone broke in, they wouldn't find it all and clean her out).

"I might need tests," she said.

"Hundred and fifty dollars," the receptionist repeated.

Maribeth counted out the money and handed it over. The receptionist printed out a receipt by hand and gave it to Maribeth.

"That's okay," Maribeth said. "I don't need it."

The receptionist raised an eyebrow. "I'll go on and leave it in the file."

"Thank you."

Maribeth started to sit down but the receptionist stood up and beckoned to her.

"Come on back."

In a small examination room, the receptionist, who was also apparently the nurse, took her vitals. Then she handed her a blue examination gown. "Dr. Grant won't be but a moment."

While Maribeth sat shivering in the gown, she began to question the wisdom of going to this Dr. Grant, who had appointments open at the last minute, couldn't afford a receptionist *and* a nurse, and, she now suspected, had probably done something to get himself ousted from the larger cardiology practice. She pictured the stooped, nefarious villain in every bad TV legal drama.

But when Dr. Grant walked in, leafing through her chart, he did not seem remotely villainous; he was actually rather handsome in that way that later-middle-aged men tended to be.

"Ms. Goldman," he said, extending his hand for a shake. "I'm Stephen Grant."

"Hi, I'm M.B. M. B. Goldman," Maribeth stumbled over the name. It felt counterfeit, even though it was her. It said so right on the chart.

"I see you're about three weeks postoperative for a coronary bypass."

She nodded and waited for him to comment, on her age, the anomaly of someone so young undergoing such a procedure, the "luck" of it being only a double bypass.

"So what brings you in?"

"Well, as you noted, I'm post-op and . . ." she stopped herself. She was about to say she was missing the follow-up appointment with her surgeon but that would open a can of worms. At this point, she just wanted someone to tell her she was okay and be done with it. "I figured I should find myself a cardiologist while I'm in town."

His eyes flitted from her chart to her. "You're not from here?"

"Not exactly."

"Where did you have your surgery? UPMC?"

"I didn't have it in Pittsburgh."

"Where did you have it?"

"I'd rather not say."

He looked at her again, a straight-on gaze. His eyes were an unusual color, almost an amber. Maybe that was what made his look so discombobulating.

"Who performed it?"

"Again, I'd rather not say."

He scratched at a sideburn. "But not in Pittsburgh?"

"No."

"You relocated three weeks after surgery?"

116

There was a hint of surprise in his voice, and she felt the hairs on her neck rise. They'd already discussed the timeline. Could they not move on to the exam?

"This seems to be closing up. The tape fell off." She tapped the incision on her chest.

Dr. Grant came closer to inspect. He had thin, delicate fingers, more suited, Maribeth thought, for playing a piano than palpating a chest. "It's healing well," he said.

"My leg's still pretty swollen." She started to roll down her support stocking, but he'd already gone back to her file, flipping through the pages, reading them carefully now. In her flimsy gown, she felt exposed. As if he were not just reading her notes, but reading her.

A piece of paper from the file fluttered to the floor: It was the receipt. He picked it up and read it, and she could see him taking in the facts — cash, no insurance. He was going to refuse her any minute.

He looked at her and she could feel the judgment. *Are you always in such a hurry?* she heard Dr. Sterling ask. She felt a sudden rush of loathing for this Dr. Grant. She understood it was transference, her anger toward Dr. Sterling, which was probably a form of transference itself. But still, she was so tired of all of them playing god. She wasn't asking for them to examine her life, her choices, her priorities. She just wanted them to check her heart.

"You know, it's my choice, not yours," Maribeth said.

Dr. Grant looked up, bewildered. "I beg your pardon?"

"It's up to me to choose if you're my doctor. Not the other way around."

She sounded like a petulant teen, defending something stupid, a purple hair streak or a terrible band she loved.

Dr. Grant seemed taken aback. He retreated to his stool and set her file down on the counter. "I assumed you chose me when you made an appointment to see me," he replied.

"Nope. I went to the place you used to work and they wouldn't take me because I wasn't using insurance. Someone there said you might."

His face clouded over. So something bad had happened at the old practice. He stood up from the stool, and Maribeth stood, too, expecting to be shown the door. But instead, he unwound his stethoscope from his neck and stepped toward her. "Would you like me to check your heart or not?" he asked.

"Sure. You can see if I still have one."

■ ■ ■ ■

After the exam, after the EKG, after everything checked out — checked out enough
that he discouraged doing blood work; she'd
need to test at six weeks once her cholesterol
levels stabilized anyhow and she could
check her iron then if she was still worried
— Dr. Grant instructed her to settle up with
Louise.

She'd known a hundred and fifty dollars
wasn't going to cover it.

"How much more do I owe?" she asked
Louise, now a receptionist again, even
though there were no other patients to receive.

"You paid when you came in."

"Right, but he did a few tests, the EKG."

"The visit costs a hundred and fifty dollars."

"He told me to settle up with you."

"Yes. Dr. Grant would like to see you
again next week. He's in Mondays, Tues-
days, and Fridays."

Next week? Dr. Sterling hadn't wanted to
see her again until her six-week mark. Was
he milking her? Doctors did that, padded
the bills with unnecessary treatments.

Except Dr. Grant hadn't charged her extra

for the tests he had run. He'd recommended against doing blood work because
of the cost. He wasn't trying to bilk her.

But there was something a little off about
him; she could tell. It should make her wary
— malpractice, probably — but, oddly, it
was kind of reassuring. He couldn't be so
godlike now. Not if he, too, was damaged
goods.

She decided then. He would be her doctor. Not because he was the only one who'd
see her, but because she chose him.

She made an appointment for the following Monday.

16

Maribeth began to sort things out. She asked Mr. Giulio where the nearest library was (in Lawrenceville) and figured out which bus would get her there. The library would have computers, which would have Google, which would help her navigate everything else.

She also thought she might write an e-mail to the twins at the library. What she would tell them, she had no idea. How did one explain what she had done? How did one not explain?

The library was about a mile away from her apartment, down a steep hill and up a smaller one. This had been another surprise about Pittsburgh, how hilly, mountainous really, it was. It made things challenging for a cardiac post-op patient. As Maribeth rode the bus, she thought that perhaps when she could make the walk round-trip, that would be a sign that she was better. Maybe then she could go home. Maybe that was what she would tell Oscar and Liv. Children liked adults to be definitive. You could have three cookies. You could watch one episode of *Phineas and Ferb.*

But when she got to the library, something stopped her from even going near the bank of computers, even though there were several empty terminals. She had already broken the most important promise a mother makes — not to leave. She could not break any more. She could not tell them when she was coming back because she had no idea when that would be.

Instead, she walked to the periodicals section, planning to read a newspaper or something edifying to make good use of her free time. The library had copies of the *Pittsburgh Post-Gazette* and the *New York Times* on a wooden table, and several magazines, including an old issue of *Frap.*

It was from last August. Inside, there was a feature on celebrities who were vocal anti-vaccination advocates, an article that she and Elizabeth had argued over in the conference room in front of the entire senior staff.

Maribeth had felt the article, at least in the form it had been in at the time, was too fawning. If they wanted to run a piece on celebrities advocating against vaccinations, she'd insisted, it needed to be critical. It needed to be a serious piece of journalism for a change. "This is a public health issue," she'd told Elizabeth.

"Be that as it may, we need to keep our tone respectful," Elizabeth had responded.

"What does that even mean?" Maribeth had asked.

Not for the first time since coming to work at *Frap,* she'd felt as if she didn't really know Elizabeth, even though they'd been best friends and confidantes since almost the moment they'd met, more than two decades ago, in that very building, in fact, in a bathroom two floors below the conference room where they now were arguing.

Maribeth had just been starting out in her career, and was not off to a particularly promising start. The day she met Elizabeth, Maribeth had been hiding in a bathroom stall, crying. She had just gotten off the phone with her former college roommate Courtney, who had told her that Jason had a new girlfriend. She and Jason had broken up — by mutual agreement — after more than two years together. But that had only been three weeks ago. The speed at which she'd been replaced, it had kneecapped her.

She'd been sobbing in that bathroom stall as quietly as she could, which apparently was not all that quiet, because she heard someone say, "You can tell me it's not my business, but are you okay in there?"

Maribeth opened the door. There was Elizabeth, brushing her teeth at one of the sinks.

"I'm fine," Maribeth had said, not fine at all.

Elizabeth wet two paper towels and held them out to the side. Like a cagey dog coming in for a treat, Maribeth approached the sink.

"You know, we just ran a profile of a woman who put a hit on her philandering husband," Elizabeth said, delicately spitting out toothpaste. She spoke to Maribeth's reflection, in deference, perhaps, to the fact that they didn't really know each other. Maribeth had been working as an editorial floater at the magazine where Elizabeth held a staff position. "She's doing ten years at San Quentin," Elizabeth continued, "so I'm not sure it's worth it in the end, but all I'm saying is it can be done."

Maribeth immediately went from crying to laughing. "He's not a philanderer, just a shithead."

Now Elizabeth laughed, too. "That's the spirit."

"Really, I broke it off. It just wasn't work-

124

ing with the long-distance."

Elizabeth smiled, as if what Maribeth said had pleased her. "Then perhaps instead of crying, I might suggest a cocktail. I know a bartender who's generous with free cosmos. I'm Elizabeth, by the way."

"I'm Maribeth."

"Two Beths."

"Oh, yeah, I guess we are."

They'd gone for drinks that night. And many nights thereafter. Until she and Jason got back together ten years later — and maybe even after that — Elizabeth had been Maribeth's person. And Maribeth Elizabeth's. And yet in that conference room, she had seemed like another out-of-touch sycophantic editor-in-chief, someone Maribeth didn't know, someone Maribeth wouldn't know, ordering Maribeth to make an article about nonvaccinating celebrities "respectful."

"Are you kidding?" Maribeth had fumed. "These people are idiots."

"They are not idiots," Elizabeth had replied. "And I am not kidding."

"If you had kids, you'd feel differently." As soon as the words came out of her mouth, Maribeth regretted them, and not just because the temperature in the conference room seemed to drop ten degrees. She sometimes wondered if the kids were the thing that had put a wedge between her and Elizabeth, even though Elizabeth had never actually wanted children and for the first year or two seemed to like Maribeth's twins well enough.

Elizabeth had rolled her eyes, something Maribeth had seen her do a thousand times, but rarely at her. "And if you were editor-in-chief of this magazine, you'd feel differently."

Maribeth put the magazine back without opening it. *Frap* had never been particularly relevant to her, but now, like her relationship with Elizabeth, it felt like Pompeii — something from the past, entombed in ash.

17

When Maribeth got off the bus near her apartment, she realized she had failed to figure out the one thing she'd really needed to do at the library: find the Pittsburgh version of FreshDirect, a grocery store that delivered.

She called information on her phone but she wasn't familiar enough with the streets here to know what was near her and what wasn't. She walked upstairs and knocked on the door. The platinum-haired guy answered.

"Oh, you wanted a phonebook. I forgot."

"That's okay. I'm just trying to find a grocery store that delivers. I'm new to the area and I don't really know what's where."

He tilted his head to the side, eyes wide, stumped, as if she'd asked him about a store that sold horse meat. "Sunny," he called into the apartment. "Does Whole Foods deliver?"

"Whole Foods?" came the reply. "Did you win the PICK 3?"

"Not me, the new neighbor wants to know." He looked at Maribeth. "What's your name?"

"M.B."

"Short for . . ."

"For M.B."

He almost smiled. Then he called back into the apartment. "M.B., our mysterious new neighbor, requires a grocery store that delivers."

"Oh, you can't ask Todd." The young woman appeared at the doorstep, shaking her head. "He's very particular about such things. I'm Sunita by the way. There's a ShurSave right on Liberty. It's walkable."

Perhaps it was walkable to someone who was not prohibited from carrying anything weighing more than five pounds. "But does it deliver?" Maribeth asked.

"They could have Channing Tatum deliver groceries, shirtless on a unicorn, and I still wouldn't shop at ShurSave," Todd said.

"See what I mean?" Sunita said, rolling her eyes. "If not ShurSave, Giant Eagle is good and it's twenty-four hours if you need something that's open late."

"It's not the hours. I don't have a car at the moment."

Todd and Sunita exchanged a look, as if surprised that someone Maribeth's age was not vehicularly sorted.

"Oh. Well, maybe we could take you," Sunita said. "Right, Todd?" Before Todd could answer, Sunita turned back to Maribeth. "We don't have a car either but Todd's daddy lets us use his whenever we want."

"Don't call him that," Todd said.

"Sorry. Do you prefer sugar daddy?"

"I prefer boss, which is what he is."

"Boss with benefits?"

Maribeth cleared her throat. "When were you thinking of going?"

"Soon!" Sunita said. "We're down to rice cakes and pickles. Todd, will you ask Miles?"

"I'll text him tonight," Todd said wearily. "We can go tomorrow."

"Work for you, M.B.?" Sunita asked.

It was funny. This time, there was no lag. She knew immediately that it was her being addressed as M.B. It was amazing, really, how quickly you could become someone else.

"Works for me."

That night, when she took out her organizer to write down a shopping list, the stub from her train ticket to Pittsburgh fell out. She flipped to the back page where she'd hastily shoved a photo of the twins before leaving. Since she'd been away, she had not been able to look at it.

She held the ticket stub, remembering how at peace she'd been on the train, when she wasn't Maribeth Klein, runaway mommy, but woman on a business trip. She had been able to leave them as that woman. Perhaps as that woman she could look at their faces. After all, she was just a traveling mother, fondly gazing at a picture of her children.

She stole a quick glimpse of the photo and found that it didn't sucker punch, after all. She put the photo away, but then she had an idea. She turned to a blank page of her organizer, and instead of writing a shopping list, she began a letter.

Dear Oscar and Liv, Mommy has had a very busy few days.

She wrote them the kind of letter she imagined the woman on a business trip might. No tortured explanations or iffy timelines, just postcard details about her day. She wrote about the puppy in a trench coat she'd seen out on her walk. How it had reminded her of the time back home when they'd seen an elderly woman pushing a poodle in a toy stroller. *Do you remember, Liv, how after that, you gave up your spot in the stroller for your Clifford doll? And how you wouldn't ride in the stroller anymore because you said Clifford needed the seat?*

Oscar had remained in the stroller for another year, and because Liv was not a fast walker, sometimes it took ten minutes to go a block. Jason thought they should just force Liv to ride in the stroller, but for once it was Maribeth counseling patience. Sure, they might be slower than a gaggle of Times Square tourists, but she admired her daughter's determination.

She finished the letter and carefully tore it out of the organizer, placing it on her nightstand. She knew she wouldn't mail it. Couldn't. At the moment, though, that didn't seem to matter.

18

Thursday evening, Maribeth met Todd and Sunita downstairs. Todd was driving an old Volvo station wagon; Sunita sat in the passenger seat. Maribeth climbed in back.

"Mind the dog hair," Sunita said. "Todd's daddy is fond of strays."

"Strays? Please. He raises championship dogs. And stop calling him my daddy!" He peered at Maribeth through the rearview mirror. "But there is Jack Russell hair everywhere. I have a roller brush if you want."

"That's okay."

They wound their way through rush-hour traffic, passing several grocery stores. Maribeth must've looked perplexed because, after a while, Sunita turned around to explain. "Todd only likes the Giant Eagle in East Liberty."

"That's not true," Todd retorted. "The Market District one has higher prices.

Anyhow, we go to this one because it's near the Indian grocery and Sunny is trying to connect with her heritage."

"*Sunita,*" Sunita said, in the tone of an exasperated parent who's had this argument many times before.

"I rest my case," Todd said.

"Sunita is your full name?" Maribeth asked.

"It is. Was until I was six. Then 9/11 happened and there were all these reprisals against Pakistanis. We're Indian but my parents were freaked out that people would think we were terrorists so I started first grade as Sunny. Because obviously then no one would know we were from South Asia."

Maribeth let that sink in. Someone being six on 9/11.

"When I started college, I switched back to Sunita. That was when I was a freshman. I'm a senior now." She gave Todd a look.

"What can I say?" Todd said. "You've always been Sunny to me." He paused. "Except when you're PMSing."

"Oh, shut up," she said.

They pulled into the parking lot and exchanged cell phone numbers. (Maribeth had to look hers up; she had a hard time remembering anything lately.) They agreed to meet back at the car in a half hour.

133

The supermarket was the kind they had in Maribeth's childhood suburb, with generously wide aisles — she'd have had no trouble angling a double stroller through here — selling everything from imported cheese to paperback novels.

Once inside, Todd and Sunita skipped left toward the produce aisle. Maribeth went right toward the refrigerated section. She vaguely knew what she was going to get, the same things she always got; she was a healthy eater, but when she reached for her favorite brand of yogurt, she did something she'd never done before: she looked at the label.

Eight grams of fat. Twenty-five percent of her recommended daily allowance.

That seemed like a lot, but yogurt was a high-protein item. Maybe that was just how it was with yogurt, like avocados, high-fat and healthy. For comparison, she picked up another brand. It had zero grams of fat.

She looked at the label on her yogurt. Was it full-fat yogurt? Had she been eating *full-fat* yogurt all this time? She scanned the package for the words *full fat,* or *whole milk,* some kind of ominous cigarette-label warning that the contents might cause death. But she found nothing like that. The label only said it was French.

Jesus Christ. She was an educated woman. She'd worked at magazines that ran countless stories about fat. And she'd been eating yogurt with eight grams of it!

She put the yogurt back and looked for a replacement. There were dozens of varieties lined up in the cooler like Rockettes. Nonfat. Low-fat. Greek. Probiotic. Soy. Maybe she should become vegan. Wasn't that what Bill Clinton had done after his bypass surgery?

Skipping the yogurts, she moved the cart a few feet to the milk and butter section. Butter was out, obviously. But what about margarine? Wait. Didn't margarine give rats cancer? Which was better? Heart attack or cancer?

She looked at milk, which she hardly used, only in cereal and for coffee. She generally just pilfered the twins' whole milk or used half and half for coffee. Once again, she read the labels. Half and half: one tablespoon, two grams of fat. Whole milk, not much better. In the course of a day, she probably had four cups of coffee (already too much, she knew) and that was four tablespoons of half and half. Eight grams of fat. That plus a yogurt was half her daily allowance.

She careened her still-empty cart toward the safe haven of the bread and cereal aisle and grabbed some granola, another of her go-to foods. Then she checked that label. Twenty-five grams of sugar per serving. She compared it to Cocoa Krispies. They had *less* sugar. Than granola. Crunchy hippie hairy-armpit granola. And added sugars, she now knew, increased your risk of heart disease.

Vegetables! Vegetables were safe. Five servings a day, raw was better, juicing was cheating. She knew all this now. And kale! Kale was the wonder drug. And blueberries. Full of antioxidants. Why hadn't she been gorging on kale and blueberries every day instead of full-fat yogurt?

By the time Todd texted her *Ready?* her basket contained a sad constellation of kale, almonds, and coffee, and she was on the verge of a full-scale meltdown.

She felt so caught out. She'd thought she'd done everything right. She'd spent her entire life making lists, following through, keeping everything in check, all to make sure this kind of thing would never happen.

And look where it had gotten her. Just fucking look.

19

Maribeth had packed only three changes of clothing, and after a week in Pittsburgh, she realized this would not do if she was going to stay any longer. She went to the Family Dollar and bought underwear and socks and then to a thrift shop right down the block from her apartment for a few pairs of jeans, some sweaters, and a pair of boots because the forecast was already predicting snow. She didn't bother looking for gems among the junk, though once upon a time, she and Elizabeth had been championship thrifters, combing through consignment stores, digging out Prada and Versace at Banana Republic prices. Of course now, Elizabeth bought Prada at Prada prices and Maribeth bought Banana Republic at Banana Republic prices. Or at least she had before she'd started shopping at the Family Dollar.

When she was finished, she had a solid, if unglamorous, wardrobe, large enough to last her several months. A passive decision that seemed to belie her rationale for leaving. Because she was no longer feeling sick. She could now climb a flight of stairs without resting. She could shower without feeling lightheaded. She had begun to walk further afield, locating other important things in her neighborhood: a coffee shop, a greengrocer, a secondhand bookstore. And yet, she had just bought enough clothes to get her through the fall.

She had written two more letters to the twins, but when she went to the library, intending to transcribe and e-mail them to Jason to pass on, she had not been able to do it.

She thought of the only other time she'd been away, when her father had had his stroke. Every time she'd called home, the twins had cried. Jason had said they'd been fine until she rang, reminding them she wasn't there. Maybe writing them would only remind them she was away. Maybe it would only make it worse.

So instead of e-mailing them, she'd bought a yellow legal pad and continued writing letters as the woman on a business trip:

Dear Oscar and Liv,

It's supposed to snow tonight. Not much. Not enough to stick, but they say it'll be the first snow of the season.

She wondered if it would snow back in New York, as well, and if so, would anyone else know about their custom of going out to the fancy candy store for the six-dollar hot chocolates to commemorate the occasion?

She didn't ask this, though. It wasn't what the woman on a business trip would ask. Instead, after her weather report, she turned back to the memories of the twins, as she had in her earlier letters.

I don't know if you remember this but last January there was a huge blizzard. They canceled school and I stayed home from work. The streets were empty and so we were walking down the middle of Church Street, because there was no traffic. Liv, you were running ahead and jumping into the drifts, squealing with delight. Oscar, you were a little more cautious, and you kept calling: "Yiv, Yiv, wait up Oskie. Wait up Oskie!"

Liv, Oscar, wait up Mommy.

139

20

When Maribeth arrived for her second appointment with Dr. Grant, she found that the price had dropped.

"Seventy-five dollars," Louise said.

"I thought it was one-fifty," Maribeth said.

"For a preliminary. This is the follow-up."

"Is that like a special cash price?"

Louise made a noncommittal mmm, mmm sound, and Maribeth started to worry. Last month she'd edited a round-up of celeb-spa secrets in which more than a few of the pedicures had cost seventy-five dollars. What doctor charged so little? Maybe an internist at an inner-city clinic but who had ever heard of bargain-basement cardiology? There were no other patients in the waiting room this week, nor had there been any the last time.

You chose him, she reminded herself as Louise wrote out the receipt.

Louise ushered her into the examination

room. There was no gown. "Don't you want me to change?" Maribeth asked.

"No need," Louise said.

Maribeth had to wonder if they'd run out of money for gowns.

Dr. Grant came in almost immediately. On a few occasions, Maribeth had seen Dr. Sterling without his lab coat but he'd always seemed like a doctor: all bowtie and bromides. Even with his lab coat on, Dr. Grant did not, although there was nothing particularly unprofessional about his appearance, except perhaps for the jeans. And his handsomeness. Were doctors allowed to look like George Clooney if they weren't playing doctors on TV shows?

He listened to Maribeth's heart and lungs, hooked her up to the EKG monitor. He checked her vitals. "You've lost some weight, but otherwise, all looks good. Why don't you come back to my office to chat?"

She knew from experience that invitations to talk in doctors' private quarters were never a good sign. It was from his inner sanctum that Dr. Simon, their IVF doctor, had always relayed the bad news that the pregnancies had not taken. Though Maribeth had always known. She could tell by the scans.

"What's wrong?" she asked Dr. Grant.

"Nothing. I'll meet you in a second. Would you like some tea?"

"No." It came out gruff. She tried again. "No thank you."

Alone in his office, she took the opportunity to snoop. There were diplomas on the wall from Northwestern Medical School and one documenting a cardiac fellowship at the University of Pittsburgh. Which was reassuring. He hadn't gotten a degree from some Phoenix University type place.

On the bookshelf were several pink breast cancer ribbons, and on his desk a framed picture of a young, smiling, light-skinned African American woman in a canoe. His daughter? Or maybe his wife. Given his age and profession, she'd be wife number two. The trophy wife.

"Sorry to keep you waiting."

Maribeth turned around guiltily as Dr. Grant strode in holding a mug of tea in both hands, a gesture that was oddly monkish. "I get cranky if I don't have my four o'clock pick-me-up." He nodded to the two chairs opposite his desk. She sat in one, he the other.

"What's wrong?" Maribeth asked again.

He set his mug down on a coaster and, still smiling, asked, "Why do you seem like you're waiting for the other shoe to drop?"

Seriously? What was it about men and shoe metaphors?

"A heart attack at forty-four," she said. "An arterial puncture during a stent procedure. Double bypass. You'll excuse me if I've become watchful for falling footwear."

She waited for him to say the usual doctorly things. How it wasn't worth getting upset about, how stress only made it worse, how she'd been through the brunt of it. But instead, he just said, "Yes, I can see why you might be."

"Because I certainly wasn't watchful before. I didn't even know I was having a heart attack," she said. "I thought it was bad Chinese food."

He blew on his tea. Maribeth could smell the bergamot. Earl Grey. "That's not uncommon."

"Really? So everyone blames the Kung Pao chicken?"

"Sweet and sour pork gets a worse rap."

"If you eat sweet and sour pork, it's your own fault."

"Is that so?"

"Yes. Read the fine print. It's in the menu."

He laughed.

The ensuing rush felt not unlike finding a twenty-dollar bill in an old coat pocket. It

143

had been such a long time since she'd made someone laugh.

"If it makes you feel better," Dr. Grant went on, "women in particular often mistake heart attacks for intestinal gas."

"No sentence with the phrase 'intestinal gas' will ever make me feel better," she said.

He laughed again. And Maribeth remembered. She used to be funny. At work, she'd been known for her wit, at least until she started at *Frap* and one too many of her comments had landed with a thud. She recalled one staff meeting early on, discussing some vein-bulgingly thin actress who'd bragged in the cover story about her penchant for "eating like a pig," and Maribeth had remarked something about how this must be the mystical air-eating pig, cousin to the flying one. Elizabeth had offered a tight smile, but not her usual guffaw. The rest of the editors had looked horrified.

As Dr. Grant laughed, Maribeth did, too. It hurt, but only a little.

"How about this," Dr. Grant said. "Heart disease with an onset in the midforties and no other risk factors is most likely a result of familial hyperlipidemia. You probably inherited this. So cut the Kung Pao chicken a little slack."

It was just like one of her jokes at *Frap*.

Thud. It deadened the room.

"I only say that because if it's heredi-
tary . . ." He reached for her file, opened to
her family history. Registered that it was
blank. "Huh."

"I'm adopted," she said, trying so very
hard to make it sound casual. "So even if I
wanted to blame my mother, I can't."

"Or your father. Heart disease doesn't
discriminate."

"How progressive of it." She stopped.
"Progressive. Ha. Get it?"

This time, no one laughed.

"You know nothing of your biological
family?" he asked.

"No." There was a sour taste on her
tongue. How had they gotten here? From
quips about Chinese food to this?

"Have you thought to look?" He held up
his hands as if to fend off an attack. "I don't
mean to get personal but you're not the first
patient who has found themselves in such a
situation. A health crisis is often a catalyst
for seeking more information."

"I've had enough drama. I'm not interested in digging up any more."

"I'm sorry. It's not my business," he said.

"No," she said testily. "It's not."

It was a lie, of course.

145

Not the part about not wanting drama. But the part about not looking. The day before she had gone to the library and finally worked up the nerve to go online, not to check e-mail but to search Burgh-BirthParents.org, a site she had discovered when the twins were born. She had not gotten any further than the homepage, full of testimonials from adoptees and birth parents who had been reunited. But she suspected she would. Why else had she come here?

21

Maribeth had not seen much of her neighbors since the disastrous trip to the supermarket. When they'd all met up at the checkout line Todd had frowned at her sad basket of surrender goods. "You could've got *that* at the ShurSave."

At the Asian grocery store, she had elected to remain in the car. She did not want to risk another panic attack. It was only after Todd and Sunita had left her there that she realized how provincial — or worse, racist — she might seem. On the ride home, they spoke among themselves, while Maribeth sat silent in the backseat. She had not made a good first impression.

But then she received a text from Todd, saying he would have the car again Wednesday and did she want to go shopping.

Yes! she texted back. This time, she would be prepared. At the library, she had looked at a few cookbooks. She now knew what she should be eating. Fish. Lean meats. Tofu. Beans. Pasta. Eggs (whites only). Leafy greens and rich-colored berries. And nonfat yogurt.

They met at five. "You can sit up front. Sunny's at a movie with 'friends,' " Todd said, making air quotes.

As they drove, Todd was silent, drumming the steering wheel with his fingers.

"Everything okay?" Maribeth asked.

"Fine," he said. "She gave me a list but I told her we wouldn't go to the Asian store, not if she's going to flake. I'm not her errand boy." He snorted. "She thinks she's learning to cook but, oh, god, I'd rather eat dirt."

"I see," Maribeth said.

"The only thing she does worse than cooking is cleaning. You should see her room. It's a disaster." He made a hard right onto Liberty. "I'm only living with her as a favor to her parents."

"Really?" Maribeth said.

"Her dad got transferred to India last year and he wanted Sunny to live in the dorms but she refused. So I was the compromise. Her family's known me forever and I might be a guy but I'm gay so I'm safe. Now I'm stuck with her."

He said all this with such eye-rolling

nonchalance that Maribeth understood the source of the blustering. Every relationship, no matter how equitable-seeming, had someone who had more power, more charisma, more something. It was hard to be the beta.

"I had a friend like that once," Maribeth said.

"A slob?"

"Not a slob. Just, you know, someone I was really close to. We even lived together."

"Did it suck?"

They exchanged a look then, fleeting but telling. "No. It was pretty wonderful actually."

Todd seemed to deflate. He stopped pounding the steering wheel and slumped in his seat. Then in a different, quieter voice he said, "The truth is, the only thing I don't love about living with Sunny is knowing that one day I won't."

Maribeth touched him lightly on the shoulder.

"Though she really can't cook," he added.

22

Dear Oscar and Liv,

Today I saw a one-man band on the street. One person was playing the banjo, harmonica, and drums all at the same time. You'd think he would sound horrible, but he sounded amazing. I stayed outside to listen to him until I couldn't feel my toes anymore and then I put two five-dollar bills in his basket, one from each of you.

It made me think about you two and the songs you sometimes make up. Remember the one about the rats? It's my favorite. I think it went like this.

Some people like dogs
Some people like cats
Some people even like mice
But no one likes a rat.

Jason had recorded the song, calling it a

proto–human rights anthem, and Maribeth had it on her phone. She wished she had a copy of it now. Not only to hear their warbly little voices (even if Liv's was stridently off-key) but also because it seemed to offer a reassuring kind of proof. Oscar played his one chord on the guitar; Liv made up charming rhyming verses. The musicality from Jason. The wordsmithing from her.

She wondered if when the twins got older they would see it that way. If they'd look at her and Jason, or at each other, glimpsing where they'd come from, where they might be going, and see it as a comfort. Or as a curse.

23

"How much did you weigh before your heart attack?" Dr. Grant asked. It was Maribeth's third appointment in less than three weeks, only this one she'd scheduled in a panic after the pair of size-eight jeans that had fit when she'd bought them at the thrift shop a week ago fell off her hips. Sudden weight loss, she knew, was a bad sign.

"I don't know. One twenty-five. Ish."

"You're one fourteen now."

One fourteen. She had not weighed so little since she was a teenager. "Is something wrong? Should we do blood work?"

"Maybe. But first, tell me: what are you eating these days?"

She was eating what she was supposed to be eating. Whole grains. Leafy greens. Chicken breasts. Low-fat. Low-sodium. Low-taste.

Even though on her trip to the grocery store with Todd she had practically had a lust attack in front of the butcher case, simultaneously remembering the taste of every steak she had ever eaten: the flank steaks her dad charred to a crisp on the grill, the *côte de boeuf* she and Elizabeth had shared in a Paris bistro, the porterhouse she'd cooked for Jason after they'd got back together.

And then she'd lost it, again, in front of the freezer case this time. She could taste, so clearly, the Neapolitan ice-cream sandwiches she used to eat for dessert every night as a kid. Starting with hard, frozen strawberry, moving on to the softening vanilla in the middle. By the time she got to the chocolate, the ice cream and the cookie crust were both squishy and delicious. "You're so lucky your metabolism lets you eat anything you want," her mother would say, sitting there, drinking her Sanka while she watched Maribeth eat ice cream.

"Oatmeal and blueberries for breakfast," she told Dr. Grant. "Kale salad for lunch. Chicken breast for dinner." Just reciting the menu killed her appetite. No wonder she was losing weight. "I'm being very vigilant."

"Vigilant?"

"To make sure I don't eat the wrong thing again."

"Diet sometimes plays a significant role,

particularly if you're overweight or you eat at McDonald's all the time. But as we discussed, given your age and your weight and your diet and other risk factors, I would hazard it's the hyperlipidemia, your body's inability to metabolize the cholesterol. You didn't do anything wrong. So you can take yourself off the hook."

"Great. I'm off the hook." She mimed removing herself from a hook, slouching down in her chair. "I'm so relieved."

"I don't know if you're a worse mime or liar."

"Hey, I'm offended," Maribeth said. "I'm an excellent mime." She mimed a wall in front of her.

He laughed. Then he looked at his watch. He was the kind of man who still wore one.

"Do you have an hour?" he said.

"All I have is hours."

"Good. Come with me."

They drove to a gourmet ice cream shop in Shadyside. He ordered her to sit down while he went to the counter. He came back with two sundaes, two spoons in each.

"Taste test," he said.

"What is it?" she asked suspiciously.

"That's vanilla with figs and balsamic," he said, pointing to one. "And that's mint chip with hot fudge and whipped cream. One yuppie, one classic. Okay?"

"You're the doctor," she said.

She stared at the ice cream.

"It won't kill you," he said.

She picked up a spoon. "You're sure about that?"

"Yes."

She dipped her spoon in the fig-balsamic sundae. "Is this part of my official treatment?"

"Yes."

"Does insurance cover it?"

"You don't have insurance. You pay cash," he replied. "Though I doubt you paid cash for that." He gestured to her chest. "I'm beginning to wonder if you're an escaped prisoner from Cambridge Springs."

"How about you don't ask me about my insurance, and I don't ask why you have all this free time to take patients for ice cream."

Something came over his face. Not anger, or resentment, or even embarrassment, but something else. It was like a veil being lowered. "I'm sorry," she said.

"Don't be," he replied. He held out his hand. "It's a deal. Now take your medicine."

They shook hands. She took a tentative bite. It *was* pretty good.

"Look," he said. "You're not dead."

"Give it a few minutes," she said.

"Give it enough minutes and we're all dead."

"Anyone ever tell you that you have an excellent bedside manner?"

"Here, try the other one." He slid the mint-chip sundae toward her. She took a bite. Also delicious.

"That one," he said, pointing to the yuppie, "is made with vegan ice cream. No saturated fat. The other one." Here he popped a bite of mint chip into his mouth. "Is your classic ice cream. Both are delicious. In moderation, both are fine."

"Except this one is full of cholesterol!" she said, pointing to the mint chip, picturing the ice cream slipping down her esophagus and detouring straight to her arteries. She pushed the sundae away. "I'll never be able to just eat ice cream again like a normal person, will I?"

"Maybe. Consider it a worthy goal." He pushed the mint-chip sundae back toward her.

She took a small bite. She tried not to think about occluded arteries, which meant she thought even more about occluded arteries. Maybe she could take a double dose of her statin tonight.

"You know what I can't help wondering?"

she asked.

"What's that?"

"What would've happened if I hadn't already been going to the doctor that day? Would I have just carried on blithely eating ice cream and then had another heart attack and dropped dead?"

He shrugged. "Not necessarily. Your chest pain might've resolved and you wouldn't have had another incident. Your chest pain would've worsened and you would've eventually gone to the ER. Or the chest pain would've worsened or not worsened and you would have a potentially serious repeat event and, as you say, dropped dead."

"There's that excellent bedside manner again."

"You don't strike me as someone who wants to be coddled."

"That's where you're wrong. I *do* want to be coddled," she said. "Just not lied to."

"Sometimes those are mutually exclusive."

She nodded. "My dad, my adoptive dad, had no idea he had any arterial disease, and then one day he had a stroke and went into a coma, and two weeks later he died. I don't know which is better, to have it hanging over you or to be blissfully unaware until the day you die."

She expected him to say that it was better

to know. It was his bread and butter, after all, letting people know, fixing things if they went wrong. But instead he said this: "I imagine it's like most things in life. You sacrifice something for the knowledge, be it peace of mind, a sense of your invincibility, or something less quantifiable."

"The truth will set you free but first it will make you miserable," she said, reciting the one inspirational poster from high school that she could remember.

"Exactly."

24

The next day, at the library, Maribeth logged on to BurghBirthParents.org and clicked on the Find Your Birth Parent tab. There was a questionnaire, basic information, name, date of birth, religion, adoptive parents' names, contact details.

As she filled in the form, it felt like filling in any online form, to register the twins for a class, or to buy diapers in bulk.

When the contact information boxes appeared, she input her new cell phone number but hesitated before listing her old e-mail address. She had not logged on to that account since she had left. Now, she imagined the pages of messages awaiting her — howlers from Jason, carefully crafted notes of concern from Elizabeth, sanctimony disguised as caring from the parents in the twins group, not to mention the usual clutter from BrightStart and the various groups and e-mail lists she subscribed to —

and shuddered. She could not go back to that. She left that part of the form blank.

She paused for a moment, her finger hovering over the submit button.

"You really don't want to find her?" Jason had asked her in college, when his own parents were divorcing. He asked it again after one of his good friends flew to South Korea to reunite with his birth siblings. He asked it yet again after the twins were born. "You really don't want to find out about your family?"

"You're my family," had been her standard reply.

She wondered if that was true anymore.

She clicked submit.

25

Maribeth knocked on her neighbors' door, feeling nervous. She had debated texting the invitation but that felt too informal. Which was ridiculous. She was not inviting them to a Yule Ball. Just to dinner.

She'd discovered a fishmonger near the library and had thought to make a paella. But the expense of all that shellfish, not to mention all that work, seemed too much for one person. And besides, the ice cream outing with Dr. Grant had been cheering. Not just the food, but the conversation. She needed to be more social, and Todd and Sunita were her only options.

She was relieved when Sunita answered the door. Even after her and Todd's moment of understanding during the last shopping trip, he intimidated her. So Maribeth was a little surprised when Sunita responded to the invitation with a shake of her head so vigorous it snapped her ponytail.

"Oh no," Sunita said. "We can't. We absolutely can't."

Maribeth felt her face grow warm. What was she thinking? Todd and Sunita were in their early twenties; she was in her midforties. She'd mistaken their overtures of friendliness for friendship, when in fact she was just an old lady they were helping to cross the street.

"Oh, okay, never mind then," Maribeth said, backing away.

"It's just tomorrow's Monday," Sunita said. When that didn't register, she added. "Monday Night Football. We play the Titans."

"Oh, football, right," Maribeth said. She was vaguely aware of such things. Jason was a haphazard sports fan at best, but her father-in-law went completely bonkers over one of the teams. The Giants? Or maybe it was the Jets.

"We're going to crush them," Sunita added.

"Oh." Maribeth didn't know what to say. "Well, good luck with the crushing."

"Wait. What are you making?" Sunita asked. "No one's cooked me dinner in a while."

"I was thinking about paella."

"Todd's allergic to scallops," Sunita said.

"No scallops in this recipe."

"Maybe you could bring it over here. If you don't mind watching the game with us."

"Really?"

"Kickoff is at seven-thirty but come earlier so we can hang out."

Hang out. "Okay."

"Be warned, Todd can be a tyrant about talking about anything but football while the ball is in play." She rolled her eyes as if to say: *Men.*

Maribeth smiled. "I'll see you at seven."

The recipe was pleasantly complicated, lots of debearding and deveining, chopping and slicing. She went about it methodically yet leisurely, a glass of red wine at her side. (One thing Dr. Grant had insisted she could feel good about.) She even bought fish heads to make her own stock.

As a briny smell filled the apartment, Maribeth tried to recall the last time being in a kitchen felt like a luxury rather than a chore. She didn't have to worry about a meal that had to be cooked, served, and cleaned in that tiny window between coming home from work and exhaustion-related meltdown (usually the kids' but not always). She didn't have to worry if Liv was or was not eating tomato sauce or rice or broccoli that week. She didn't have to worry if seeing the shrimps with heads on in the kitchen would traumatize Oscar. She didn't have to perform a cost-benefit analysis of a multipot meal: tastiness of food versus time spent cleaning up.

Even cleaning the kitchen felt gratifying. A cutting board was dirty. It was washed. Now it was clean. The simple satisfaction of it. It made her happy in a very basic way, much like editing once had.

At seven, she brought the steaming platter next door. Sunita answered, wearing an oversized Steelers jersey, her eyes blackened with those marks football players wore for reasons that mystified Maribeth. Todd appeared behind her. He was dressed exactly the same. Maribeth had seen Sunita in sports jerseys but Todd had always been dressed on the preppy side.

"It's for luck," Todd explained, picking up her look. "Otherwise the Steelers lose."

"It's true," Sunita said. "We lost the Super Bowl in 2011 because Todd was trying to impress a guy and wore J.Crew."

"Youth," Todd said, shaking his head.

"Here, this is heavy," Maribeth said, nodding toward the platter.

"Oh, right. Put it down on the table," Todd said.

"It's hot. Do you have a trivet?"

"Grab a catalog or something, Sunny," Todd said.

Sunita snatched a magazine from the pile of mail. It was a recent issue of *Frap*.

"I haven't read that yet," Todd said.

"You're not missing much," Maribeth joked.

"You read *Frap*?" Todd arched his eyebrows and Maribeth suspected she had just scored another point with him.

"I've been known to."

"See?" he said to Sunita. To Maribeth he said, "Sunny gives me no end of shit, even though the girl has never met a BuzzFeed Harry Potter quiz she didn't take."

"You cannot compare HP and your silly magazines."

"Oh, give it up. It's two against one. And M.B. reads it and she's smart. She's probably a visiting professor or something."

She glanced at the issue of *Frap,* the cover growing soggy from paella steam. "A consultant."

"A *consultant* reads it," Todd said. "So no giving me shit."

"But then what would I live for?" Sunita said. "M.B., do you want the grand tour before the pregame?"

"Sure."

"I already warned her what a slob you are," Todd said, and he exchanged a conspiratorial look with Maribeth.

The apartment was a lot like hers, the same aging appliances in the kitchen, the same dirty carpeting in the living room, the same generic oak-veneer dining table. Yet it looked completely different, perhaps because it looked lived in. There were chili-pepper lights strung along the windowsill, a bookshelf teetering with paperbacks and school texts. There was what looked like a shrine to the Steelers: a framed front-page newspaper article trumpeting a Super Bowl win, a few bobble-head toys, a placard that read, I BLEED BLACK AND GOLD. There was a smattering of framed photos of the two of them, younger, softer-faced, and endearingly awkward.

Sunita's bedroom was, as Todd had warned, a mess: a jumble of throw pillows and brightly colored wall mosaics, a pile of clothes spilling out of the closet.

Todd's bedroom by comparison was spartan: a bed that would pass a military inspection, a framed poster of the periodic table of the elements done up to look like a Warhol, and an enormous bulletin board full of movie ticket stubs that had been artfully arranged to look like a flower. Maribeth went to inspect.

"We see a lot of movies," Todd said. "I figured if I was going to spend all that money, I might as well have something to show for it."

"Do you like movies?" Sunita asked.

"I do, but I don't go often enough." When she'd taken the job at *Frap* she thought she would use at least a couple of the Fridays to sneak away to an early matinee. But she hadn't. Not once. She glanced at the stubs, which were mostly from recent films, none of which she'd seen: *Skyfall. Pitch Perfect. American Hustle. Identity Thief. The Hunger Games. Ted. Harold and Maude.*

"Harold and Maude?" she said in surprise.

"I know," Sunita said. "He dragged me to that at the Row House. It's really weird. Have you seen it?"

Not since college. Not since the first night with Jason.

After Maribeth had taken Courtney up on that dare to profile Jason for the college newspaper, she'd gone to the radio station office, prepared to spend exactly one hour with some ugly music snob.

But after talking to him, she found a reason to continue the interview the following day. And then he insisted that she sit in on one of his shows, to get the full experience, he said.

It turned out that everything Maribeth had expected about Jinx had been wrong. Sure, when she first admitted she didn't like Nirvana, he'd ribbed her a little — "Who raised you?" — but it was all good natured. She could tell straightaway that he didn't judge what people liked so long as they liked something. His whole thing was that he loved music. Deejaying wasn't a way to be cool, or discerning, but his way of expressing the love.

And he wasn't ugly. Not in the least. When she'd first seen him at the radio station office, she'd thought he was cute: that mop of hair, the hazel eyes, those plummy lips. When he got excited about some track he was playing her — because when she didn't recognize a band he was referencing, he would drag her into an empty studio to educate her — he'd close his eyes and bite his lips, and Maribeth would lick hers as if in response. By the third day of the interview, after she'd watched him spin records for his show, she had upgraded her assessment from cute to beautiful, and she had chapped her own lips from licking them so frequently.

Normally writing was agonizing for Maribeth — it was why she preferred editing —

but she wrote the article about Jason in a frenzy of inspiration and filed it immediately. When she saw it in print the next day, she understood what she'd written. Not a profile, but a mash note, circulation 11,500.

"On an average day, Jason Brinkley flits around campus anonymously, a sort of Clark Kent in jeans and a T-shirt. But when he gets in the booth, in this case the radio broadcast booth at WLXR, he transforms into Jinx, a musical Superman," she read out loud to Courtney from their dorm room. She skimmed further down, unable to stomach the thing. Then she got to the kicker. "In an era of practiced cynicism, when everyone pretends to be too cool to care, Brinkley is that rare exception, someone who truly cares and is all the cooler for it." She threw down the paper. "Why'd you make me do this? I hate you. No, I hate me." She put her head in her hands. "Kill me now. Please."

"It's kind of sweet," Courtney said. "Sensible Maribeth, crushing so publicly."

Maribeth crumpled the newspaper and threw it into the bin. "I'm staying home today. I can't risk running into him."

She was still hiding out in the dorm that night when Courtney persuaded her to come to the movies. "A late showing of

Harold and Maude. Who will be there?"

Almost no one, it turned out. Except for Jason Brinkley, sitting by himself, holding a bag of popcorn and a box of Jujubes. It wasn't a setup — Courtney had never met Jason — but Maribeth felt a tickle in her stomach, heralding some kind of fate at work, though she was too tongue-tied to say a word to him during the movie or on the walk back to campus. Instead, she just listened to him and Courtney rave about the film's soundtrack.

They lingered outside her dorm. Courtney gave them a look and went on ahead. "I have a kind of writing question for you," Jason said to Maribeth.

"Okay," she said cautiously.

"I like to title my mixed tapes. It's an important part of the process. I'm working on one I was thinking of calling 'Too Cool to Care,' but I didn't know if the inherent contradiction was clear enough, or if it was overkill." He shot her a mischievous grin that in the coming years would become more familiar to her than her own smile. Maribeth understood then who the tape was for, and that if a gushing article was a reporter's declaration of love, then a mixed tape was the deejay's equivalent.

"It's nicely ambiguous," Maribeth told him.

"One more question," he said, still grinning. "If I'm Superman, does that make you Lois Lane?"

Her whole body flushed with pleasure. It was so rare in life for things to play out exactly how you fantasized. "Only if you shut up and kiss me," she said.

"I've seen *Harold and Maude*," she told Sunita and Todd. "But it was a million years ago."

The pregame started. Sunita brought out a tray of deviled eggs, the whites an unappetizing gray. "Steelers eggs," she explained. "You have to eat at least two or we lose."

Maribeth must have shown her panic because Todd laughed. "I think that's only true if you're a Steelers fan."

"So I take it you're both big fans."

"Since birth," Todd said, tapping his chest.

"Me too," Sunita said. "When my dad moved here, he said becoming a Steelers fan made him feel more American than getting his citizenship." She shook her head. "When he heard he was being transferred back to India, his first concern was what would happen to me. His second was, how would he watch the games?"

"Thank god for satellite," Todd said.

"I know, right?" Sunita said. "Sometimes he phones if he disagrees with a ref's call."

"Some things never change," Todd said. To Maribeth he explained: "If you're from Pittsburgh, Steelers love is in your blood. Whether you're a Yinzer or a transplant from India or gayer than a bag of rainbow dicks."

Maribeth almost said something. That she *was* from here.

The TV chimed. "Ohh. It's almost kick-off," Sunita said.

"Did you tell her the rules?" Todd asked.

Sunita nodded. "No extracurricular talking when the ball's in play."

"Got it," Maribeth said.

They filled their plates with paella and sat down to watch. During commercials, they explained the ins and outs of the play and went on at length about the starting quarterback, with whom they were both enamored. "When he retires, we're dead," Todd said.

"Please," Sunita said, smacking him with a throw pillow. "It's called *team* for a reason. And people used to say that about Terry Bradshaw."

"Right, and when he retired, look what happened?" Todd replied. "Let's just hope that 2014 is our year."

It became a pleasant blur. The food, the wine, the bickering, the drone of the commentators, the constant replays. By halftime, Maribeth was feeling warm and drowsy, and during the last quarter of the game, she drifted into a gooey sleep. Maybe it was the reminder of *Harold and Maude* but when Todd gently shook her awake, for a brief moment she thought she was back home, on the couch, and it was Jason who was rousing her, ready to lead her back to bed.

26

Maribeth was walking to the secondhand bookstore on Liberty to buy a new book, something she'd been doing so regularly that the bookseller had taken to buying her old books back from her, essentially becoming her personal library. Which was handy because the actual library would not issue a card without a local ID, which she did not have and could not get without blowing her anonymity.

That morning, she'd finished a thriller that had come out the year before — she remembered seeing it everywhere on the subway — and, today, if it was still there, she would trade it in for that buzzy British novel she'd meant to read but hadn't, even though she'd been sent multiple copies by the publisher. Back in New York, the only time she had to read was before bed. (Her subway commute was always spent scrambling to read all the work e-mails she'd missed.) Once she got into bed, however, no matter how good the book, after two or three pages, her eyelids would grow heavy, and the next thing she knew, it would be morning — or the middle of the night if one of the twins was having a nightmare — and her book would be back on the night-stand, a bookmark in its pages, put there by Jason, presumably, to keep track of her glacial progression.

But here she was racing through books, reading with a voraciousness she hadn't known in years. Some days, she sat in a café for hours on end reading. Other days, she went to the Lawrenceville library, took a book from the stacks, and sat in the rotunda by the windows, flipping the pages as the afternoon light waned.

She'd just turned onto Liberty when the phone rang. It rang a few times before Maribeth realized it was hers. Though she'd had the phone for nearly three weeks, it had never rung before. Only Todd and Sunita had her number, and they always texted. Dr. Grant's office had it, too, but no one there ever called to confirm appointments.

"Hello?" she said.

"I'm looking for Maribeth Klein."

It was such a familiar request, it took a moment for the wrongness of it to sink in.

No one who had this number should be asking for that person.

"Is this Maribeth Klein?" the voice repeated. It was older. Female.

"Who is this?" Why was a woman calling? Was she a private investigator? Had Jason hired a PI to track her down? Would Jason do such a thing?

"Oh, sorry. It's Janice Pickering from BurghBirthParents.org."

Maribeth exhaled, unsure if she was relieved, disappointed, or both.

"I'm calling about your online form. Is this a good time?"

"Hold on." It was noisy on the avenue. Maribeth ducked into a pharmacy.

"Right. Sorry. Hi. Did you find anything?"

Janice Pickering laughed. "Oh no. We're not there yet. But I can help you if you want to search for your birth parents. I'm very familiar with the process."

"Can you tell me how it works?" she asked.

"It's somewhat involved to get into over the phone."

"Okay. Should I come into your office?"

A pharmacist in a white coat asked if Maribeth needed help, then saw she was on the phone, and gave her a scolding look. *Sorry,* Maribeth mouthed.

"It's better if we just meet at your house or a café," Janice was saying.

"Café," Maribeth said.

"I'm free this afternoon. Are you closer to Mount Lebanon or Squirrel Hill?"

Maribeth had no idea where Mount Lebanon was. Squirrel Hill was nearby, she thought. "I live in Bloomfield. I don't have a car, but I can figure it out by bus."

"Oh, if you don't have a car, I can come to you. You're in Bloomfield, you say?"

"Why don't we meet in Lawrenceville," Maribeth suggested. She didn't know why but she wanted a buffer. She named a coffee shop near the library and they agreed to meet at five.

She hung up and apologized to the pharmacist. It was actually a good thing she'd stopped in here. She had a three-month supply of her statin and her beta blocker, but she might need a place for Dr. Grant to call in refills for the semifictitious M. B. Goldman. She wondered vaguely if ordering prescription drugs under a false name was a crime. Also, she seemed to have developed a rash on her neck. She showed the pharmacist, who said it looked like eczema and gave her a tube of cortisone cream.

■ ■ ■ ■

Janice Pickering was twenty minutes late to their meeting, spilling folders and apologies all over the place. "I had to run home for my files and then there was an accident in the tunnel. In opposing traffic but, you know, rubberneckers."

"Don't worry about it," Maribeth said, putting away her new novel. She'd already read half of it. "I feel bad I made you schlep."

"Oh, I'm used to it. We bought the house in Mount Lebanon because of the schools, but I wound up working in Squirrel Hill, so I'm always back and forth."

"Mount Lebanon? Where is that?"

"A suburb across the river. Quick as can be when there's no traffic."

"I see. Well, can I get you a coffee? A scone?"

"Oh, it's after four. I won't sleep if I drink coffee now."

"Tea maybe."

"Mmmm, what about one of those caramel lattes, if I get it decaf? Do you think I should?"

"Why not?"

"Oh, go on then."

Maribeth got in line for the drinks. When she returned to the table, Janice had her folders neatly fanned out. Maribeth handed her the cup, from which she took a loud slurp, sounding not unlike the twins snarfling down their first-snow hot chocolates.

"Oh, my, that is decadent. You're sure it's decaf?"

"Says so on the cup."

They drank their drinks and made their small talk. Janice asked Maribeth where she was from. "New York," she answered. It didn't seem worth the trouble of lying when so much of what they were going to do together — were they going to do this together? — required personal details. Besides, Janice, with her dove-gray hair falling out of its bun, did not seem like an undercover PI. And it was ridiculous to think Jason would've hired one in the first place.

"Children?" Janice asked.

"Yes, two. And you?"

"Grown now."

"And where do you work?"

"At a school for special-needs children. Not so far from here. I'm a social worker."

Maribeth smiled and nodded. "So," she began. "This is your second job?" School social workers must make terrible money.

Janice laughed. She had the tiniest foam mustache on her top lip. "Oh, this isn't a job. It's a hobby. Or maybe a calling."

"Oh, so BurghBirthParents.org is what, exactly?"

Janice set down her cup. "I suppose it's me."

"Oh." Maribeth felt let down. She'd psyched herself up for this, and now she was having a tea party with someone's grandma.

"Tell me, did you come to Pittsburgh to look for your birth mother?"

"I'm not really sure," Maribeth said.

"I understand. It's a big step to take after spending so much of your life thinking about it."

"I haven't spent so much of my life thinking about it," Maribeth said.

Janice frowned, as if she didn't appreciate the tone. Or maybe she didn't believe this. No one did. Not Jason. Not even her parents. When Maribeth was in elementary school, the Broadway musical *Annie* had been all the rage. Some of her friends had gone with their parents into the city to see it and returned singing "Tomorrow" on a loop, as if they were constantly auditioning for the play. Maribeth learned all the songs secondhand and asked, later begged, her parents to take her to see it. But they never did.

In fifth grade, a friend offered Maribeth an extra ticket to go with her family, but Maribeth's mother refused to let her go. There was a huge row. Maribeth couldn't understand. Some kids hadn't been allowed to see *Grease,* because it was racy, but her mother had been okay with that. What was wrong with *Annie*?

Finally, her father explained it: "*Annie* is about an orphan trying to find her parents."

"So?" Maribeth asked.

"Your mother is worried it'll put ideas in your head."

Maribeth had known she was adopted for a few years by then, but until that moment, the idea of another set of parents hadn't entered the picture. "I don't care about them," Maribeth had told her father, in one final futile attempt to see the play.

"Can you explain how the process works," Maribeth asked Janice. "I read the laws have changed."

"They have and they now favor the adopted child's right to know her background. That doesn't mean your birth parent will want contact, or even be alive, I'm afraid, but we can almost always find the trail, find out where you came from."

Almost always. Pretty definitive. "How do we start?"

"Do you know what agency you were adopted from?"

"No."

"Do you have any memories of going to picnics or parties? A lot of the adoption agencies had those each year."

"We moved to New York when I was little, once my dad finished dental school here. All I know is that I was born in Pittsburgh."

Janice flipped through a file. "This says that you're Jewish."

Maribeth stiffened. She'd almost left that part blank, wondering if someone was going to challenge her Jewishness, as had Brian Baltzer, a lawyer she'd once dated. After they'd been seeing each other for about a month, he informed her that if they ever got married, Maribeth would have to convert, because though she'd grown up going to Hebrew school and had a bat mitzvah, she couldn't be sure she was Jewish "by blood." They broke up shortly after that.

"I don't see what that has to do with it," Maribeth said.

"It narrows it down," Janice replied. "It might mean that your birth mother was Jewish, and if that's the case your adoption most likely went through the one Jewish

182

adoption agency in town."

"Oh."

"But. I'm getting ahead of myself. If you were adopted through any of the currently operating agencies, Jewish or otherwise, it's much more straightforward. They have all their back files. We ask them to do a search. If there's a match, they can reach out to the birth family on your behalf."

"That sounds easy."

Janice smiled indulgently. "It's more straightforward. Nothing about this process is easy."

"What if it wasn't through any of those agencies, the ones that are still around?"

"That's a good possibility. Many adoption agencies have shut down. Or your adoption may have been facilitated through a private doctor or lawyer, so we might want to petition a separate search through the Orphans' Court."

"The Orphans' Court?"

"Yes. This drink really is delicious. What was it called?"

"Caramel mocha."

"Decaf?"

"Yes, decaf," Maribeth replied. "It's really called the Orphans' Court?"

"Yes," Janice said.

They were silent for a while, Maribeth

thinking, Janice noisily savoring her drink.

"Okay, so about this search? What does that entail?"

"You submit a request in writing to the court. A judge reviews it and issues an order and a search is initiated. An authorized search representative goes through the records, attempting to find a match. I'm an authorized search agent so you can designate me as your representative."

"Okay. Let's do that."

"Let's put a pin in that search. Your adoptive family being Jewish might really shrink the pool."

Last summer, she and the twins had hunted fireflies in Battery Park. When Oscar had caught one by the wing, he looked terrified, like he didn't know what he'd done. It was precisely how Maribeth felt now.

"What happens? If we find her?" she asked.

"Contact is made. A kind of general letter, followed up, if she's willing, by a letter from you. And then you and she take it from there."

"What if she's dead?"

"There's always next of kin."

"And what if she doesn't want anything to do with me?"

Janice took a few deep breaths, as if Maribeth's negativity was off-putting. "That also could happen," she admitted. "And so you put it out there and have faith. Just because you've been dreaming of this for a long time doesn't mean it's mutual."

"I already told you. I *haven't* been dreaming of her," Maribeth said.

Janice frowned, her tiny milk mustache sloping downward.

"I only mean, it's been a sudden decision, precipitated by health issues. I'm really just looking for a genetic history, that kind of thing."

"But why then did you come all this way to find her? You could've done that from New York."

Maribeth sighed. "That part is complicated."

Janice smiled kindly. "It usually is."

It was after six by the time she and Janice finished, but the night was mild so Maribeth decided to walk back to her apartment. Her birth mother had always been a shadowy, abstract figure. Maybe she was out there, maybe she wasn't, but there was no way of knowing so why bother obsessing about it. It was not unlike how Maribeth felt about God. She supposed this made her a birth-mother agnostic.

But now, there might be actual proof of her existence. How old would she be? Sixty-five? Seventy? Did she think about Maribeth? Did she wonder if they had the same eyes? (Maribeth's were gray.) Or hair? (Maribeth's was brown and curly and starting to gray at the temples.) Did her knee do that clicking thing when she first woke up in the morning? Did she have a funny laugh? Did anyone ever call it a "sexy seal bark"? which was how Jason used to describe hers. Did she have a Jason? Had she been married? Divorced? Did she have other children?

And what of Maribeth? Why had she given her up? What would make a mother do that?

You might ask yourself the same thing, she thought.

27

She continued writing letters to the twins, the stack of pages on her nightstand growing. One afternoon, she stopped into a stationery store in Shadyside and dropped forty dollars on a package of Crane's paper and another twenty dollars on a fountain pen. It was her most decadent purchase since she'd left home.

She couldn't remember the last time she'd written letters on paper like this. Her wedding thank you cards? When the twins were born, she'd e-mailed thank yous for the gifts. Not very classy but she was lucky to manage even that. These days, thank you notes tended to fall to the bottom of the pile, except for those to Jason's mother, who got offended if her gifts were not properly, and promptly, acknowledged.

It felt good to write on paper that smelled like old libraries. The pen scratched noisily across the page as it filled up with words. It seemed to imbue her letters with more substance.

Dear Oscar and Liv,
There are lots of museums where I am. Last week I started exploring some of them. First I went to an art museum, and then yesterday I visited a natural history one. It had so many dinosaur fossils, but no blue whale. Do you remember when we saw the blue whale at the Dinosaur Museum? Do you remember what you said, Liv?

The Dinosaur Museum was what they called the Museum of Natural History, because when they visited, it was mostly to see the giant dinosaur skeletons. But on this particular day — which had been that rarest of birds, a Sunday free of birthday parties and playdates and classes — the four of them had explored further afield, looking at the moon rocks and then the Hall of Ocean Life, where the enormous blue whale hung from the ceiling.

We were all lying down, which you two thought was crazy, and we were looking up at the whale. And Liv, you said, "At school, we learned the blue whale has a

heart so big you can walk through it."
And Oscar, you said, "I want to walk
through someone's heart." And I
squeezed your hands and said, "You
already walk through mine."

They still did. Though she didn't write
that. A woman on a business trip would
have no cause for such sentimentality, no
need to prove the capacity of her flawed
heart.

28

A week after what she'd come to think of as the ice cream intervention, she had another follow-up with Dr. Grant to check her weight. She'd gained two pounds, which seemed to please Dr. Grant, and had gone grocery shopping with Todd and Sunita without any drama, which had pleased her.

As they were finishing up the exam, she asked Dr. Grant about her neck. "I thought it was eczema. I've been using this cream but it hasn't helped," she said. "I've changed soaps, shampoo. I looked online and now I'm worried it's a vitamin deficiency." Talking about it made not just her neck itch but her entire body. "I was thinking you could refer me to someone who wouldn't be averse to my, um, insurance situation."

"Hmm. I might know an understanding dermatologist, but why don't I take a look first." He patted the stool. "Have a seat."

She sat down and leaned over. He parted

her hair, and for a second the itchiness was replaced by the warmth of being touched by another human.

"So the good news is that it's not a vitamin deficiency," he said.

"And the bad news?"

"You appear to have lice." He paused. "A rather robust case of it, I might add."

She dropped her head into her hands. "I used an entire bottle of that RID shampoo." She scratched her head again. "That stuff is literally poison."

"But it only kills the live bugs, not the eggs. You have to pick those out." He scratched his temple as if the talk were making him itchy, too.

"Oh, yes, I'm familiar with the process." She tried to imagine combing herself out as she'd done the twins. She remembered that horrific day back home. Niff passing judgment. Walking through the rain. Liv shoving her. Her hitting Liv.

She started to cry.

"It's not that bad," he said. "Lice don't discriminate. It doesn't mean you're dirty."

"It's not that . . ."

"What is it then?"

"I just feel as if it will never end."

She kind of detested herself. Whatever self-pity points she'd earned had already been spent. And then some. "I'm sorry." She stood up and wiped her eyes, prepared to leave, even though her favorite part of the appointments was fast becoming the talk after the exam in his office. "I have to go find one of those combs." She imagined getting it through her rope of shoulder-length hair. "Shit."

"I have a better idea," he said. "Let's go upstairs and I'll get them out for you."

"You?"

"Yes, me."

"Do they teach nitpicking in medical school?"

"No. But I have a daughter and she had them a few times."

"But you need a special comb?"

"Says who?"

Niff Spenser.

"You just need a good pair of eyes and a fair amount of patience," he said, "and while my eyes aren't what they used to be, my patience is improving with age."

She looked at him. He was serious.

"I don't think I can let you do this. It's too . . ." Intimate, she wanted to say. "Icky."

"I'm familiar with icky. I am, after all, a doctor. And a father."

This made her smile.

And when, in a softer voice, he added,

"It's okay to ask for help, you know," it made her relent.

He told Louise he was done for the day. There were no other patients in the waiting room and, obviously, none coming. Maribeth wondered, not for the first time, if she was his only patient. Outside, she headed down the walk, toward his car, but he went in the opposite direction, up the pathway toward the front porch of the house.

"You live here?" Maribeth asked.

"Yes."

"Oh."

He opened the door, sweeping Maribeth inside with an after-you gesture. She walked into a grand foyer; the light streaming through the stained glass transom colored the dust eddies blue and gold. To the right was a mahogany staircase, to the left a parlor with built-in bookcases and a fireplace with a neat stack of logs next to it.

"Come on through," he said.

Come on *through*. Her friends back home might say "come on in" but no one said "come on through" because few abodes were large or deep enough to warrant a "through." Except perhaps for Elizabeth and Tom's townhouse, but she had not been there since the Christmas party last year when she was ushered in by a coat checker.

She followed him down a long, narrow hallway, the walls covered with framed photographs, through a dining room, the table piled high with mail and medical journals, and into a bright, open kitchen with top-of-the-line stainless steel appliances and fire-engine red laminate cabinets. It looked like a showroom, pristine, as if the kitchen had never been sullied by the messy act of cooking.

He slid open a pocket door on the far side of the kitchen. Inside was a powder room. "We'll do the deed here," he said.

Maribeth raised an eyebrow.

"The lice," he said, coloring slightly. "Let me fetch some tools."

He returned, carrying a magnifying headlamp, a towel, a fine-tooth comb, and a bottle of olive oil.

"Are you going to lecture me about the benefits of a Mediterranean diet?" she joked.

"Yes." He handed her a towel. "It's best when applied directly to the hair."

"You're going to put that on my head?"

"We'll leave it for an hour. The oil smothers the bugs." She remembered the Wilsons' babysitter Joanne putting coconut oil on the twins. Perhaps it wasn't cheating after all. "Then I'll pick the nits out."

"How did you become such an expert?"

"Well, that's somewhat involved. My daughter, Mallory, hated to get her hair braided. She said it hurt. She wanted to wear her hair down. But her mother, Felicity, insisted she wear it in braids," he said as he massaged the oil into Maribeth's hair.

Maribeth was only half-listening now. His touch was having a strange effect on her, at once soothing and exhilarating. Though he had laid hands on her before — he was her doctor, after all — this felt different somehow.

"Mal had these beautiful curls so I told Felicity she should let her wear it down. She called me soft-hearted and said that if I wanted to be in charge of managing the mess, it was on me. So I did. We developed a nice bath-time ritual, Mal and me."

She pictured him giving a little girl a bath, gently combing her hair. "You sound like a good father."

"Not particularly. I was gone a lot and we made this special time. And then when she was maybe seven or eight, Mallory came home with her first case of lice. Felicity said if Mal's hair had been in braids, it wouldn't have happened. So it was my responsibility to get rid of the lice." He paused, as if remembering something. "Needless to say, those nitpicking sessions were a little less pleasant." Then he smiled sadly. "Oh, how she screamed."

"Yes, I know something about that." Maribeth stopped, realizing that she'd given another bit of herself away. Because who but a parent would say that? Then again, who but a parent would have such a robust case of lice to begin with?

If this new information registered, Dr. Grant didn't show it. He continued to massage the oil through her hair and she relaxed back into it.

"The irony is," he said, "Mallory wears braids all the time now."

"Does she still live here?" Maribeth asked dopily.

"All grown up and moved out."

"So you live here alone?"

"I should sell it. It's too big a house for one person to rattle around in." He sighed. "But I've been here so long. I'm stuck, I'm afraid."

By the time her hair was saturated, she felt almost liquid. When he announced he was finished, she was a little sad. She would've liked this to go on forever. He offered her a cup of tea, which she declined. He said he had to run back down to the office and he'd be back.

Alone in the house, Maribeth went into the hallway to look at the gallery of pictures. There was Dr. Grant in his younger days, his hair more pepper than salt. There he was with Mallory. And there he was with Felicity, dark skinned, angular boned, bright laughing eyes. She was a beautiful woman. Or had been. She must be dead, Dr. Grant a widower. No divorced man would display so many family photos, or speak so affectionately of an ex.

She looked into the kitchen again. It was almost new. And very much a woman's kitchen. Yes, a widower. And a recent one.

The hour passed quickly. When he returned, she was back in the bathroom. "Options: you can shampoo it out here or I can just comb it with the oil and you can shower later."

She couldn't bear the thought of showering here. "I'll shampoo later," she said.

"Okay." He put on his glasses. "Let's see what we have." He ran a comb through her hair. When it snagged, she jolted.

"Sorry," he said. He tried again. The comb snagged again. Maribeth tensed even more. It really hurt. She began to sympathize with Liv.

"Here's the source of your misery." He flicked the comb against his thumbnail, and

197

showed her a tiny insect. She inspected it, fascinated. In an odd sort of way, it was like a piece of her children had been traveling with her. Which wasn't to say she didn't want to get rid of the lice.

But that was proving to be a challenge. Dr. Grant couldn't seem to get the teeth of the comb through her unruly hair. "It's very tangled," he said.

"I know. It's a disaster. I haven't had time to deal with it." This was a lie. There was a salon on her corner that advertised twenty-dollar blowouts; she could've had one every day if she wanted to. Instead, she shoved her hair into a ponytail, often falling asleep with it in a tangle at the base of her neck. She was, as her mother might say, allowing herself to go to pot.

He hit another snag. "Wow, it's almost dreadlocking in places."

"You know what?" she said as he attempted to detach the comb. "Let's cut it off."

"If I managed Mallory's hair, I can manage yours."

"Not all of it. Just hack a hunk off. To here." She pointed to the top of her neck. "Do you have some scissors?"

"Not haircutting scissors."

"Any old kind will do."

"I really can handle this. I don't think cutting your hair is necessary."

She wasn't sure if it was necessary but right now it felt urgent.

"And you might regret it," he added.

She had not cut her hair short since the summer before senior year of college, when, inspired by Demi Moore in *Ghost,* she'd gotten a pixie. Her mother had warned her she might regret that — curly hair and short cuts did not mix, she said — but Maribeth had loved the jagged look of it. Or at least she had until she'd seen Jason's expression upon returning to school a few weeks later. "You cut your hair," he'd said mournfully, as if she'd amputated a limb.

"I won't regret it," she told Dr. Grant. "Look, if you don't want to do it, just give me some scissors. I'll hack off the four or five inches and we can carry on."

They stared down one another's reflections in the mirror. And then Dr. Grant dropped the chunk of hair he'd been holding and left the bathroom.

As soon as he did, she thought of the pink ribbons in his office. They'd seemed so incongruous on his bookshelves. She'd glimpsed more on the bookcase in the parlor.

They were breast cancer ribbons. Felicity

must have died of breast cancer. (She now remembered she still had not gotten a mammogram.) Maybe Felicity's hair had fallen out from the chemo. Maybe he'd had to preemptively shave it for her. Maybe he'd shaved his own head in solidarity. That was why he hadn't wanted to cut her hair. And now she'd practically bullied him into it.

Sometimes she really did think her heart no longer functioned. Sure, the muscle beat fine, but the feeling part of it was completely damaged.

"Never mind," she called out in a reedy voice. "It's okay."

"Why? You lose your nerve?" Dr. Grant returned snapping a pair of surgical scissors. He did not look the least bit mournful.

She couldn't help but grin. "No."

He stood behind her, fingering the greasy locks. "Should we rinse it first?" he asked. "So I can be more precise."

"I've spent most of my life trying to tame my hair," she said. "I think I'm just going to give in to the mess."

He liked that. She could tell. "Where to then?" he asked.

"Here." She pointed to a bony vertebra at the top of her neck.

"That's C-5, if you want to be anatomical

about it." He gathered her hair into a pony tail and twisted. It hurt but pleasantly so, the force paradoxically draining her of any remaining tension. She felt like a kitten, held snug by the scruff.

"Ready?" he asked. "One, two."

Three.

She heard the wet slap of hair dropping to the floor, felt a tickle of breeze against her newly bare neck.

She looked up. The itching had stopped, though she knew she must still have lice. And her face, it looked lighter, less haggard. For the first time since the surgery, she felt like putting on some lipstick.

"Better?" he asked.

She didn't answer. Only smiled.

"Shall we finish the job?"

"Go forth."

He tidied up the cut as best he could with the oil in it and then he picked out the nits. As he did, they talked easily. He told her more stories about Mallory, who had graduated from college last year and was in California, making her way in the working world. She in turn told him about initiating the search for her birth mother.

Beneath the chitchat, Maribeth sensed a whole other conversation taking place. One about the family she'd left behind. One about the family who'd left him behind. It was as though they already knew, as though they'd mutually decided to bypass huge chunks of their history and get straight to the heart of the matter.

29

Maribeth, Todd, and Sunita were driving to their weekly shopping trip when the conversation turned to plans for the upcoming holiday.

Thanksgiving was in four days, a fact that Maribeth had managed to ignore until a few days before, when she'd looked out her living room window and seen a balloon turkey wearing a Steelers cap and realized the holiday was imminent. She'd been gone almost four weeks. How had that happened?

It wasn't that she was unaware of time. But with no deadlines, no staff meetings, no potlucks, no playdates, no school week, no work week, the indicators changed. She had a few repeating events — trips to the library, shopping with Todd and Sunita, checkups with Dr. Grant — but those weren't what demarcated time anymore. Rather, she noted the days passing by the way her leg no longer swelled if she went an entire day without wearing a support stocking, or how back-drawer words (ubiquitous, semiannual) were becoming easier to pull up. Or by the stack of letters to the twins, which had grown as thick as her thumb.

"I'm not sure what I'm doing," she told Todd and Sunita. "What about you?"

"Sunny's parents will be enjoying the traditional Thanksgiving ritual of naturalized Americans living in Hyderabad," Todd said. "And my family will be enjoying the traditional Thanksgiving ritual of the broken home."

Sunita patted him on the shoulder. She turned back to Maribeth. "His parents split up five years ago. He's not over it."

"I'll never be over it." He sighed dramatically. "Dad's spending the holiday with Barbie Wife and Mom is off with her new boyfriend in *Altoona*." Todd winced. "I don't want to go to Altoona."

"I don't blame you," Maribeth said, even though she'd never been to Altoona and for all she knew it could be the Shangri-La of the Keystone State.

"We were thinking of inviting over a bunch of friends who don't have anywhere to go," Sunita said.

"An orphans' dinner," Maribeth said. She used to host them all the time, first with

Elizabeth, and later, with Jason. Epic meals, with ten, fifteen, sometimes twenty people crowded into the loft. Raucous games of charades and Balderdash. Lots of wine. Everyone sprawled on the floor watching movies. A midnight buffet of seconds that decimated any hope of leftovers. (Jason had taken to roasting a second turkey the Friday after just to have sandwich fixings.)

"Yeah, an orphans' dinner. I like that," said Todd. "Only we don't know how to cook a turkey."

"And we thought if you weren't doing anything," Sunita said, "you could come, too."

"And make the turkey?" Maribeth asked.

"No," Todd said. "We don't want you to give us the fish; we want you to teach us to fish, sensei."

"And we want you to come, too," Sunita added. "But we weren't sure if you were, you know, an orphan."

That morning, Janice had called with disappointing news. The Jewish adoption agency had no record of her. It was a minor setback, and yet it had unmoored Maribeth. For a moment, she had this panicky feeling that her existence had never been registered. "No, no, no. It just means you were adopted through some other avenue," Janice had reassured. "We'll check the other agencies and initiate that search with the Orphans' Court."

Maribeth contemplated Todd and Sunita's invitation. She wasn't sure what she wanted to do about the holiday, but as to the question of her orphanhood, that would appear to be a yes.

30

Janice was late. She'd told Maribeth to meet her at four by the fountain in the courtyard of some municipal building downtown, but at four-fifteen, the leaden sky was darkening and there was still no sign of Janice. Maribeth shivered, and scowled, trying not to stare at the couple on the bench opposite her, who were engaged in some serious heavy petting. She felt the pelt of the first icy raindrop, the weather a perfect reflection of her mood.

Janice arrived a half hour late, apologizing for her delay, which she attributed to a printer malfunction. Given that what she was printing had been Maribeth's paperwork, Maribeth could hardly complain.

"Perfect timing, too," Janice said. "It's about to rain."

"Yes," Maribeth said, looking at the couple, who did not seem to mind the rain one little bit. "Let's go inside." She started toward the building but Janice steered her back toward the street.

"The Orphans' Court is across the way," she explained. "I wanted to meet here because it's one of my favorite spots in the city. Isn't it lovely?"

"Maybe when it's not raining," Maribeth said.

"Oh, dear. If you subtract points for rain in Pittsburgh, nothing will be lovely. The courtyard is so peaceful. You'd never guess it used to be a jail."

Another couple entered the courtyard, holding hands and pausing to exchange a long, wet kiss.

"And what is it now?" Maribeth asked. "A hotel that rents by the hour?"

Janice laughed. "A courthouse, but the marriage registry is right around the corner. You know how young love is."

"I seem to faintly recall," Maribeth said.

More than faintly. There'd been a similarly kissy couple in front of her and Jason when they'd applied for their marriage license in New York. Maribeth had averted her eyes but she could not avert her ears: the lip-smacking, the cooing.

"What is it about lines that makes people lose all inhibition?" Maribeth had whispered to Jason.

"Relieves the boredom," Jason had replied. "We can do it, too. Give us a kiss, Maribeth Brinkley." He leaned in, lips puckered.

"Maribeth *Klein*," she'd replied, pushing him away.

"There's still time to change your mind. Maribeth Brinkley. Sounds nice."

"Sounds Waspy."

"When we were in college you said you couldn't wait to get rid of your culturally confused name."

Well, yes. It was a peculiar name. Klein, so Jewish. Maribeth, so goyish. At least she didn't have it as bad as a girl from her Hebrew School named Christine Goldberg.

"That was then," she said. "People know me now professionally as Maribeth Klein."

"You can still be Maribeth Klein on the masthead."

"I'm *not* taking your name!" Her voice was sharp, cracking through the echoey hall. Even the PDA couple came up for air to see what was going on. In a softer voice she added, "I mean, what if we split up? Then I'm stuck with it."

He didn't say anything for a while, just stared at the couple in front of them who now had their hands in one another's back pockets. Then, in a quiet voice, he said, "We're getting our marriage license and you're thinking about breaking up?"

"I'm not. The waiting in line is making me nervous," she'd said.

What she didn't say: *though we did break up once before*.

The Orphans' Court was housed in a stately historic building, full of deep rich woods, marble, and brass, all of it looking freshly polished. Two bronze lions stood sentry over the entrance and a giant stained-glass window of a woman floated over the lobby. It was apparently from a famous artist. "The name of that one is *Fortune at Her Wheel*," Janice said, as they waited for the elevators. "Which is fitting to our endeavors, no?"

Maribeth didn't answer. She felt sick with nervousness, as if the elevators would open onto the fifth floor and her birth mother would be there waiting.

But there was just another lobby, pretty if a little shabbier than the one down below. Janice announced herself and Maribeth, and after a short wait, a woman came out to collect their paperwork and have Maribeth sign a form.

"That's all?" Maribeth asked after the woman returned to her office, saying she'd be in touch.

"For now," Janice replied.

A bleakness had fallen over Maribeth. This whole process was just dispiriting. Half of her wanted to get far away from Janice, from all of this, and the other half didn't want to be alone.

They found a deserted café and Maribeth ordered a coffee for herself and a decaf pumpkin spiced latte for Janice. Then they huddled into a corner table.

"Are you okay, dear?" Janice asked, patting Maribeth on the hand.

Maribeth nodded.

"I imagine this stirs up a lot of feelings, thinking about your birth mother. And everything is worse around the holidays." She paused and slurped her drink. "You might think about starting your letter."

"My letter?"

"The one you'll write to your mother when you locate her, explaining who you are, why you're looking for her. It might help you process."

"Did it help you?"

Janice stirred her drink with the wooden stick. She had not been forthcoming with her own story but it was obvious to Maribeth that she too had searched for her birth mother.

"Yes, it did," she said at last.

"I don't know what to say," Maribeth said.

"Just speak from the heart. Tell her about yourself, your family. Whatever feels true to you."

Maribeth tried to imagine writing the letter. She knew she was supposed to be the tearful abandoned daughter, full of questions, but really, all she wanted to know was if anyone else had had heart disease. It was as much for her children now as for her.

"You know," she told Janice. "I think I conceived my children on Thanksgiving."

"You did?"

Well, she couldn't say for sure it was *on* Thanksgiving. And the procedure by which Dr. Simon had implanted the fertilized embryos into her uterus could only be called conception in the most science fiction of contexts. It was their fourth, and last, IVF try. They were out of patience, time, money. They'd had to ask Jason's mother for a few thousand dollars to cover this last one. Nora had given them the money, but in return, had reallocated a diamond tennis bracelet that she'd apparently willed to Maribeth to go to Lauren instead.

The implantation had taken place the Tuesday before Thanksgiving. When it was over, Dr. Simon had patted Maribeth on the belly. "Third time's a charm."

"It's the fourth," Maribeth had said glumly.

She didn't think it would work. She'd been abstaining from drinking but that year she got rip-roaring drunk on Thanksgiving. She woke up the next morning, puking. "I think it took," Jason said. "It's too soon. I just drank too much," she'd replied. But a few weeks later, she tested positive. Even then, she didn't believe it would stick. She'd been pregnant before and had always miscarried before the sixth week. When the ultrasound showed two beating hearts — they'd never had heartbeats before — Jason had joked that it was the getting drunk that did it. "Maybe we should've been doing that all along," Maribeth had said, laughing. "Getting wasted and humping in the backseat of our parents' car."

Telling Janice now about the false starts, the misses, put a lump in her throat. She swallowed it down with her lukewarm coffee. "The thing is, when my kids were born, when I saw them, I thought, *Yes. This was why.* It was like all those other zygotes that didn't implant had been impostors. *These* had been my children all along."

She looked up, surprised to find tears glistening in Janice Pickering's eyes.

What a fraud Maribeth was, peddling a

story of loving motherhood. Look at her now. Her strength was back. And she was still here.

"I wonder if that's even true or if I just needed to believe it was," she said.

"Are those two things really so different?" Janice asked.

31

She tried. She tried to write her birth mother a letter. But it felt like writing to Santa Claus, as an adult, and a Jew. What was she supposed to say?

She had no idea. So she put the letter aside and instead wrote to the twins.

Dear Liv and Oscar,

The Thanksgiving decorations are up here. Across the street, there's a turkey made of balloons, not like Macy's balloons but actual balloons. Do you remember last year when, Oscar, you asked why there were no presents on Thanksgiving? I think Daddy said it was the one holiday the corporations hadn't co-opted and I think I'd said Hanukkah and Christmas were right there so we didn't need to have presents on Thanksgiving, too.

But the real truth is that we got you

215

two on Thanksgiving. It's not when you were born but when you were conceived. (One day that will make sense.) So how could any present compete with that?

She laid down the pen. Because what she wanted to write was that she was sorry. Sorry for ruining this Thanksgiving. Sorry for ruining every Thanksgiving so far.

She had not lied to the twins. She really did consider them the ultimate Thanksgiving gift, the source of so much of her gratitude in life. Which was why it was so bewildering that every single Thanksgiving since they'd been born had been awful. One year worse than the next.

The first Thanksgiving they'd all trekked up to Jason's sister's — the orphan dinners discontinued without any discussion. Lauren's kids had wanted to hold the twins and Maribeth hadn't wanted to be that mom, the one who was obsessive with the hand sanitizer, and as a result, Oscar and Liv had come down with matching colds, and Maribeth had spent the holiday holding, walking, and nursing two cranky infants. "The days are long but the years are short," one of Jason's aunts had said. Which she'd found hard to believe given that the weekend alone felt like it might last a year.

The following Thanksgiving, her parents had come to visit and to "help" with the food prep and childcare, no small feat as Oscar and Liv were now fifteen months old, heat-seeking missiles of destruction. Maribeth had left others in charge for twenty minutes to take a shower, and when she'd come out, Oscar had managed to tip over the cooling turkey. It had taken a half hour to rescue the bird, an hour to calm Oscar. When they went around saying what they were grateful for, Maribeth, feeling spiteful, had said, "Pass."

Which she regretted. Particularly because by the following year, her father was gone. Which was why she and Jason and the twins had flown to Florida to be with her mother. Upon their arrival, her mother had announced that after fifty years of preparing food for others, she had retired from kitchen duty. Maribeth, she said, was welcome to cook the meal. Maribeth had stayed up until two a.m. the night before finishing a freelance story so she wouldn't have to work over the holiday and had spent eighteen hundred dollars they couldn't really spare on the airfare. She knew her mother was in mourning, but that didn't prevent her from wanting to kill her. They wound up eating the most depressing meal in history at a near-empty restaurant in downtown Boca.

Last year, they went upstate to see Jason's father, and it hadn't been bad. Now working at *Frap,* Maribeth had been forced to bring work with her, but Jason and Elliott had kept the kids entertained so she could focus on work and the cooking. On the drive home, she was trying to finish up an edit. Glancing in the rearview mirror, she'd caught a glimpse of Liv coloring and smiled for a moment, savoring the connection, mother and daughter, hard at work.

"Did you have fun?" she asked.

"No. You worked. You always work," Liv said. Her tone was mild but that made the accusation punch even harder.

She put the article aside for the rest of the drive, and that night she stayed up late trying to finish it.

"Come to bed," Jason said.

"In a minute," she replied, tapping the page with her pen.

"I thought you did that in the car." When she didn't answer, he said. "Liv?"

There was something to his tone. Simultaneously scolding Maribeth for letting a three-year-old best her, and admiring the three-year-old for being that powerful. "She's going to give us a run for our money, that one," Jason added, smiling.

People often said this. Though usually it was directed to Maribeth: "She's going to give *you* a run for your money."

As if she didn't already know.

32

Thanksgiving morning, Maribeth decided to show her gratitude by taking a bath. It had been nearly seven weeks since her surgery, and she remembered from the brochures Dr. Sterling had given her that six weeks post-op was like the twenty-first birthday for the cardiac patient, the date after which many previously forbidden activities — sex, bodily immersion in water, strenuous exercise — were permitted.

As she waited for the tub to fill, Maribeth inspected her naked figure in the mirror. Though she had gained some weight back, she was still thinner than she'd been in years — she could tell by the daylight blinking between her thighs — but it wasn't an enviable skinny. And even if it had been, there were the scars. She had three of them now: the pucker on her leg, the angry welt up her chest, and the pale white smile of her C-section.

"Scars are just tattoos with better stories." Again, she was reminded of what Jason had told her when she'd first showed him her crosshatch of stitches after the twins were born. She'd been worried he'd think she looked disfigured (she thought she did). And then he'd said that lovely thing.

Her scars now were worse. Or would be. They didn't even look like scars yet, more like wounds. If they had stories to tell, they were still being written.

Maribeth eased into the tub, grabbing a couple of the magazines Todd had given her yesterday when she dropped off the Thanksgiving shopping list. She'd promised to help them dress and stuff the bird, but after that, they were on their own. She was skipping Thanksgiving this year.

She was skimming an important piece of reportage about the fashion evolution of Nori Kardashian West when she heard the pounding at her door.

"M.B., are you there?" It was Todd.

"Yeah, hang on." She heaved herself out of the tub, toweled off, and threw on her dirty clothes.

Todd and Sunita were at the door, staggering under the weight of the most enormous turkey she'd ever seen. It looked like a defrocked poodle.

"I thought you wanted to put it in at noon," Maribeth said. "Though that thing is huge, so maybe you'll need more time."

"A *lot* more time," Todd said.

"It's completely frozen," Sunita explained.

"Didn't they have any fresh birds left?"

"It was fresh last night."

"What happened?"

"It was too big to fit in our fridge so Sunny thought we should leave it on the windowsill," Todd said.

"We wouldn't have had to get such a huge bird if Todd had gone shopping earlier in the week when there was more selection, like M.B. said we should," Sunita said, her tone equally scornful.

Last night it had dropped to the twenties. Maribeth gave the bird a good knock. Yep. Frozen solid.

"What do we do?" Sunita asked.

"Defrost it somehow," Maribeth said.

"It doesn't even fit in our sink," Sunita said.

She thought of her bath tub. "Maybe try the tub."

"We thought of that. Ours doesn't have a stopper."

"Mine does. Better bring it in."

The bath was still full, the water grimy with gray bubbles. Todd wrinkled his nose.

"I don't mean to be picky, but I think Fred deserves a fresh bath."

"Fred?" Maribeth asked.

"He named the turkey," Sunita explained.

She drained the water, quickly scrubbed the basin, and filled it with fresh water. Todd gently laid the turkey in. "That'll warm you up."

"You do realize it's dead?" Sunita asked.

Todd covered the bird's wings with his hands. "Obviously. But *he* doesn't know," he mock whispered.

Maribeth went to get herself a cup of coffee. When she saw her range, with a half-sized oven that was the same as Todd and Sunita's, she went back into the bathroom.

"I'm afraid you guys have bigger problems than Frozen Fred."

"What?" they asked.

"I don't think he'll fit in the oven."

"Oh, I didn't even think of that!" Sunita ran up the stairs. Maribeth heard the sound of her oven door creak open, then slam shut, then Sunita yelling: "Gah!"

"There's no way," she said when she returned to the bathroom. "Not even if we take out the racks. And we have like fifteen people coming."

"Can't you get a new turkey?" Maribeth asked.

"The store hardly had any birds left," Todd said. "It was why we had to get such a huge one."

"Try a different store," Maribeth suggested.

"But we already blew all our money on groceries. We spent more than a hundred dollars."

"I can pay for the bird."

"But you're not even coming," Sunita said.

"Also, we don't have a car," Todd said. "Miles left for Philly today."

"I guess we could see what the markets around here have," Sunita said.

"I'm not going to the ShurSave," Todd said.

"Maybe we can cook it in someone else's oven?" Sunita said. "Your mom's house."

"We'd have to get it to the suburbs. How?"

"Take the bus."

"On Thanksgiving? With Fred?"

"I suppose we could just cancel," Sunita said.

They looked so crestfallen. Maribeth couldn't bear it.

"I may know someone who can help," she said.

"Really?" They looked at her with such sweet hopefulness.

She left a message with the service. "Not

an emergency," she repeated, not wanting to alarm him. But when he called back within ten minutes, she knew he had assumed the worst.

"It's not a medical emergency; it's a poultry one." She told him about the turkey, presently being defrosted in her tub.

"Ahh, clever. It's what they do for hypothermic patients."

"Good to know our practices are medically sound. Now we just need a place to cook it. Neither of our ovens will hold it. And I thought of you, well, because you have that huge kitchen. But you're probably going somewhere."

"I'm not going anywhere," he said. "Tell me where you are, and I'll pick you and the turkey up."

"Fred," she said.

"What?"

"The turkey's name is Fred."

33

Dr. Grant arrived by noon. Sunita and Todd wrapped the half-thawed Fred in a garbage bag and lugged him to the curb.

"You're sure you don't want us to come?" Sunita asked. "I feel like we've fobbed the whole thing off on you."

"Do you know how to cook a turkey?" Maribeth asked.

Sunita shook her head.

"I'll handle the bird. You do everything else. I'll come back when it's done."

"Okay, but you have to come to the dinner now," Sunita said. "Your friend, too." She waved at Dr. Grant. "Thank you," she called.

Maribeth said, "We'll see."

Dr. Grant had already preheated the oven and pulled out a roasting pan.

"My, you're prepared."

"I'm very comfortable being the sous-chef."

Maribeth peered into the oven. It was spotless. She and Sunita had already made stuffing and put it in a Ziploc bag, and Maribeth had packed an extra onion, because she'd suspected, correctly, that Dr. Grant wouldn't have one.

She instructed Dr. Grant to chop the onion while she salted the bird's cavity and prepared to stuff.

When she had spooned in all the stuffing, she asked: "Do you have any olive oil left, or did it all go in my hair?"

"I think I have some. Or butter."

"Butter! And you call yourself a cardiologist!"

He smiled and handed her a bottle of olive oil. "The entire thing drips in fat so I'm not sure it makes a difference at this point."

While the onions sautéed, she hunted for some dried herbs in the pantry. They were covered in dust. "Do you think herbs expire?" she asked.

"If they do, then they have."

"When was the last time you used your kitchen?" she asked.

"This morning. I made tea."

"When was the last time you used your oven?"

"Why? Is it not working?"

"It's working fine."

"Does heating up pizza count?"

"No."

"Then about two years ago."

So, Felicity had died two years ago.

"Mallory's not coming home for Thanksgiving?" she asked as she poured the oil and onions onto the turkey and massaged them into Fred's still chilly skin.

He shook his head. "I'll see her in a few weeks for Christmas when I go out to California."

"And you really weren't doing anything today?" she asked, sprinkling herbs and salt over the bird.

He seemed transfixed, as if he'd never seen anyone prep a turkey. "Louise has been on my case to come over. But I feel like one of her church projects." He grimaced. "I had planned to watch football all day."

"You can still do that."

"I might do."

"Do you have any twine? Or anything to tie the drumsticks together?"

"Hang on. I've got just the thing," he said and went into his office, returning with a pack of surgical sutures.

She used the sutures to tie the legs together. "Unless you prefer to do stitches."

"I yield to the expert," Dr. Grant said.

She gave the pepper mill a few final twists and then began to lift the roasting pan toward the oven.

"Allow me," Dr. Grant said.

"I'm past six weeks," Maribeth said.

"This is about chivalry, not infirmity."

"In that case." She stood to the side.

When the bird was in the oven, she set the timer. It was twelve-thirty now. It would take at least five hours to roast, possibly longer because it was not fully defrosted. Really, it ought to be basted once an hour, though it wouldn't be the end of the world if it went without. "Should I go and come back?" she asked. "Or I can stay here and babysit the bird if you want to go somewhere. I don't want to put you out."

"You're not putting me out. And I have nowhere to be," he said. "You can leave the bird if you have somewhere to be."

"I have nowhere to be either," she said.

By the time Fred was ready, it was getting near six, and Maribeth was somewhere on the road between tipsy and drunk. Around three, she and Dr. Grant had gone down into his basement wine cellar and picked out several bottles for the dinner that by some unspoken agreement they had both decided to attend. Somewhere around four, they had uncorked a bottle of Rioja. Somewhere around five, she'd stopped calling him Dr. Grant.

"Oh, thank god," Todd said when they arrived bearing Fred on a platter. "We thought we were going to have to eat the nut loaf."

"Nut loaf?" Maribeth asked.

"Sunny's friend Fritz made a nut loaf because he thought she was vegetarian because she's Indian. And because he totally wants to jump her bones."

"Hush, he does not," Sunita said. She turned to Dr. Grant — Stephen — and held out her hand. "Hi, I'm Sunita. Thank you so much for helping us out."

"I'm Stephen," he said. "And you're welcome."

"And you brought wine! Excellent!" Todd said, gesturing to the bottles in Stephen's hand. "All Sunny's philistine friends brought beer. And nut loaf."

"Shut up about the nut loaf already," Sunita said.

"Can I have a glass of that?" Todd asked Stephen, pointing to the Shiraz.

"I feel like I should perhaps card you first."

"He acts immature but he's of age," Sunita said.

"Then show me to your corkscrew."

"Follow me," Sunita said.

As soon as Stephen was out of earshot, Todd nudged Maribeth in the ribs: "Who's the silver fox?"

"A friend."

"Hmm, mmm. A *friend*? Is he the friend you cut your hair for?"

He was the friend who *cut* her hair, but she didn't say anything.

"Your grin gives you away," Todd said.

She bit her lip, though what was there to give away? He had been her doctor, and he had become her friend. It seemed official now, though had it not been heading in that direction? Consider her appointments: increasingly short physical exams, followed by ever-longer conversations in his office after. And those conversations — metaphysical, intellectual, philosophical, meandering — they'd become the highlight of her week. She couldn't remember the last time she had talked to anybody like that.

"He's just a friend. Like you and Sunny are friends."

"So he's gay?" Todd asked, misunderstanding.

"Not that I know of."

"Then why exactly is he just a friend?"

■ ■ ■ ■

After the meal, after the bottles of Australian Shiraz and Chilean Pinot and a very expensive French burgundy had been sunk, after everyone had gone around reciting what they were grateful for — nearly all the locals had said something Steelers related; Maribeth, drunk by then, had blurted "not being dead," to much laughter; Stephen had said "the unexpected" to much confusion; and Fritz had said his statistics class, to much derision, until Todd asked wasn't that the class where he had met Sunny, and then poor Fritz had gone as red as the cranberry sauce. After Sunita and Todd tried to snap the still-wet wishbone and knocked over a candle, after half the group had decamped to the living room to watch the tail end of the Eagles game, after the other half had gone to the kitchen to haphazardly do the dishes, Maribeth flopped onto the couch and Sunita sat down next to her, kissing her on the cheek and saying that it was the best Thanksgiving she'd had in ages, and Maribeth had said, "Me too." Only then did she think of Oscar and Liv.

It was the first time she'd thought of them all day.

34

The hangover came, as hangovers will, the following day.

Maribeth woke to a weak light peeking in the cracks of her shades. Her head was pounding.

She reached for her phone. It was past noon. She'd been lamenting her inability to sleep late like this since having kids, but now that she'd done it, she remembered that sleeping late, like unconsciousness, happened for a reason. Because your body knew you couldn't handle being awake.

Staggering to the bathroom, she put her head under the tap and drank. Then she brushed her teeth, and put on a pot of coffee. While it brewed, she pulled up the shades and squinted. Outside the sky was gray and flat, threatening snow. Not that anyone seemed to care. Even the humble streets of Bloomfield were buzzing with Black Friday shoppers.

She lowered the shades and padded into the kitchen, where she cooked a pot of oatmeal, but as it bubbled and burbled on the stove, it looked like vomit. She felt perilously close to throwing up. She tossed the oatmeal in the garbage and made some toast instead.

She picked up her latest book, a collection of postmodern short stories, another big book she'd meant to read — and though she'd been thoroughly enjoying it two days ago, today she found herself reading the same paragraph over and over.

It was not a day for reading. It was a day for surrendering. She poured the coffee, put the toast on a plate, and gathered all the blankets in the apartment into a nest on the couch. Then she channel surfed until she landed on something bland and mindless, one of those Lifetime-type movies, though she didn't actually get Lifetime, only the network channels and a few weird off-brand cable stations that seemed to come with the reception. She was watching it for about ten minutes before she realized that the story revolved around an alcoholic mother who had abandoned her four children.

She should've changed the station, but she couldn't look away. She was riveted by the melodramatic scene of the wayward mother sobbing in a phone booth — the phone booth dating the film much the way her request for a Yellow Pages had dated her — hitting herself with the receiver after her collect call home was denied. Tragic as this scene was, Maribeth knew there would be a happy ending. This mother would be redeemed because she was the one on-screen. It was when the mother was not present, when she never got any air time, when she was defined only by her absence, because she'd missed court dates or forgotten birthdays, that you understood implicitly that she was a villain, her sole purpose a vehicle for someone else's redemption.

When the commercial came on, Maribeth wondered about the made-for-TV movie of her own life. Which mother she would be? The answer came to her, immediate and obvious. The mother who had upped and left home a month ago, who had not uttered a word to her family, had not even bothered to see if her four-year-old children, whom she claimed to love more than anything else in her life, were okay. Who had got drunk and had a wonderful Thanksgiving last night even though her children were probably crying in her absence. The mother who had not called those children once, had not even sent a single e-mail.

Sure, she'd written letters. But those letters would never appear in *her* movie. They would not be submitted as evidence to her defense, proof of her love, flawed though it might be right now.

In Maribeth's made-for-TV movie, she was the villain.

35

The library was generally quiet when Maribeth visited in the late mornings, but when she dragged herself over later that day, it was jammed with teenagers, who had not only taken possession of all the computers — the ones in the teen section and the ones for general use — but of the library itself. They were talking to one another in nonlibrary voices, monopolizing all the computers to watch YouTube videos. As Maribeth hovered, waiting for a terminal to open up, the teens regarded her with the sort of suspicion that mothers at playgrounds reserved for lone men.

She had no idea what she was going to say to her children. She only knew that she had to say something, she had to communicate to them that she wasn't *that* mother. She was one of the good mothers, the one who fought her way back to her children. Only how could she tell them that and explain why she wasn't coming home? If walking to and from the library had been her barometer of health, she had reached that. She could climb that hill. But now that she could, she had seen all the other peaks beyond it. And she knew she wasn't ready to go back.

But she would be. She needed Oscar and Liv to know that. She needed them to know that she wasn't the villain, the one who would desert them forever.

When a computer finally opened up in the teen section, Maribeth swooped over to it just before a young girl with pink bangs and a pierced lip got there. "Hey," the girl said, angrily. "You're not allowed over here."

Maribeth ignored her and launched Gmail. She had not gone this long without checking e-mail since she'd had e-mail, and the anticipation and fear were sending waves of panic through her. It was so much worse than that time after she'd gone offline at Tom and Elizabeth's retreat. She could only imagine what Jason had written as the days of her absence added up. And oh, god, what if her mother had found someone to send an e-mail for her?

It was almost a relief when the first screen was all junk: ads for Black Friday sales, credit card offers, pleas for year-end charitable donations. She deleted them and brought up a fresh page of messages. There were notices about Career Day at Bright-Start, endless threads about the best organic baby food on TribecaParents, and double jog strollers for sale on the twins' e-mail list, but nothing from Jason.

She went back five, then ten, then fifteen screens' worth of messages. Two, three, four weeks. There was nothing from Jason. She did a search, for both his personal and work e-mail addresses. The last e-mail from Jason Brinkley was from late October. Two days before she'd come to Pittsburgh.

She had left, in precarious health, two and a half weeks after having emergency bypass surgery. And he had not e-mailed her once. Not to ask: Are you okay? Not to yell: Fuck you. Not to beg her to come home or order her to stay away.

She started to laugh, only it wasn't really a laugh, because two seconds later, she was crying. The snarky teenagers were looking at her with something like concern now.

"Are you okay?" the girl with the pink hair and the pierced lip asked.

"He didn't fucking e-mail me."

The girl looked startled. Maybe it was the profanity. Or maybe she'd never seen a grown-up so spectacularly losing it before.

But after a second, the teenager regained her equilibrium and rolled her eyes. "Guys are such dicks," she said.

36

Friday night, she stewed. All that trouble — paying cash for everything, keeping herself hidden, the false identity — for what? She was playing hide-and-go-seek . . . with herself. Nobody was looking.

By Saturday morning, though, she had convinced herself, they had to be. She had missed an e-mail or it had gone to her spam folder. Given when she had left, how she had left, why she had left, surely, someone would send up a flare.

She returned to the library that afternoon. It was less crowded and she got a computer right away. She logged onto Gmail, paging through each screen. There was nothing. She checked her spam file. Nothing. The trash. Nothing. She checked her work account in case he'd accidentally e-mailed her at the wrong address, but there was nothing from him there either. She logged on to her Facebook page. Old get-well messages and random tags from people unaware of what had happened, but from Jason or Elizabeth, nothing.

It was like she didn't exist.

She sat there refreshing the screen, unable to comprehend this. She told herself she would wait until three o'clock, and if there was no message, she'd leave. Three o'clock came. Then four. Then five.

Nothing.

By the time the librarians blinked the lights to announce closing in ten minutes, her sorrow had iced over. One month gone and not a word. She opened a new message window. She began to type in his name. Google autofilled it.

I was under this crazy impression that in spite of everything you might actually give a shit.

The cursor blinked at the end of the message. A little voice in the back of her head warned her not to do it. It was the same voice she'd heard more than twenty years ago, when she was about to send Jason a drunken e-mail after she'd found out about the new San Francisco girlfriend. *Didn't let the sheets get cold, did you?* she'd written.

He never replied to that e-mail, and she'd

regretted sending it. But that didn't stop her from sending this one now.

37

Maribeth ran into Sunita on the stoop as she got home from the library that day.

"Hey, we just got back from the Holiday Market," Sunita said.

"The what?" Maribeth asked.

"That Christmas thing. I texted to see if you wanted to go."

"Sorry. I was at the library."

"Did you get any books?"

"Oh, I was just using the computer." *Using* probably wasn't the right word. Staring glazed in front of it, like those old ladies in front of the nickel slots. "How was it?"

"Lame. But next week is Handmade Arcade, which is awesome. It's like Etsy in a convention center," Sunita said. "You should come."

"We'll see. I might have to go back to the library."

"If it's a computer you need, you're always welcome to borrow my laptop."

"Really?"

"Sure."

"Could I maybe borrow it now?"

"Of course." Sunita went into the apartment and returned with her laptop. "The Wi-Fi should work from your place."

Furtively, as if she were about to watch porn, Maribeth brought the computer into her apartment. She launched her e-mail program and left it open all evening, refreshing the page while she attempted to distract herself with a short story collection, and when that didn't work, resorting to the TV again. There was a *Modern Family* marathon on but the show's irreverence was making her murderous so she changed to a *Friends* rerun but that depressed her, because it reminded her, in its bright-TV version, of her old existence with Elizabeth. (Well, they had a loft. And they were young.)

By the time Maribeth had moved on to *The Good Wife,* the slow boil of her anger had cooked down to a sludgy resignation. What had she expected? This was how it always was. Maribeth fought with words. Jason fought with silences. Just because she wanted it to be different didn't mean it would be. As her dentist father used to say: "If wishes were gumdrops, I'd be a rich man."

At two in the morning, there was no more TV to distract herself with. Maribeth felt drained and jittery. She needed to try to sleep. She started to close the e-mail window, but then couldn't stop herself.

So you're punishing me? she wrote. *I'm not surprised. I just hoped that for once you'd be the bigger person and rise to the occasion. Wrong again!*

38

Sunday morning, Maribeth woke up with Sunita's laptop lodged next to the pillow. Seeing it, remembering the e-mails she'd written — and not even while drunk; she didn't even have that excuse — she winced. It was great that Google now gave you a minute lag time to take back e-mails you'd mistakenly sent, but couldn't they invent technology that let you take back e-mails the morning after?

She grabbed the laptop and brought it into the kitchen, shoving it inside the cupboard under a package of brown rice. Then she went back to bed and stayed there until she heard footsteps upstairs.

Though it was not yet ten, Todd answered the door fully dressed, in what appeared to be his catering uniform plus a boater hat.

"She's making me go to the flower show at the Phipps Conservatory in old-timey clothes," Todd whispered. "Save me!"

Sunita appeared in a flapper dress and a pair of jeans. "Oh, please, you were all over this." She looked at Maribeth. "You want to come?"

"No thanks."

"Are you sure? It'll be fun."

"I'm positive." Maribeth did not want to linger or chat. She just wanted to return the computer; it felt as lethal as a loaded gun. "Thanks for the loan. Bye."

Just as she'd closed the door to her apartment, her phone started to ring. "I appreciate the offer," she said, assuming it was Sunita, "but I'm really not interested in going to a flower show today."

There was a pause. And then, "But this is so much worse than a flower show."

"Oh, Dr. — Stephen." She paused to untangle the names, and the new reality in which Dr. Grant — Stephen — called her. "What could be worse than a flower show?"

Another pause. "The mall."

When she didn't say anything, he continued. "On Black Friday weekend."

"Yes. That's worse than a flower show."

"Now that we've cleared that up . . ." he trailed off. In the background, she could hear the sound of the TV. "Remember that time I cooked your turkey?"

"Technically, it wasn't my turkey."

"Right, Fred belonged to the kids. I was just invoking some quid pro quo."

"And this quid pro quo involves a mall on Black Friday weekend?"

"I know. It's an uneven bargain. I'd still be in your debt."

"I think if we're keeping tabs, I'm still in the red. But why exactly do you want to go shopping *this* weekend?"

"To get Mallory her Christmas gift."

"You do realize, in spite of the hype, you have four weeks until Christmas."

"I want to get it out of the way. So I don't panic again."

"Panic?"

"Last year, I left it too late and panicked and got her a leather jacket from the Home Shopping Network."

"Nothing wrong with that."

"Unless you're a vegan who is very serious about animal rights. Mal thought I was making fun of her and got very offended in the way that twenty-one-year-olds will." He sighed. "She sold it on eBay and got herself kayak lessons so maybe it worked out in the end. But I'd like to avoid another disaster this time around. Hence, the mall. It's what people do, right?"

Maribeth rarely had cause to enter a mall (score a point for New York City). But when she did, while visiting her mother, for instance, she became immediately irritable; the crowds made her claustrophobic, the number of stores made her dizzy. A mall on Black Friday weekend sounded like a nightmare. But perhaps it was a testament to just how wretched the weekend had already been that when she told Stephen she would be happy to go with him, she meant it.

"We're going to the Ross Park Mall," Stephen informed her as they drove across the Thirtieth Street Bridge. "Have you been?"

"Have I not made my feelings about malls clear?" she joked.

"They say this is the best one in Pittsburgh."

"That's like telling someone they have the best cancer."

Her hand flew up to her mouth. Cancer. Which his wife had died of. What was wrong with her?

"Well, there are better cancers," Stephen replied, taking it all in stride. "Thyroid, prostate, highly curable."

She wanted to change the subject before she stepped in it again. "Tell me about Mallory. What's she like?"

"Twenty-two. Smart, ambitious, bossy. By her own admission. She has a tattoo that says Bossy Bitch, but with that number sign in front of it?"

"A hashtag?"

"If you say so."

"So she's a feminist, and maybe a wee bit shortsighted."

"Aren't all young people shortsighted?" he asked.

"I suppose so."

"And if she's shortsighted, good for her. In many ways she had to grow up too soon."

Maribeth assumed he meant losing her mother. If Mallory was twenty-two now, she would've been twenty when Felicity died. That wasn't great, but twenty . . . it was better than four.

"She wants another tattoo but I can't bring myself to fund one as a gift."

"What else does she like?"

"She majored in public policy but with a minor in theater." He smiled proudly. "So she likes performances: plays, concerts, dance. That's what Felicity used to get her, tickets to opera or ballet, and they'd go together."

"Why not do that?"

"I feel like I'd be intruding on their thing. And I hate opera."

"What about a donation? Maybe to a cancer charity," she said, mentioning the c-word intentionally this time, in a more sensitive manner.

They pulled into the massive parking lot and started searching for a spot. "Now you're just trying to get out of going to the mall," he said.

Maybe. It was packed, judging by the dearth of parking spaces. They circled twice before finally resorting to stalking a family back to their car.

"I feel like a cheetah tracking its prey," Maribeth said.

"I know," Stephen said, as he pulled to the side and put on his blinker while the family loaded shopping bags into an SUV. "If anyone takes the spot, you go out and eat them, okay?"

"Oh, no. I'm just here for gift advice." The family was piling into the car now. "I'm actually good at it. I used to edit holiday gift guides."

"Really?"

"Yep. Back in my other life."

Maribeth's temples began to pound as soon as they got inside and saw the line for Santa's Village snaking past the food court. The children, faces sticky with extorted cotton candy, were already sugar-high out of their minds, and their poor parents all

252

seemed ready for a good long nap that would not happen for another month.

Ahh, the holidays. Maribeth was a little relieved to have no part in them this year. Not that she ever had much to say about Christmas, aside from buying Jason's family their presents and organizing the trip to whichever one of his relatives they were celebrating with. "Well, it's not really *your* holiday, is it?" Lauren had said a few Christmases back when Maribeth had suggested that maybe, just maybe, her buying five presents per twin was overkill.

They passed various stores, Maribeth calling out suggestions: Crate and Barrel for a knife set? Tumi for a suitcase? Kate Spade for a handbag? Stephen vetoed everything. Mallory didn't cook. She traveled with a backpack. Designer bags were too bourgeois, and also, leather.

They were standing near the entrance to Nordstrom when Maribeth heard the strongest Pittsburgh accent she'd encountered so far calling, "Dr. Grant. Dr. Grant? Is that you? Look Donny, it's him!"

An elderly couple in matching tracksuits barreled toward them. Unlike pretty much everyone else in the mall, they carried no shopping bags, only water bottles holstered into fanny packs.

Stephen plastered on a bright toothy smile. It made him look, Maribeth thought, like a doctor, just not her doctor.

"Don, Susan, good to see you," he said. There was a round of back-patting and handshaking.

"Who's your *friend*?" Susan asked.

"This is M.B. M.B., Don and Susan were my patients."

"We had matching heart attacks," Don said, smiling at Susan adoringly. "Five years ago, one after the other."

"My heart attack gave him a heart attack," Susan said.

"My doll baby." Don's line was accompanied by a dramatic clutch of the chest.

It was kind of sweet, this practiced shtick. It was also obvious by the way they delivered their lines to Maribeth that it occurred to neither of them that she might be a patient, that she too might have had a heart attack.

"You both look well," Stephen said. "And I haven't heard from you, which I take as a good sign."

"Because you're not at the practice anymore. We're with that Dr. Garber now," Don said.

"Don!" Susan scolded. She lowered her voice. "We don't like him as much. We would've followed you to the new place but we didn't know and then all of our records and insurance are with the old place."

"It's fine," Stephen said.

"I don't want you to think that we thought . . ." Susan trailed off. "It was all just so sad."

"I appreciate that," Stephen said, though Maribeth noticed his doctorly smile was fraying at the edges. "You're here doing your walks?"

"We come three times a week," Susan said. "Just like you told us to. Usually it's not as crowded."

"I said it would be," Don said.

"I thought it would be worse if we came early," Susan snapped.

"You look well," Stephen said again, starting to pull away.

"We are. And my cholesterol, you wouldn't believe," Don said. "It's at 140 and my LDL is very low and my HDL is high. What were the numbers, Suse?"

"That's wonderful," Stephen said.

"You should see the grands," Don said, pulling out a battered billfold.

Maribeth sensed it, then, his discomfort, his need to get away, and above all, his sadness. She'd been curious about what had happened with his old practice but had resisted trying to find out. Now, she was glad not to know. It felt, somehow, like protecting him.

"We should go," Maribeth said, linking an arm through Stephen's. "I'm late."

Stephen looked momentarily confused. "Right. So you are. Don, Susan, good to see you both."

"You, too. Dr. Grant. I'm glad you're doing better," Susan said. "Life marches on. It must."

As Maribeth and Stephen left Don and Susan and escaped into Nordstrom, Stephen's mood clouded over and Maribeth's spirits, as if finally admitting defeat, plummeted as well. A piano player was going to town with Christmas carols, and an army of overly made-up young women was politely, but aggressively, offering fragrance samples. It all made Maribeth dizzy. She had a sudden flashback of nearly passing out at Macy's while she and Jason registered for their wedding (or, rather, as Elizabeth registered for them — she'd come along to offer "technical support" and had gleefully aimed that little gun at gravy boats and Nambé salt shakers while Maribeth and Jason shuffled behind her).

In women's apparel she stopped in front of a rainbow display of cashmere. "How about a sweater?" she asked. "Cashmere's good for cold weather but also more temperate. Very flexible."

"I don't know," Stephen said. "Feels a little conservative for Mal."

"How about arm warmers?" she suggested. "A little more funky. They'll keep her warm in the Pittsburgh winters." She was no longer conversing. She was speaking in *Frap* copy.

"Maybe. If she ever came home."

"Oh?"

"I usually go there."

"Where's there?"

"San Francisco."

"I fucking *hate* San Francisco."

She'd said it loudly and several shoppers turned around with disapproving expressions, as if this were not Nordstrom but the Sistine Chapel, and it was not Golden Gate City she'd maligned but God.

"What did San Francisco ever do to you?" Stephen asked.

She had such a visceral memory of that one horrible trip to see Jason there. It had only been a few months since he'd announced his intention to move to San Francisco after graduation. Maribeth had been shocked. Not just because it was the first she'd heard of it, but because only a few weeks earlier, Jason's sister, Lauren, had come to visit and had taken Maribeth out for an early twenty-second birthday lunch. "Look," Lauren had told her after they'd ordered, "Jason asked me to take you out so I could sneakily get your ring finger sized but I have no idea how to do that without you figuring it out so can we just go to the jeweler after this and you pretend to be surprised later?"

"Surprised? About what?"

"Mom gave Jason her engagement ring," Lauren said. "You know, now that the divorce is final she doesn't want it anymore."

"And he wants to give it to me?" It took a minute for the implication to sink in. Jason was going to propose? They'd discussed moving to New York City together after graduation — her to work in magazines, him to get a job as an A&R scout for a record label — and maybe getting a place together down the line and, yes, there was a permanence to their talks of the future. But getting married?

They had her finger sized and then nothing happened. Her birthday came and went; no proposal. Spring break came and she and Jason went to New York City together so she could do informational interviews with human resources reps. No proposal.

As the weeks went by and still no proposal came, she found herself growing anxious, wondering if *now* would be the moment. She began to anticipate it. And then she began to anticipate it eagerly.

She'd been anticipating when Jason told her that he'd decided to move to San Francisco.

"But I can't move to San Francisco," she'd said, misunderstanding at first.

"I know that," he'd replied.

"Wait. Are you breaking up with me?"

"What? No. It's not about you." Jason had rushed to explain how the tech scene was starting to heat up and there might be a future in Internet radio and he might be able to deejay. Now was the time to take a risk, he said, when he was unencumbered.

Unencumbered? She'd felt so humiliated, so caught out. How could she have been thinking *forever* when Jason had been thinking *San Francisco*?

But then they didn't break up. They graduated and she moved to Manhattan and he went to San Francisco, and she got a job as an editorial floater at a magazine publisher and he got work as a temp. They kept in touch, e-mailing, calling each other when the rates were low. When he suggested Maribeth visit for Labor Day weekend, she wondered if he was finally going to propose. She used her brand new credit card to buy a ticket.

Maribeth knew from the minute he picked her up at the airport that it wasn't going to happen. Their kiss was awkward. Everything about the weekend was awkward, that aborted proposal stomping around like the elephant in his tiny room. (Lauren must've told him that she'd told Maribeth. Maribeth wanted to ask, but couldn't.) Neither one knew what to do, what to say. So they compensated by having a ton of sex — which wasn't that great either — and then Maribeth got a bladder infection. Her old college roommate Courtney was about to start graduate school at Berkeley and said she could hook her up with some antibiotics so Maribeth had borrowed Jason's car to go see her. "I can tell things with you two are still going strong," Courtney said, winking and handing over the Cipro. Maribeth hadn't said anything.

It was on the way back to Jason's place that Maribeth had gotten hopelessly lost. Market. Divisadero. The Presidio. She kept going in circles, trying to find Golden Gate Park, which was the one landmark she knew. The afternoon fog was rolling in off the

Pacific. She had no idea where she was and now she couldn't see. Alone in the car, she began to cry. It seemed like she would drive around, in the fog, on an endless tank of gas, lost and alone, until she withered and died.

Not long after she got back to New York, she called Jason and told him that though she still loved him, the long distance wasn't working. He agreed. They broke up. It had all seemed, at the time, very mature. Very amicable.

And then three weeks later, Courtney called to tell her about Jason's new girl-friend, and Maribeth had had her meltdown in the bathroom.

"I don't know," she told Stephen. "I just hate it there."

They left the mall empty-handed, and empty. That night, when Maribeth climbed into bed, she pulled the pillow over her head and cried. It had been another miserable holiday weekend. Thanksgiving, after all.

39

Monday morning Maribeth woke up to someone knocking on her door. She peered through the peephole. It was Mr. Giulio, coming to collect the rent on the first of the month.

She counted out eight hundred-dollar bills for him and after he left she went about counting all the cash she had left. Twenty-one thousand and some change. At this rate, she could probably last at least a year in Pittsburgh. She never had any intention of staying away that long, but the past weekend had forced her to face up to some ugly truths. She had left not only her children but also her marriage. She had always planned to go back. But what if there was no back for her to return to?

And what happened then? When the twenty-one thousand dollars ran out? How had she not thought about the implications before? Because she had not just walked out on her family; she had left her job, her career, too. She'd burned the last bridge to what had been her city on a hill since she was thirteen years old and received that first copy of *Seventeen* (Brooke Shields on the cover) and had known with a strange-but-comforting certainty that when she grew up, she would somehow do that.

Elizabeth used to tease her about her single-minded ambition. Maribeth remembered one day, about two years after they'd met, when they discovered they'd both been invited to a seminar about the future of magazines put on by one of the big industry trade groups. After the coffee and rock-hard Danish networking portion of the event, Elizabeth whispered: "We came. We schmoozed. Let's shop. I heard about a Lacroix sample sale in Chelsea."

They hadn't gone shopping but instead had gone to Central Park, where they'd laid out on the fresh grass of Sheep Meadow, kicked off their heels, and basked in the spring sun and the chance to spend time together during the workday.

"I feel bad," Maribeth said after a while. "That we ditched. Those seminar invitations are hot tickets."

"You hardly need a seminar to tell you about your future," Elizabeth had teased.

"You already have it all in your lists."

This was true. In high school, Maribeth had told a guidance counselor about her desire to work at a magazine one day and the counselor had advised her to take journalism classes and write for the school newspaper and attend a college with a journalism program and maybe one day do an internship at one of the magazines in New York City. Maribeth had copied it all down — newspaper, journalism, college, internship, New York City — and over the years had followed the plan meticulously, writing many more lists in the interim.

And it had worked. After graduating from college, she'd landed the position as a floater — her $16,500 a year salary barely covered her rent and subway tokens — until she nabbed her first permanent job at a cooking magazine. She spent a year and a half there until she was hired as an assistant editor at a women's business magazine, which was where she currently worked. She planned to stay there another year and jump to another publication if she hadn't been promoted to associate editor by then.

"I can tell you your future if you want," Elizabeth said. "You'll work your way up the masthead and within ten years, fifteen tops, you'll be an editor-in-chief."

Maribeth didn't answer. That was exactly what she hoped, exactly what she had written in her lists.

"As for me, I'll be one of those sad, forty-year-old waitresses. Like the actresses who never make it. Don't get me wrong. I'll work at a nice restaurant and make good tips but I'll have foot problems and I'll never be able to get the smell of grease completely out of my hair."

Maribeth laughed and playfully kicked Elizabeth's leg. "You're so full of shit," she said. In the two years since they'd met, she and Elizabeth had both risen at the same pace. Elizabeth was now an assistant editor at a trendy new men's magazine. "You'll run your own magazine, too. You know you will."

"Nah. I don't, actually. I'm not a natural editor like you. I can't make copy sing or come up with the quippy display copy and cover lines. You're a genius at cover lines. This stuff is in your blood. I'm just some art history major who lucked her way into an internship." She shook her head. "One day, they'll all figure out what a fraud I am."

"Everyone feels that way. And you have other strengths. You have a nose for trends, for seeing what the next big thing on the horizon will be. You have vision. You can't learn that in J school."

Elizabeth had flipped over onto her elbows, plucking tiny flowers from the grass. "Maybe," she said. "Just promise me if you become an editor-in-chief and I'm some pathetic waitress, you'll hire me."

"So long as you promise me the same thing."

"Don't be absurd," Elizabeth said. "You're far too clumsy to be a waitress."

They laughed. And then they promised.

Maribeth and Elizabeth had each climbed from assistants to associates to senior-level editors. And then their paths diverged. Elizabeth met Tom, got married, became an editor-in-chief. And Maribeth became a mom, had a heart attack, and ran away from home.

In every issue of *Frap,* there was a profile called Unsung Heroes that highlighted an "ordinary" woman with an "extraordinary" story. Usually, these women experienced some great crisis, and instead of being beaten down, they "took stock" and "reevaluated" and "rose to the occasion" to "beat the odds" and always wound up so much better and wiser than they had been before.

Readers loved this section — Maribeth

suspected it was because it was the only place they ever saw women larger than a size eight — but she found it to be the most disingenuous part of the whole magazine, even worse than the gift guides in which $10-million-a-movie actresses gushed over their favorite $60 artisanal salts. It wasn't that the stories were made up — they were true, or, at least, truthy — but their rictus need to skim coat a happy ending onto every shitty situation . . . she couldn't stand that. It was the magazine's version of Jason's "everything will be fine."

Maybe one day it would be fine. Maybe one day she would get past all this and figure out some great second act. Maybe then she might look back and see that all the destruction she had brought down on her family, on her marriage, on herself, had been worth it. Because she would be extraordinary. Because she would be a real-life hero.

But standing here now, amid the wreckage of her own making, it was nearly impossible to imagine.

40

Dr. Grant — Stephen? she wasn't sure what to call him in his official context — had sent Maribeth to have a blood test. They discussed her results at her next appointment. The numbers, he said, were excellent. The statins were working. Her iron levels were fine. She did not need to schedule another follow-up unless she felt she needed to.

"So this is it?" she asked.

"This is it," he said.

She half-expected some official pronouncement. "You are healthy and are hereby relieved of duty." Perhaps he might tap her on the shoulder with a stethoscope. But instead he kept absentmindedly offering her tea, even though she had never once accepted his offer of tea because she didn't drink tea. (It made her teeth feel unpleasantly squeaky.)

"So maybe I should let you get on with your day?" Maribeth said, though she was well aware there was no busy day for either of them. She didn't have much to do on a good day and she never planned anything for the afternoons of her appointments with him because the meandering conversations tended to bleed into the dinner hour. And she now knew — the run-in with Don and Susan had made it even clearer — that he had few other demands on his time. But she was officially healthy. There was no need to keep this up.

"Oh, okay," he said. He seemed a little out of it himself. Or maybe not out of it, but not like the man she'd spent Thanksgiving with or had gone to the mall with. "Before you go, I have something for you. It's upstairs in the study."

She stood to follow him, but he motioned for her to stay put, which also felt like a demotion. She was no longer invited into the private space. "I'll be right back."

He returned with a thick creamy envelope, her name, or rather his version of it, written on the front.

"I'm intrigued," she said.

"Don't be. They're guest passes to my health club. Five of them. They expire at the end of the year so I thought someone might as well use them."

Health club passes. How terribly sensible.

269

What had she hoped for? Tickets to Bermuda? He was, at the end of it, her doctor. And after today's appointment, not even that.

They shook hands. "Thank you," she said. "For all you've done." She felt bereft. Was this it? After the ice cream and the hair and the horrible shopping trip and the talks? Was this the end of it?

"You take care of yourself," he said. "Join the gym. Remember ice cream won't kill you."

Yes, this was it. And why wouldn't it be? He had gotten her where she needed to be. But hadn't he done more? Hadn't they been more?

She wanted to acknowledge that, to hear him acknowledge it. There was something between them. Something that transcended doctor and patient. Something that transcended friendship. Even if today marked the end of it, she wanted some indication that it had been there. Because why else had he been so good to her? Why else had she let him be?

She tucked the envelope into her bag. At reception, she said good-bye to Louise. "Call if you need anything," Louise said.

At the bus stop, Maribeth took out the envelope and opened it. Perhaps there would be a note inside, something private between them. But there wasn't, just the passes. The club was obviously a nice one. The passes were printed on thick card stock, with diploma-fancy embossed script reading, *For Guests of the Grant Family.*

She ran her finger over it. *For Guests of the Grant Family.* And so there it was, an acknowledgment, after all, even if it was unintentional. He had lost his family. She had lost hers. In different ways, and for different reasons, she and Stephen were both orphans now.

41

The next day, Maribeth arranged to take a tour of the health club. It was nice, all the newest machines and every kind of class, from yoga to kickboxing. But it was the swimming pool in the basement that called to her. She wasn't sure why but it felt like this, more than an elliptical machine or a vinyasa class, would ease the itchiness that was growing inside of her. Swimming felt new. Or maybe it was because she was sinking and wanted to see whether, if forced to, she might swim.

The club was in Squirrel Hill, catty corner to the library there. Maribeth decided to stop by, because it was on her way and she'd not seen it before and she'd heard it had an extensive collection. She was not going to touch the computers. Absolutely not.

Five minutes in, she touched the computers. She checked her e-mail. There was nothing from Jason. Of course there wasn't.

She was furious anew, but this time at herself. It was her own fault for opening this Pandora's box. For five weeks, Jason had not e-mailed her but she had not known about it and had been fine. For five days she had known and had been a basket case.

The next morning she woke up and resolved to avoid all computers and e-mail and the temptation of the library. Instead, she would try swimming. She took a bus to Target to procure a bathing suit and a pair of goggles, then took another bus over to the club.

A Mommy and Me swim class must have just gotten out because a parade of towel-swaddled toddlers was being shepherded into the locker room. Maribeth recognized the look on some of the mothers' faces: a sort of shell-shocked glaze. Because who in their right mind thought it was a wise idea to mix helpless children and deep water?

Maribeth had taken precisely two swim classes with the twins. At the first one, Liv kept trying to unhook the flotation brick strapped to her chest, while Oscar cried every time he felt even the tiniest splash. The teacher, a balding Israeli, had suggested she take turns with the twins, but Oscar cried when she left him on the deck, and while unsupervised, Liv had wandered over to the deep end and jumped in.

Later that week, Maribeth had recounted the story to Elizabeth, who had snorted with laughter. "It's not funny," she'd told her friend.

"It's a little funny," Elizabeth had replied.

Maribeth failed to see the humor. All those years of trying to get pregnant, she'd dreamt of doing something like this: swim class with her babies. Now it turned out, like so much else, to be a bust.

"Why don't you ask Jason to help?" Elizabeth suggested.

Now *that* was funny. Jason's salary was paying for the lessons. They could not afford for him to take time off to swim.

"I could come," Elizabeth said.

This time Maribeth had laughed out loud, assuming Elizabeth was kidding. But the next week, there she was, at eleven on a Thursday morning. In her Chanel bikini and Brazilian-blowout hair, Elizabeth was a tropical fish amid all the guppy moms in their fraying Lands' End one-pieces. But she'd been great with the kids, excitedly bobbing in the water with Liv, distracting Oscar with songs, while dishing the latest gossip to Maribeth about her new boss, a legendary, seventy-five-year-old editor-in-chief who still believed in the three-martini lunch. It was a welcome change from all the talk of sleep training and Music Together classes.

But the following week, Elizabeth canceled. She had forgotten she was taking Friday off for a long weekend with Tom and she could not skip out Thursday. She was so sorry. Maribeth was disappointed, but she understood. After a whirlwind courtship, Elizabeth and Tom had only recently gotten married — on a yacht, off the coast of Capri; Maribeth had not been able to attend.

Maribeth told Elizabeth to enjoy the time with Tom and then didn't go to swim class that week. But then the following Wednesday night, Elizabeth called to cancel again. Her boss had invited her to one of his three-martini lunches and she couldn't refuse. "I promise I'll be there next time," she said.

"Oh, don't worry about it. We went last week and I managed just fine," Maribeth lied.

The next day she dropped the class.

Maribeth waited until the Mommy and Me brigade cleared out before stripping down to her suit. The high neckline covered most of the scar on her chest but there was no hiding her leg.

It was only after she'd stashed everything in her locker that she realized she had not brought a lock. She carried a couple of hundred-dollar bills at all times — contingency cash, and also her nest egg in case some clever thief got into the apartment, found all her hiding places, and cleaned her out.

Across the aisle, a woman in a swimsuit was locking up. "Do you know if they sell locks here?" Maribeth asked.

The woman stared at her through blue-tinted goggles. "Maribeth?" she asked.

Her first thought was that Jason, upon receiving her e-mail, had tracked her to Pittsburgh and sent someone to tail her. Her second thought was that this made no sense, given he had not attempted to contact her once in the previous four weeks nor responded to her messages.

Even after the woman pulled off her goggles and swim cap, it took Maribeth a minute to realize it was Janice.

"Golly, what a treat to bump into you," Janice said. "I didn't know you swam!"

"I don't. Not really. A friend gave me guest passes and I thought I'd try something new. But I didn't bring a lock."

"Why don't you share my locker?"

They walked back to Janice's locker. Maribeth stuffed her things inside.

"I was going to call you this afternoon," Janice said as they went down the stairs to the pool deck.

"You were?"

"Yes, I wanted to e-mail you over the weekend, but I didn't have your address."

"Oh, I don't use e-mail much these days. I can give it to you. Why? Did you find something?"

"Not yet. I need more information. Your parents' social security numbers would be helpful. Or a copy of your birth certificate."

"Oh. Okay." Her birth certificate was at home but she thought she might have that other information in her e-mail archives. "You could've called."

"I didn't want to interrupt you over the holidays in case you were with family."

"I wasn't. With family."

"Oh, me neither," Janice said.

"What did you do?" Maribeth asked.

"Mostly paperwork."

"Oh. I'm sorry." Maribeth wasn't sure why she should feel guilty, but she did.

"No, don't be. I roasted a turkey breast, which is the best part anyhow, and I even have leftovers for sandwiches."

They'd arrived at the pool. Maribeth had assumed lunchtime would be off-peak, but all five lanes were full of swimmers. "It's so busy."

Janice snapped her bathing cap low over her ears and adjusted her goggles. "This is nothing." Maribeth expected Janice to get into the slow lane, which was where the older people were swimming, but she set out toward the faster lanes. "Have a good swim," she called over her shoulder.

Maribeth stood above the slow lane. The three people circling in there seemed to be going terribly fast. Maribeth spent a good few minutes trying to figure out the etiquette of inserting herself into the flow. It reminded her of being fifteen, in driver's training, trying to work up the nerve to merge into freeway traffic for the first time.

When there was a break in the swimmers, she got in and tried a sort of breast stroke but soon found that her still-healing underarm muscles restricted her range of motion so greatly that she was hardly moving. A swimmer swooped up suddenly behind her.

"Sorry," she called.

She switched to a doggy paddle and made it to the end of the pool, where she held on to the side while she caught her breath. Another swimmer came up behind her. "Are you swimming?" she asked. Maribeth wasn't sure if what she was doing could rightly be called swimming. It felt more like not-drowning, but before she could think of an answer, the swimmer did one of those neat little underwater turn-kicks and took off (not remotely slowly, Maribeth couldn't help but notice) in the other direction.

Once she'd caught her breath and once there was a decent gap between her and the other swimmers, she pushed off again. This time she tried the crawl, *crawl* being the optimal word in describing her painfully slow stroke. Two swimmers passed her before she reached the other end of the lane. In the time it took her to complete the next length — having to stop and stand halfway through — all the other swimmers in her lane had passed her. She could feel their impatience radiating through the water. Slow lane or not, she understood, she shouldn't be here. She was the old lady do-ing thirty-five on the freeway.

By the time she reached the other end — she had done four lengths at this point — her breath was raggedy, perilously close to hyperventilation. She felt panicked and must've looked it, too, because the lifeguard jumped down from his perch and in a voice that carried across the pool deck asked, "Ma'am, are you in crisis?"

She was forty-four years old and had suffered a heart attack and undergone bypass surgery. She'd run away from home and neither her husband nor her best friend had tried to contact her. And she couldn't swim. Yes, she was in motherfucking crisis!

"I'm fine," she gasped.

She managed to heave herself out of the pool and get herself back upstairs without collapsing. Up in the locker room she realized that all her things were stowed in Janice's locker. And she had forgotten to bring a towel.

She was on the bench, shivering, when she felt a towel being draped over her shoulders. "There you are."

Maribeth couldn't answer. It wasn't just that she was still breathless and shaking, it was that she had been caught out again. She could float, she could tread water, she could paddle, she could even approximate the strokes, but she couldn't actually swim. How had she not known this?

"Let's get you warmed up," Janice said, guiding her toward the communal showers. She stood under the water a long time, letting the heat soak the cold and sorrow and emptiness out of her. When she finally dried off, she felt as wrung out as if she'd been swimming hard laps for days.

Janice was already dressed and packed up.

Maribeth apologized.

"What are you sorry for?" Janice asked.

When Maribeth didn't answer, Janice asked, "How long since your surgery?"

She was briefly surprised. But of course, she was now naked, her medical history was etched in relief all over her skin. "Seven weeks."

"Why, that's no time at all."

Even if she could swim, it was a certain kind of hubris, perhaps the same sort that made her think she could run away with no repercussions, to think she could simply get into the pool and go.

She handed Janice back her towel. It was white, like a flag of surrender.

42

Later that afternoon, Maribeth logged on to her e-mail to search for her parents' social security numbers. She really had given up on hearing from Jason. When she saw his message, for a brief second she wondered if he'd done that on purpose, waited the exact number of days that it would take her to go through the stages of grief and then just when she was starting to feel, if not okay, then resigned, drop an e-mail.

But that was paranoid.

Also that was way too much effort for Jason.

There was no subject line, but there was a little paper clip icon in the attachments field. Had he written her a letter begging her to come home? Had he sent divorce papers?

Okay. Take ten calming breaths. One, two —

Her hands flew to the keyboard, opening

the message, downloading the attachment. She began to read. The first line was sickeningly familiar.

She felt vomit rise in her throat. She pushed herself away from the table. She did not want to puke on a library computer.

After five weeks away and nearly a week since she'd e-mailed him, Jason's response was to send back the note that she had written to him the day she'd left home. Just like that. Return to sender.

This was what she meant to him? *This* was what her absence meant? So little that he had nothing new to say? All he could be bothered to do was to throw her words back at her?

She hadn't remembered exactly what she'd written on that rushed morning, but seeing that first line again . . . She closed the window, deleted the e-mail, and emptied the trash, erasing all traces.

Except she couldn't erase what Jason had done. She couldn't believe he'd done that.

But as she sat there, her tears drying into itchy streaks, she could. Why *would* Jason respond? Why would he offer to carry any of the load when he never had before? Why would he start now, after she'd done this unforgivable thing, relinquishing all rights to martyrdom, transferring them so neatly to him. On a platter. Just like always.

She didn't know why she'd hoped for more, but she had.

She didn't know what she'd expected, but not this.

43

Dear Liv and Oscar,
~~I'm sorry~~
~~Don't hate me~~
~~I'll always be your mother~~
~~I had to~~
~~I left because~~

44

The next day, she was back on the couch, in her nest of blankets, the TV bleating away. Janice called to invite her swimming and she said no. Todd and Sunita texted that they were going on the weekly shopping trip that night and she didn't respond. Janice called again to ask if she'd had any luck getting that information she'd requested and she put her off. Todd called and she didn't answer. Janice called a third time to say that she had some potential news and why didn't they meet at the pool tomorrow to discuss. Maribeth said maybe. Sunita texted, asking her if she wanted to go to that hipster craft fair on Saturday. Maribeth didn't respond.

You okay? Sunita texted.

"I don't know," she answered out loud.

And then Stephen texted. *Checking in to see how you're doing. Also, starting to panic about*

Mallory's gift. Almost bought her a banana chair.

It was the first time she'd smiled since, well, since the last time she'd seen Stephen.

She thought about the craft fair, which Sunita had described being like an Etsy flea market. It actually sounded like the kind of place they might find something for the discerning Mallory.

Step away from the banana chair, Maribeth texted back.

She kicked off the blankets.

Screw Jason.

45

When Janice said she wanted to meet Maribeth at the club to discuss news about her birth-mother search, Maribeth figured it was a matter of convenience. The pool was around the corner from the school where Janice worked and she often swam on her lunch break. "Make sure you bring flip-flops this time," Janice said. "You don't want to catch a fungus." Maribeth had little intention of swimming again, but in deference to Janice, she did pack a bathing suit.

In the locker room, Janice started to undress and Maribeth started to undress with her because not to felt weird.

"Some potentially exciting news but I don't want to get your hopes up too much. It's not certain," Janice said.

"What?" Maribeth asked.

"Allegheny Children's Home, one of the oldest, still-operating adoption agencies in Pittsburgh, has a record of a baby girl with your date of birth."

"Is that me?" Maribeth asked.

"It might be," Janice replied. "We could use more information to verify. Your parents' social security numbers would be helpful."

"I'll get that as soon as I can," she promised.

"Once we have that, we can try to confirm. And the Orphans' Court search is underway but I'd expect that to go on into the new year."

Maribeth sighed.

Janice patted Maribeth on the arm, then glanced down at Maribeth's bare feet. "Did you bring the flip-flops?"

"No. But I don't think I'll swim today."

"Oh, nonsense. You brought your suit didn't you?"

"Well, yes, but . . ."

"And here, I brought an extra pair." She handed Maribeth some orange shower shoes. "If they fit, you can keep them."

"But I don't think I'm going to swim."

"Try them on. Do they fit?"

They were a size or two big but they would do.

"Perfect," Janice said. "As for your swimming, I was thinking, I could give you some tips."

"Tips?" Maribeth began to suspect that

the meeting at the pool had not been a matter of convenience. She had been played.

"I was a lifeguard for years. I'm not certified anymore but I've taught more than my share of children to swim."

"I'm not exactly a child," she said.

"I know," Janice said. "But I'm sure I can teach you, too."

Five minutes later, Janice was presenting Maribeth with a kickboard.

"Really?" Maribeth asked.

"I find it's good to start at the beginning."

"But I thought I just needed tips, like you said, on my form. Because I'm recovering from surgery."

"True. But good form sometimes means unlearning bad habits," Janice said.

"What bad habits?"

"Oh, nothing specific."

"But it's not as if I've never swum before." She may not know how to swim properly but she could swim. Sort of.

"Sometimes the best way to master something is to start at the beginning."

Any minute now Janice was going to turn into Julie Andrews and start singing.

"Fine." Maribeth reached for the kickboard.

Janice held onto it. "Not so fast. Do you

know how to kick?"

She was insulted. She knew that much. "Of course I do."

"It's just that most people kick with their knees bent like this." She mimed kicking with her fingers bent at the knuckle. "But really you should keep legs straight and kick from your hip like this." She kicked with straight fingers.

Maribeth didn't say anything. She had always kicked with bent knees.

Janice demonstrated and then handed the board to Maribeth. "Don't forget to point your toes, graceful like a ballerina."

Maribeth started kicking. The board flipped over and she went with it. Graceful like a water buffalo.

"Here," Janice said, taking the board back. "Hold it in front of you and keep your elbows straight. Then kick from your hip crease. Lightly. No need to fight the water."

After a few tries, the board stopped wobbling so much, and after a few more, she was able to kick straight. She went up the length of the pool, then back. Up. And back. Her hamstrings and calves started to burn and her pointed toe sent her foot into a spasm. None of it was graceful, none of it was fun. But for a moment or two there, she did zone out enough to forget about her birth mother and about Jason and the kids.

Then Janice took the kickboard away. "That's enough for today," she said.

"But I only kicked," Maribeth said.

"And that's plenty for one day," Janice repeated.

Well, at least she was not on the verge of passing out this time. Up in the locker room, Janice reminded her to get the information about her parents. Maribeth promised it by Monday. Which was when they agreed to meet for their next swim lesson. Maribeth wasn't sure how she felt about that, but it seemed too late to back out.

46

Saturday morning Maribeth texted Stephen. *Pick me up at 11 or meet at the craft fair?*

A minute later, her phone rang. "I can't make it," Stephen said.

He'd been so keen to go when she'd suggested it a few days ago. "Medical emergency?" she asked.

"In a matter of speaking." He did not sound right. His voice was not just hoarse but raw, as if he'd been drinking glass.

"Are you sick?"

"If I am, it's by my own hand."

"What do you mean?"

He coughed. "I am hungover, M.B. Very, very hungover."

"I'm coming over," she said.

"I'm not fit for company," he said.

"I don't expect to be entertained."

"I'm just in very bad shape."

"Didn't you once tell me that it was okay

293

to ask for help?"

The line was silent. Then he said: "Come over."

He was gray. His hair, his skin, his rumpled, sour-smelling T-shirt, all of it gray. She knew he was nearly sixty, but this was the first time she'd thought of him as old.

The source of his misery was sitting out on the counter: three empty wine bottles and a half-full pint of something else.

Maribeth could see he was embarrassed by the booze, by having her witness it. So she brushed right past, brusque as can be, as if she were the cleaning lady and this were an unpleasant business but nothing unusual.

She took the bottles out to the recycling bin, wondering if this was the scandal. A binge alcoholic cardiologist. Word would travel fast, if not to her.

Back inside, he was hunched over a mug of coffee.

"Warm that up for you?" she asked.

He shook his head.

"Can't keep it down?" she asked.

Another sad, little-boy shake of the head.

She dumped the coffee and poured a glass of water and set it before him. "Do you have any Alka-Seltzer?"

"Upstairs. Bedroom nightstand."

As she climbed the stairs, the treads groaned, as if the whole house were suffering. She found the large master bedroom, its king-size bed rumpled and unmade, and paused at the threshold. She could smell him, his usual scent of bergamot and leather, mixing with the spoiled-cheese aroma of vomit.

Walking lightly on the balls of her feet, she went to his nightstand. (She assumed it was his; it was cluttered with medical journals.) She opened the drawer; inside were more medical journals, a deck of playing cards, a Kindle, some Post-it notes, but no Alka-Seltzer.

The nightstand on the other side of the bed was bare, save for a framed wedding photo covered in a film of dust. Now Maribeth truly felt like an interloper as she opened the drawer. There, next to a package of Kleenex and a dog-eared collection of Junot Díaz stories, was an open box of Alka-Seltzer.

Had Felicity used it to settle her stomach during the chemotherapy? Had she read the Díaz stories to take her mind away from the bleakness of her present? The uncertainty of her future?

The master bathroom smelled strongly of

vomit. Holding her breath, she rifled through the medicine cabinet, found a bottle of pain reliever, and went back downstairs.

Stephen sat at the counter, staring into space, the glass of water untouched. She dissolved the Alka-Seltzer and tapped his hand. She placed three tablets of Tylenol in his palm. "Swallow," she commanded. "Drink."

He drank the water, eyes closed, in one gulp. Maribeth resisted the urge to say "good boy." When he belched, the fumes were strong enough to give her a contact buzz.

"Better?" she asked.

A grimacing attempt at a smile. "A little."

"I'm going to make you eggs, something greasy. It'll absorb whatever booze is left in you."

"Who's the doctor now?" he said weakly.

"Do you have eggs?"

He nodded toward the refrigerator. It was mostly empty. But it did have half a dozen eggs, some half-and-half, and some butter.

"How about hot sauce?" she asked.

He nodded toward the pantry. She shuffled around and found several specialty bottles of CaJohn, a Trinidadian brand. She wondered if that was where Felicity was from. Or maybe they got it on holiday there. Or maybe they just liked hot sauce.

"We're two for two," she said. "Going for a trifecta. Bread?"

"Try the freezer."

She found some hamburger rolls and set them out to thaw. She beat the eggs with half-and-half and salt and pepper, heated the skillet, and melted a pat of butter and poured in the eggs.

"How come my kitchen only smells good when you're here?" Stephen asked.

"I'll take it as a sign of progress that you think food smells good." She popped the rolls into the toaster oven, gave the eggs a toss with the spatula, sprinkled on the hot sauce.

"Where did you learn to cook?"

"It's only scrambled eggs, Stephen. Pretty basic."

"But you know how to cook properly. I can tell."

"I do. I learned from a magazine."

"How industrious."

"Not from reading it, from working at one. My first job was at a cooking magazine. Before that I could make macaroni and cheese from a box."

"How'd you get a job at a cooking maga-zine then?"

"I faked it. The week before my interview I read cookbooks and food magazines and watched cooking shows, so that by the time I showed up, I was Julia Child."

"How long did you work there?"

"Long enough to give me an appreciation for cooking."

"I see that."

"That's what I loved about magazines. You become an expert in something for a few years. Budget travel, world affairs, celebrity lifestyles."

"Jack of all trades."

"Master of none." Which was true. She was highly skilled as an editor and basically a dilettante at everything else. Except now she wasn't even an editor anymore.

She folded the eggs onto the plate and started to douse them in more hot sauce. He raised his hand. "I think maybe that's enough."

"You have to trust me," she said. "I don't understand the scientific reasoning why spicy cures hangover, only that it does."

"Perhaps we should author a paper on it."

"Then we have to test it first."

She put the plate in front of him. He made a face.

"One bite. You just said it smelled good."

He picked up the fork, took a small bite,

chewed, swallowed.

"See," she said. "You're not dead."

"Give it a few minutes," he said.

"Your sense of humor is returning. Try a second bite. Keep it small."

"You're an excellent doctor." He smiled weakly. "Or maybe I should say, nurse."

She raised an eyebrow. "Demoted after one bite?"

"Promoted," he countered. "Nurses are the true healers." Then as if to convince her, he added. "Felicity was a nurse."

"Oh," she said. "Was that how you met?"

"No, she worked in pediatric oncology."

"Oncology." Maribeth shook her head. "How ironic."

Stephen took a bigger forkful of eggs. "I think this might be working," he said. "And ironic, how?"

Maribeth wondered if the question was some sort of rejoinder, scolding her for intruding on their private affairs. But he was the one who brought her up. Maribeth stammered something about the irony of an oncology nurse dying of cancer.

Stephen's fork clanked against his plate. "Felicity didn't die of cancer."

"She didn't?"

"What gave you that idea?"

Maribeth's face, neck, arms went hot. "I

don't know. She was just so young and pretty." She heard how ridiculous that sounded. "And you had those pink ribbons in your office."

He almost smiled. "Mallory works for the Breast Cancer Survivors' Network. She's an event planner. That's me showing school spirit. I'm sorry. I assumed you knew. Because everyone around here knows. And because of what you said that day in the ice cream parlor."

What had she said? Something about a deal, him not digging into her secrets, and her not digging into his.

"I didn't know," Maribeth stammered. "I mean, I don't."

"It's no mystery. It was in the newspaper, after all. I'd have expected you to do a more thorough job of vetting me."

She shook her head. She hadn't googled him once. She'd decided that if he had done something terrible, she didn't want to know about it.

"She died in a car accident. Which wasn't noteworthy. Many people do. Except this one happened to be my fault."

Her heart did something strange, an undulation stopped cold by a thud, which she understood had nothing to do with her coronary disease. "Your fault?"

"Perhaps not in the legal sense. But that doesn't change anything, does it?" He made a bitter guffaw, so un-Stephen-like, Maribeth thought. It was a sound much more at home coming out of her own mouth.

"What happened?"

"Bad luck. Bad karma. Who knows?" He waved his arms, as if accusing the universe. "We'd gone to see one of her former patients play with an orchestra in Cleveland. She was always doing things like that, attending school productions or weddings or concerts of former patients, and I was dragged along. This was a point of contention. I thought our job was to treat the patients, get them well to lead their own lives, not weave them into ours. But Felicity continued to collect her survivors. Sometimes she lectured me that I would be a better doctor if I wasn't so clinical. So removed, she said." He barked out another bitter laugh.

"In any case, I'd gone, reluctantly, to the orchestra, and then after we'd been — or rather, she'd been — invited to a gathering where this oboist patient of hers would be, and I had no choice but to go along. I wound up sitting at the bar while Felicity made herself the life of the party, as always. We didn't get on the road until midnight, which meant we wouldn't be getting home until two.

"In the car, I was angry with her about how late it was, and she was chiding me for being in such a rush when I had nothing to do the next day, and then she got upset with how fast I was driving, and things got nasty and I was distracted, so when the traffic backed up in front of us, I didn't see it. I slammed on my brakes but couldn't stop in time."

"Oh, god, I'm so sorry."

"No," Stephen said, holding out his hand. "That wasn't it. We were fine. It was just a fender bender."

The dread in Maribeth's stomach solidified. "What happened?" she whispered.

"What happened was that instead of pulling onto the shoulder or putting on my hazards, I spent the last moments of Felicity's life berating her for making me get into a crash. I was yelling at her when the car plowed into us from behind. I didn't even have my brake lights illuminated because I'd thrown the car into park."

"Oh, no, Stephen. No."

"I wound up with a concussion and dislocated shoulder. But Felicity." He paused to clear his throat. "Her side of the car . . . it wasn't even a car anymore."

He continued telling Maribeth this most

terrible of tales: sitting opposite Felicity, caged in by the wreckage, begging her to hold on, seeing that she couldn't. Maribeth started to cry.

He handed her a napkin and carried on, dry eyed. She had the sense that he wasn't talking to her anymore, but toward her, using her as a cover, so that he might withstand telling the story to himself. Much the same way she wrote to the twins.

"After, I took a month off work, and when I came back I'd already lost some patients. And then I lost some more because I became, I suppose the term was *gruff,* though I'd always been gruff, but I guess I just became something untenable.

"Maybe that was why the rumors started. Felicity was beloved. I was not. She was dead. I was not. There were whispers of my being drunk. I wasn't, though I certainly have been many nights since." He gestured toward the sink where the empties had been. "But people seemed to smell my wrongdoing. Or perhaps they didn't want any part of the whole sorry business. Who can blame them? The practice began to suffer. It was suggested I take a leave, though we all knew it was permanent."

He pushed away his plate of eggs. "Perhaps it was for the best. Medicine requires a certain level of delusion, a belief in one's invincibility. But watching Felicity die, being right there and not being able to do a goddamn thing to stop it, well, it robbed me of that, too."

And so this was it. Not a malpractice suit. Not binge drinking. Not even a scandal, at least not the kind she'd thought. It was a damaged heart, eating away at itself. This was something she understood.

Stephen was quiet now but his hands were shaking. Maribeth cupped them in hers, held them firm until the shaking stopped. Then she kissed him.

47

Before her swimming lesson on Monday, she stopped at the library in Squirrel Hill to search her e-mail archives for her parents' social security numbers. Since she had deleted the message from Jason without replying, she was not expecting to hear anything more. But there it was, another e-mail from him, the subject line an ominous P.S.

As in, P.S. I hate you? P.S. Don't come back? P.S. You are the worst mother in the world?

p.s. You seem to think I'm punishing you. For the record, it was Thanksgiving and we were in the country and then Oscar got sick so I was home with him and those e-mails were sent to my work account so I only saw them on Monday night. You'll forgive me if I took one goddamn day to absorb it all seeing as you haven't uttered a word for a month.

For Christ's sake, Maribeth, I'm leaving you be. I'm doing EVERYTHING you asked me to do. I don't know what else you want me to say.

She checked the date. It had been sent the day after she'd received the first e-mail from him. Two days before she had kissed Stephen.

She had been thinking about that kiss with a strange mix of tenderness and confusion, but now those were joined by a retroactive guilt. Because would she have kissed Stephen had she received this second e-mail from Jason? Had she kissed him to spite Jason? It hadn't felt that way. If she'd been thinking of either of the spouses in that kitchen, it was Felicity.

She read the message again. They were in the *country*? And what was wrong with Oscar?

Is Oscar okay? she typed immediately, and without thinking, hit send.

Jason must have been at his desk because his reply was immediate. He is fine.

Jason was never one for specifics. Not one for sweating the small stuff, though Maribeth could never get a bead on what qualified as the big stuff for him. For instance,

306

did her running away count?

But Oscar being sick was a concern. Was it his ears? His tubes? Oscar had been a late talker — everyone had assumed it was because Liv had a tendency to answer questions for both of them — until Lauren noticed him saying "What?" a lot and asked if they'd had his hearing tested. It had turned out Oscar's ears were so full of fluid he could barely hear, and that was why he wasn't talking. Maribeth had been mortified, by her failing Oscar, by Lauren catching it before she did. ("Come on," Jason had said, "she has four kids.") Oscar got ear tubes and speech therapy and had caught up, but over the summer, the tubes had fallen out, and the ENT said they needed to make sure the fluid didn't build up again.

She wrote back a longer e-mail: Was it Oscar's ears? Had Jason made an appointment with the ENT? Had he spoken to the speech therapist? Now that she had an opening, she asked more general questions: about the children's mental state, their physical state, their pediatrician appointments, their haircuts. When she finished, she had filled an entire screen with queries.

Jason's reply came too quickly for him to have answered properly. They are doing fine, he wrote.

Can you be more specific? she wrote back.

Oscar is fine. Liv is fine. I'm taking care of things. We are all fine.

Fine? Everything wrong with Jason Brinkley could be boiled down to that one innocuous word. It was one part wish fulfillment, two parts laziness. Yeah, everything was fine. Because she was there to make sure it was.

But she wasn't there now, so how exactly were things fine? He claimed he wasn't punishing her but when she and Jason got into a fight, this was exactly what he did: became a turtle, all hard shell. It was the perfect protection, the perfect weapon. She lost every time.

She understood that she deserved his anger. She wasn't trying to weasel out of it. She was not seeking forgiveness or absolution. She just wanted to know where she stood. For once, to know where she really stood. Because how could she even think of going back without knowing this? With the ground always shifting under her, how could she ever hope to regain her footing?

Fine? How could she trust such an insubstantial word? How could she trust such an insubstantial man? Who never said what he really meant. Did he mean fine as opposed to drowning, or fine as in thriving?

But then a jolt of understanding hit her like a fist to the gut. What if Jason was saying something else entirely? That they were doing fine. Without her.

48

Pittsburgh was not as cold as Maribeth had expected — she'd been anticipating piles of snow — but as winter approached, the blue skies seemed to disappear under a constant shroud of gray that chilled her to the bone. Maribeth had brought her winter coat but it was no match for the long, windy waits at bus stops, and she found herself lingering in her apartment, watching more TV, and feeling generally itchy and sad. Until one day she broke down and went to the fancy Goodwill in Shadyside and spent fifteen dollars on one of those puffy parkas that she and Elizabeth had always sworn never to wear.

Before leaving the store, she put on the new coat, stuffing her stylish but insufficient one in the plastic bag. As soon as she got outside, she understood she'd been doing it wrong. Wearing the parka was like walking in a sleeping bag. The cold nipped at her nose, her earlobes, but had no purchase with the rest of her. How in the world had she survived forty-four years without one of these things?

After her next swimming lesson — more time with the kickboard to work on rotary breathing — Maribeth felt so snug in her new coat, she decided to walk back from Squirrel Hill to Bloomfield through Shadyside. This was the chicest neighborhood she had found in Pittsburgh so far, the one with packed Asian fusion cafés, organic coffee shops, artisanal ice cream stores, and many boutiques. Aside from the stationery, she had not bought anything in Shadyside, had not really bought anything beyond necessities here. But sometimes, when she was missing home and needed a New York City hit, she liked to walk through the area.

Today as she window-shopped down Walnut, she stopped in front of a cosmetics chain. There was a sandwich board sign in front advertising makeovers.

One of the employees came to the door. She was beautiful in a Björk sort of way, jutting cheekbones, green, slanted eyes. "Minimakeovers are free," she said. "Or you can have a full makeover with fifty dollars worth of products."

Since her haircut and lice comb-out,

Maribeth kept meaning to buy herself a tube of lipstick, maybe a new mascara, or to get the haircut professionally cleaned up. Like so many things she kept meaning to do — go to the movies, take herself out for lunch — she had not. Straying from her ascetic existence for even the most minor indulgence felt wrong.

But why was she punishing herself? If they were doing so fine without her? She followed the young woman inside to a swivel chair before a large, lit mirror.

"Are there any products you like?" the young woman asked. Her nametag read Ash.

"Not really." Most of her products were pilfered from the beauty samples closet at work; Revlon one day, La Mer the next.

Ash pulled Maribeth's hair back with a headband, and for a brief moment, Maribeth saw another face in the mirror.

"You have a great skin tone, so I would go minimal," Ash said. "Maybe a tinted moisturizer, a pale lipstick, a touch of mascara."

It felt so good to be touched, Maribeth felt herself surrendering. If Ash had recommended a full on Goth makeover, she probably would have said yes.

Ash returned with a few products and swiveled Maribeth toward her as she dabbed drops of each onto her wrist to match tone.

"You really have gorgeous skin, and a lot of collagen left," Ash said. She pulled up the skin along Maribeth's jawline. "Do you know if you have Scandinavian in your background?"

Maribeth shook her head. There was a pleasant buzzing in her chest. "I don't know."

"I'm told Scandinavian skin ages really well, because the sun there isn't so strong. Did your mother's skin stay so young?"

"I don't know," Maribeth said. "I mean I do, but I don't. I'm adopted."

"Me too!" Ash said, a huge smile lighting up her face. "I was born in Kazakhstan."

"Kazakhstan?" Maribeth said. "I'm not even sure where that is."

She laughed. "It's in Central Asia. Between China and Russia and Mongolia."

"Sounds far."

"I know. When I graduate next year, me and my parents are going to visit."

"Will you try to find your birth mother?" It was the kind of personal question Maribeth never would've dreamed of asking a month ago.

"I doubt it. I was found in a box outside an orphanage in the middle of the night. I just want to know where I come from, you know?"

Maribeth nodded. "Yes, I know. You're lucky your parents are so supportive."

"They're even more excited about the trip than I am. They had to stay in Almaty for two months to get me and they loved it there so they're thrilled to go back."

Maribeth had been unable to locate her parents' social security numbers in her e-mail files and for a second had thought of asking her mother. And then she'd remembered all those veiled remarks growing up. The drama about seeing *Annie.*

And there was the time she and her mother had gotten into a huge fight when Maribeth had missed curfew because her friend Stacy's car had broken down. Her mother had grounded her for a week. Maribeth had tried to explain it wasn't her fault but when her mother had refused to reconsider she had packed a bag and stormed out. She hadn't gone far, all of ten blocks to Stacy's house, where she was invited to have dinner. Halfway through the meal, her father had arrived, apologizing for the interruption, but telling Maribeth she needed to come home. Now.

They rode back in a stony silence and when they pulled up into the driveway, her father said, "Your mother thought you ran away."

"Good!" Maribeth had said, gratified that she'd scared her mother and ready to go back into the ring for another round. Because her mother was being so unfair!

"She thought you ran away to find her," her father had clarified.

It had taken a moment to realize who the *her* was. Her birth mother. And then all of the fight had gone out of Maribeth. She'd gone back inside and, at her father's insistence, apologized to her mother and accepted the terms of the punishment.

"That moisturizer is perfect on you," Ash said. "I'm going to do a brown mascara and then a pearly plum sheer lip gloss, unless you want something more dramatic."

"Whatever you think."

"Look up and to the right." Ash expertly applied the mascara and casually asked Maribeth if she knew her birth mother.

"I don't. But I think I'm close to finding out who she is."

"That's so cool! Rub your lips together. Now blot." She handed Maribeth a tissue. "I'll bet she'll be so glad to hear from you."

"I'm not so sure about that," Maribeth said. "Maybe she doesn't want to hear from me. She did give me up." And then realizing she was speaking to someone dumped in a box, she added, "I'm sorry."

"Oh, that's all right. The way I see it, it had to be the hardest thing in the world for my mother to leave me at that orphanage, right? And besides, who wouldn't want to hear from you? You're so pretty." Ash dramatically swiveled Maribeth around to face the mirror.

The makeup had transformed her face, made it look different, younger. When she stared at her reflection, she saw that face again, like hers, but not. And though she had no way of knowing this, she felt that she'd just caught a glimpse of her mother.

49

Dear Oscar and Liv,

Do you remember last summer when we walked by that truck with all the dogs that needed homes and, Liv, you asked the woman how to buy one and she said that dogs were not for sale but up for adoption? So Oscar, you said, "Can we take one?" And the lady said, no, you needed to fill out forms and pay. And then Liv, you said, "But you just said the dogs weren't for sale." And she said that dogs in pet stores were for sale. These dogs were up for adoption because nobody wanted them.

Maribeth hadn't been so sure that this was the best explanation for it, but she wasn't going to get into it. Besides, by then the twins had moved on from the nuances of adoption to begging for a dog. (Out of the question; their building didn't allow them and their landlord was just waiting for an excuse to evict them and raise the rent.)

But they must have brought it up again with Jason because a few nights later, before bed, he asked her why she hadn't told the twins that she was adopted. "It hardly seemed like an apt comparison, their mother and an unwanted pit bull. Besides, they're too young," she'd said. She could tell by his silence that he disagreed.

There is something you don't know about me. When I was a little baby, the mother who gave birth to me couldn't keep me. So she put me up for adoption and Grandma and Grandpa became my parents. They are my parents. But I have other parents, too. I don't know anything about them. And now, for the first time, maybe I want to. So I can know more things about me, and also about you.

50

They were in a holding pattern with Maribeth's birth-mother search, Janice said, until they had additional information about her adoptive parents. It was frustrating because Maribeth knew exactly where that all was, at home, on her laptop, in well-organized files.

She could just ask Jason.

He might ignore her.

Then again, what did she have to lose at this point?

Strange request, she wrote. Do you think you could get my parents' social security numbers for me? She told him where to find everything.

He sent her the information the same day. Maribeth forwarded it to Janice. Jason had not commented or questioned why she needed any of this and she did not *need* to explain, but somehow felt compelled to. Jason might have operated in the land of the opaque. But Maribeth liked clarity. Even now. Even with him.

In case you were wondering, I'm not applying for a new passport or anything. I'm looking for my birth mother.

And because it no longer seemed much of a threat to disclose her whereabouts — it was clear no one was going to drag her back — she added: In Pittsburgh.

I figured you might be, he wrote.

That surprised her. Even for someone intuitive, it would've been a leap, and Jason was not intuitive.

So you knew I was in Pittsburgh?

He replied, How would I know anything, Maribeth? I just suspected. From your note.

What had she said in her note that had implied that she was coming here? She'd been in an emotional fugue state when she'd written it, and last week when she'd seen the first line, she'd had a sickening déjà vu. It was the same sort of gut-plummet regret she'd experienced all those years ago when she'd opened the college newspaper to her profile of Jason.

My note? she fished.

Jason replied, Yeah. Your note. Which I still can't get over. It's not even the whole, out-of-the-blue Dear John part of it, though that wasn't fun. But your implication that you have some claim on terror because you're a mother . . . I know what you were getting at but, Jesus, Maribeth, did you really think that? Do you still think that? Even now?

She didn't know what she thought because she didn't know what she'd written. But what did she know, what she could feel pulsing through the computer's monitor, was Jason's anger. And it was the strangest thing because though it was what she had been imagining, resenting, dreading, since his silent treatment — since she'd left, really — now that it was here, all she felt was relief.

51

Allegheny Children's Home had a record of a baby girl born March 12, 1970, adopted by a Mr. and Mrs. Seth Klein.

Janice broke the happy news after their fourth swim lesson — kickboard again, to work on her arms — while they were taking a leisurely steam. Upon hearing the news, Maribeth passed out.

She was fine. It wasn't her heart. It was the heat. And the shock.

She was fine. Really.

"I should've waited until we got out, but I couldn't keep it in. I saw the e-mail on my phone when I went to the locker to get my toiletry bag," Janice said, wringing her hands. "I thought the steam room would be a *relaxed* place to tell you. I feel just awful about it."

The club manager was not helping matters. "I'll need a doctor's note for you to use the steam room," he said. "That was very irresponsible."

"It was *my* fault," Janice said. "The steam room was my idea."

"I'm an adult, Janice. It's not your fault." Maribeth turned to the manager "And a doctor's note, really?"

"It's for legal purposes," the medic who was examining her explained.

"In fact, I'd feel more comfortable if you had a note before you returned to the club," the manager said.

Fine. She was seeing Stephen tomorrow for lunch.

Once Maribeth was deemed in no imminent danger, she was allowed to get dressed. "Let's get out of here," she told Janice. "I'll buy you something frothy and decaffeinated."

"Only if you let me treat. Seeing as I made you faint."

They went to a nearby Commonplace Coffee. Janice was still self-flagellating and therefore would only order a tea. "I never should've let you go in the steam room," she said.

"I'm fine. I'm a big girl," Maribeth said. Though in truth, she felt rather like a little girl, waiting to see what was in that big wrapped box. "So now what happens?"

"Allegheny Children's Home has the intake file and they just have to redact it and give us a copy."

"Redact it?"

"Yes, they'll cross out names and identifying details. And then, if you want, the agency will reach out to your birth mother and see if we can initiate contact."

"When can I get the file?"

"Maybe in a week. But there's more."

"What?"

"Your birth mother spent her confinement at the Beacon Maternity Home."

"What's that?"

"It was a home for unwed pregnant girls. A lot of young women spent their pregnancies there. We forget how taboo it was until recently."

"Isn't that the Children's Home what's-it?"

"No, that's the adoption agency, where *you* would've gone for several months while the adoption moved through the courts."

"Months?" Maribeth had always thought it was faster than that. She was born, she was adopted.

"It usually took several months," Janice explained. "Sometimes up to a year."

In her childhood home, there used to hang a series of framed photos in the hall —

Sears portraits of the early years, replaced by school portraits once Maribeth started kindergarten. But the pictures began when she was a year old, already with a shock of hair, and four baby teeth. Maribeth had always assumed it was because the photos were a yearly event, a marker of milestones. Now she wondered if it was because there were no other pictures before then.

How long had Maribeth's mother known that Maribeth was to be hers before she *was* hers? What was that like? To know she was out there but not be able to hold her? Feel her? Comfort her? Was she scared that her birth mother might change her mind? Might take her back? Maribeth remembered being pregnant with the twins and how reassuring it was always to have them with her, inside of her. She felt that she'd been their mother long before they were born.

"We're getting close," Janice said. "It might be you find all the health information you need in the narratives, but if you want more . . ." she trailed off.

Did she want more? She didn't know. Maybe. Maybe it was okay to want more.

"I'm not sure," she told Janice.

"Well, if you do," Janice said, "it's time to start that letter."

52

She and Stephen met for lunch at a bistro in an up-and-coming neighborhood called Highland Park. The place was airy and bright and the waiters recited specials with ingredients like duck confit and locally sourced lamb.

Stephen told Maribeth about settling on a Christmas gift for Mallory. "I decided to buy us tickets to something after all. A musical, which is something Felicity would not have taken her to, but I think Mal will like it," he said. "*The Book of Mormon.* We're going on New Year's Eve. It'll be over by ten, and then I can go back to my hotel like the geriatric I am, and she can go out."

"Sounds like you found a great gift," Maribeth said politely.

It was the first time they'd seen each other since the kiss and perhaps that was why everything was so formal, so nice.

She told Stephen about passing out in the

steam room. She had assumed he'd find it an amusing anecdote, but instead he was alarmed. If he'd had his doctor bag with him, she suspected he would've examined her on that spot. (Not that Maribeth knew if he even had a doctor bag; he just seemed like the kind of old-fashioned physician who would.)

"It's nothing," she reassured him. "It was just the . . ." She stopped short of saying *shock*. She did not want to tell him that she'd found her birth mother. It felt too intimate now that they were skirting a different kind of intimacy. "The heat," she finished.

"You have to be careful," he said.

"I know. They won't let me back in the club until I get a note from my doctor." She paused. "That's still you, right?"

"If you still choose me."

"What?" She had not mentioned Jason, his existence, let alone the fact that they were back in touch. And Maribeth had kissed Stephen once. She did not know if that warranted a discussion about choosing.

He gently reminded her of her own statement from their first appointment. "Oh, yes. I still choose you," she said. But the statement felt perjurious now.

"I'll fax over a letter," he said. "I know

the manager."

"Thank you."

"You're welcome."

They carried on like this, low voices and safe conversation, until Stephen called for the check.

Outside, the sky was bright and the air smelled of snow. The shopkeepers were salting the sidewalks. Stephen offered her a ride home but Maribeth preferred to walk. There was a park nearby and she liked the looping trail around the reservoir. It was up a steep hill but she could handle those now.

Before they parted, there was an awkward pause.

"I keep thinking I'm not going to see you again," Maribeth admitted. "Now that we don't have weekly appointments."

"We can do this weekly," he said. "Or more often. I have time."

"I did wonder about that. Do you have any other patients?" Now that they were outside in the raw cold, it was like they could be themselves again.

"Most of my patients were ones who loyally followed me from the old practice and I don't take on many new cases, but yes, I have other patients," Stephen said. "I just had Louise schedule you last."

"Why?"

"The same reason I eat dessert last."

"You just skipped dessert."

He smiled. "It felt redundant. And at that first appointment, you seemed like you needed, I don't know, a soft place to land."

"Is that why you had me come weekly? And why you charged me so little?

"I charged what the standard Medicare reimbursement would be."

"You still didn't answer the question."

"And you still haven't told me who you really are," he said.

"All I've been doing is telling you who I really am."

He didn't look entirely convinced. Which, she supposed, was fair enough.

"Are we going to talk about that kiss?" he asked.

"What kiss?" she asked.

He held her chin in his hand. The kiss that followed was as delicate and fleeting as the snowflakes that were starting to fall.

"That one," he said.

53

She wrote five drafts of a letter to her birth mother. Each one worse than the last.

My name is Maribeth Klein and forty-five years ago you gave me up for adoption. I am not angry. I am not seeking explanations or recrimination, but mostly answers. Recently, I suffered a heart attack and —

It sounded like a cover letter. She tore it up.

I am the daughter you gave up for adoption. I've had a good life. I'm not angry. Four years ago, I became a mother myself and there are things in my own children I don't recognize —

Why bring up the twins? What if she wanted to meet them one day?

On March 12, 1970, you gave birth to a baby girl. That girl was me. I don't know why I haven't tried to get in touch with you before. I'm not angry or upset. But recently, I . . .

This all felt wrong. And why did she keep insisting she wasn't angry?

Upstairs she heard a roar and a woot. It was Sunday. It must be a football game. Todd and Sunita had not invited her to watch, but she knew she would not be unwelcome, and she needed the distraction. She shoved the notepad underneath the scrapbook she'd just bought to hold her letters to the twins and went upstairs.

Todd opened the door, wearing his jersey, eyes blackened. "This game is going to kill me."

"Is it close?" she asked.

"I can't handle the stress. I hate the Falcons."

"Is that M.B.?" Sunita called.

"Yes, I believe she came to watch football with us. Is that right?" Todd asked suspiciously.

"I'd love to. But do you mind if I check my e-mail first?"

He made a *pfff*ing sound. "Can we dispense with the charade and admit that you're using us for our Internet."

"I'm using you for your Internet the way that you're using me for my cooking abilities."

He grinned. "Doesn't it feel good to come clean?" He nodded toward the laptop. "Help yourself."

She sat down and Todd returned to the living room. It had been three days — and one more kiss — since the e-mail from Jason and she had yet to respond. It wasn't exactly avoidance. She just didn't know what to say. Where to start. *I'm so glad you're mad at me because at least we're not pretending* didn't feel quite right.

But she didn't have to think about how to reply because when she logged on to her Gmail, there was already a message from Jason waiting. The subject line was "Full Disclosure."

Remember when you were pregnant and I had all those dreams? Maybe you don't. I tried to downplay them. I didn't want to scare you but they were very vivid, Maribeth. So vivid that I went to a therapist. She said the dreams meant I was afraid of losing you to the babies. But I said, no, I really thought you were going to die, could feel the terror of it.

Once you had the kids and didn't die, the dreams mostly went away and I quit therapy.

When that doctor came out to get me in the waiting room to tell me there'd been a problem with your procedure, I thought he was going to tell me you were dead. The look on his face, Maribeth, was like the grave. I thought my own heart stopped. I really did. He said you weren't dead. You were having emergency open-heart surgery. But still, terror.

So I guess that's what got me most upset about your note, aside from you leaving. Your suggesting that I didn't understand terror. Maybe I didn't feel that same way you did that day when the twins were babies, but I felt the love, and I've known the terror.

— Jason

p.s. Fuller disclosure: After you came out of your surgery okay, I called up that original shrink, planning to let her have it, ask for my money back because my dreams had been prophetic. Dr. Lewis called me back, listened to me rant, and then asked if I might like to come back in and talk about some things. I've been seeing her ever since.

p.p.s. Dr. Lewis was the one who told me that if I were going to challenge your whole staking the claim on terror business, I needed to come clean about all this.

"Touchdown!" Todd and Sunita screamed.

"Falcons? Ha! More like sparrows," Sunita yelled. "M.B., you're missing the game."

"I'll be right there," she said.

Jason was in therapy? Her Jason? In college, when his parents were in the midst of their split, he had fallen into what Maribeth thought was a depression. She'd implored him to talk to someone at the counseling center, but Jason had said he couldn't stand to listen to himself like that. It seemed so indulgent. "But you're a deejay," Maribeth had said. "You listen to yourself talk all the time." "That's different," he'd said.

Jason was in therapy. Had been when she was pregnant. Had been even before she'd left home.

"Are you going to watch *any* of the game?" Todd yelled from the living room.

"They seem to be doing okay without me," Maribeth said.

"You really are using us for our Internet."

334

"I thought we'd established that."

She read the message again and logged off without replying.

She went into the living room just as Todd was turning off the TV. "Excellent timing. It's over."

"Did we win?"

"You can't say 'we' when you didn't watch," he said.

"*We* won," Sunita said. "Don't mind him. And you can use the computer whenever you need to. Did you find what you were looking for?" she asked, exchanging a look with Todd.

Jason had been so scared she was going to die that he'd gone to therapy. Back then and again now.

Why hadn't he told her?

What else hadn't he told her?

"I'm not sure," she answered.

54

From: MBK31270@gmail.com
To: jasbrinx@gmail.com
Subject: Therapy?

I wish you'd told me.

From: jasbrinx@gmail.com
To: MBK31270@gmail.com
Subject: Therapy?

I don't know why I didn't. It's a good question for my therapist.

From: MBK31270@gmail.com
To: jasbrinx@gmail.com
Subject: Therapy?

Is it wrong that the idea of you in therapy is oddly gratifying to me? I wish I could say it was purely altruistic, that I'm glad you're getting healthier/happier. (And if you are, I am.) But really, I like the company. I like that it suggests that maybe I'm not the only damaged one in the family.

From: jasbrinx@gmail.com
To: MBK31270@gmail.com
Subject: Therapy?

I think Dr. Lewis would take issue with the idea that being in therapy = damaged. That said, I will fully acknowledge that I have fucked up. We are a family of fuck-ups. Except maybe not the kids. They're fuckups in training.

From: MBK31270@gmail.com
To: jasbrinx@gmail.com
Subject: Therapy?

Fuckups in training sounds like a band you would've championed back in the day.

From: jasbrinx@gmail.com
To: MBK31270@gmail.com
Subject: Therapy?

I like that. The Fuckups in Training. We'll take our act on the road and be like the Partridge Family. Oscar can play guitar. Liv can sing.

From: MBK31270@gmail.com
To: jasbrinx@gmail.com
Subject: Therapy?

Have you heard Liv sing? You and Oscar handle vocals. Liv will be Reuben Kincaid, only much, much scarier.

From: jasbrinx@gmail.com
To: MBK31270@gmail.com
Subject: Therapy?

Liv manages, Oscar and I handle music? Are you in this lineup?

From: MBK31270@gmail.com
To: jasbrinx@gmail.com
Subject: Therapy?

I'm not sure. Shirley Partridge was a widow. So one of us has to die. I'm the more obvious candidate.

From: jasbrinx@gmail.com
To: MBK31270@gmail.com
Subject: Therapy?

That's not funny, Maribeth.

From: MBK31270@gmail.com

To: jasbrinx@gmail.com
Subject: Therapy?

I'm sorry. A therapist might say I deflect discomfort with humor.

From: jasbrinx@gmail.com
To: MBK31270@gmail.com
Subject: Therapy?

Every time the phone rings, I think someone is calling with bad news about you.

From: MBK31270@gmail.com
To: jasbrinx@gmail.com
Subject: Therapy?

No wonder you never pick up.
(Sorry. I could probably use some therapy, too.)

From: jasbrinx@gmail.com
To: MBK31270@gmail.com
Subject: Therapy?

Pretty much everyone in the world could use some therapy, I'm learning.
And, for the record, I pick up on the first ring now.

55

Janice had still not received the report from Allegheny Children's Home. And after several lessons, Maribeth had still not graduated from the kickboard.

"Some things take time" was Janice's explanation for both.

Maribeth had no control over when the report would come in, but after several lessons, she felt fairly certain she was ready to swim on her own.

"Practice makes perfect," Janice said.

"Yes, but sometimes you can overthink things."

"You're not the first person I've taught to swim, Maribeth."

"I know, but I'm just getting impatient."

"Okay. If you think you're ready, have at it." She set the kickboard on the pool deck.

"Fine, I will."

"Okay. I'll just go do a few laps," Janice said.

Janice had been forgoing her own swimming to help Maribeth. Maribeth could at least be a little less of an asshole about it. "Have a good swim," she said belatedly.

"You too," Janice replied with no apparent hard feelings.

The slow lane was almost empty, which was good. Every time a swimmer came up behind Maribeth, that ancient part of her brain that still feared predators kicked into gear and made her panicky.

She pushed off, with her straight legs, kicking from her hip crease, her rounded arms, her barely lifted face. All the things she'd learned. *See Janice? See what a good student I am?* About three strokes in, she breathed in when she was meant to breathe out and swallowed a mouthful of water and went sputtering. After a bit of recovery time, she tried again, and it seemed to be going okay until she drifted out of her lane and into the path of an oncoming swimmer. "Watch it!" the swimmer hissed.

"Sorry!" Maribeth overcompensated this time by kicking and stroking so furiously she banged her head into the wall.

She swam back to the other end, pointing her toes so violently her foot cramped. She also got water up her nose. By the time she had completed a lap, she was panting.

341

As she rested, she caught a glimpse of Janice in the fast lane, slicing through the water with abundant grace.

Maribeth watched her for a few minutes. Then she pulled the kickboard off the deck and got back to work.

56

Todd and Sunita were in a fight. Maribeth could tell straightaway when she met them by the car for their shopping trip. Todd always drove; Sunita always sat in the passenger seat and played radio deejay — Miles's car had no iPod hookup. But this time, Todd was up front, Sunita was in Maribeth's seat in the back, and both of them were glowering.

"You're shotgun tonight, M.B., because Sunny is being a —"

"Because Todd's having a temper tantrum," Sunita interrupted.

"You don't *have* to come. Me and M.B. can go on our own. We have before. You can find your way to the Asian market. Maybe ask Fritz for a ride."

"Maybe I will." She started to undo her seatbelt.

"Hang on," Maribeth said. "Take a breath. What's going on?"

"Todd's all pissy because I went out with Fritz."

"On a date," Todd added, as if that sealed the indictment.

"Yes, fine." Sunita threw up her hands. "On a date."

"That you didn't tell me about."

"That I didn't tell you about."

"When it was our night to watch *Outlander.*"

"We can DVR it. I don't see what the big deal is."

"I never flake on you to be with Miles."

"Oh, I'm sorry, is Miles your boyfriend? I wouldn't know because you hardly let us in the same room together."

"Exactly! So you don't feel left out!"

"Oh, so it's for my sake?" Sunita flung herself against the backseat.

"Yes!" Todd retorted. "Because everyone knows that the number one friendship killer is a romance."

"That's the dumbest thing I've ever heard."

"Is it? Ask M.B. I bet she'll tell you differently."

Maribeth felt momentarily exposed, as if they'd watched the filmstrip of her life. But of course, Todd was just assuming she knew this because she was old and therefore had

Life Experience.

"Well, I did have a best friend, and then I fell in love with a guy, and it did complicate things."

"See?" Todd said.

"Complicated doesn't mean the friendship was ruined," Sunita said.

"That's *exactly* what it means," Todd replied.

They were both looking at her.

"Right?" Todd prodded.

"I'm not sure what it means," Maribeth said. "Elizabeth, that was my friend, she was really protective when this guy and I got together but over time she warmed up to him. We all were friends. Eventually she even helped him pick out my . . ." she stopped herself. "My birthday presents."

What she'd almost said was that Elizabeth had helped pick out Maribeth's engagement ring. And this more than anything else had felt like the official Elizabeth Ford Seal of Approval, the completion of a slow thawing and eventual warming between Elizabeth and Jason, or rather Elizabeth toward Jason, though he did seem a little scared of her even though Maribeth had never told him what Elizabeth had said when he'd gotten back in touch, via a Facebook message, nearly ten years after they'd broken up, which was: "Don't respond. Don't talk to him. Don't give him the time of day. He broke your heart once. He does not deserve a second go."

But by the time they got engaged, the three of them were friendly, even friends. They sometimes went out together, to meals and plays, and one August rented the same summer share on Fire Island. After Jason proposed and Maribeth accepted, Elizabeth was the one to throw them an engagement party at her apartment. It had been a beautiful, opulent affair, full of personal Elizabeth touches. She'd hired eclectic musicians Jason would like — a mandolin and a stand-up bass player — and instructed the caterers to serve all the food in shot glasses because Maribeth had a thing about having to balance plates while standing. Though it had been a party for her and Jason, Maribeth had felt like it was for the three of them. Especially when in his toast, Jason had cracked a joke about Maribeth being such a catch that he was willing to move across the country, accompany her to a Maroon 5 concert, *and* put up with the fact that she was already married.

Most of the guests had chuckled politely, not quite getting the joke, perhaps thinking it was some reference to the TV show about

bigamist Mormons that had just begun air-
ing. Maribeth glanced at Elizabeth, who
winked and tapped the gold filigree ring
Maribeth had bought her for her twenty-
fifth birthday, a piece of jewelry that until
Tom and his big fat emerald came along,
shc'd worn on her ring finger. Maribeth had
fingered her own engagement ring, a sap-
phire eternity band. She never found out
what had become of Jason's mother's old
ring; neither it, nor the aborted engagement,
had ever been discussed. Not that she really
cared. She preferred this ring so much more.

"So what happened?" Sunita asked. "With
the friend?"

In spite of what she'd just said to Todd,
sometimes she had held Jason responsible
for her and Elizabeth's drift. It was Jason
who had brought them together. And Jason
who had split them apart. Not because of
anything in particular that he'd done, but
because you couldn't have it both ways — a
husband and a wife.

Though when she thought back to that
engagement party what she remembered so
vividly now was how reassured she'd felt.
She was marrying Jason, as she'd wanted to
since college, but wasn't it good to know
she'd had Elizabeth, too? She pictured
them, her little trio, like a three-legged stool,

as sturdy as anything in life.

But then one leg had broken off. And then another. And then everything else toppled over.

57

From: MBK31270@gmail.com
To: jasbrinx@gmail.com
Subject: Closer

We found her. My birth mother. The report should be here any day now. I'm not sure what I'll find. She could be dead of a heart attack for all I know. Part of me thinks it might be easier if she is. It would be less complicated. I would have found out what I needed to know. Definitively.
I'm a horrible person.
DO NOT tell my mother about this.

From: jasbrinx@gmail.com
To: MBK31270@gmail.com
Subject: Closer

You're not a horrible person. You're just human. And anyway, I don't think you really mean that.

And don't worry about your mother. She's being taken care of.

From: MBK31270@gmail.com
To: jasbrinx@gmail.com
Subject: Closer

Taken care of? Is she locked in the pantry? And you're probably right. Because if my mother — the other one — died of a heart attack, then I'd worry even more about what I passed on to the twins. It would seem inevitable then.

From: jasbrinx@gmail.com
To: MBK31270@gmail.com
Subject: Closer

My father had a heart attack. It's on both sides. You don't get to take all the credit. And nothing is inevitable.

From: MBK31270@gmail.com
To: jasbrinx@gmail.com
Subject: Closer

That's for sure.
I don't want all the credit. I just don't want all the blame.

From: jasbrinx@gmail.com
To: MBK31270@gmail.com
Subject: Closer

I think there's more than enough of that to go around.
After your surgery, I didn't step up like I should have. I thought I had but now I can see that I didn't. I'm sorry.

From: MBK31270@gmail.com
To: jasbrinx@gmail.com
Subject: Closer

Wow. I think I like this Dr. Lewis.

From: jasbrinx@gmail.com
To: MBK31270@gmail.com
Subject: Closer

I figured that out all on my own. In my defense, I didn't really get all that you did around here until I had to do it myself.
The shrink says that maybe I needed everything to be like it always had been because otherwise I had to think about the alternative, which was what might happen to you. And that was too hot to touch.

From: MBK31270@gmail.com

To: jasbrinx@gmail.com
Subject: Closer

The terror?

From: jasbrinx@gmail.com
To: MBK31270@gmail.com
Subject: Closer

Yeah. The terror.

58

Maribeth hadn't really meant it when she'd said she was using Todd and Sunita for their Internet. She genuinely liked them. But she had been taking advantage of their Wi-Fi and laptop generosity a lot since Thanksgiving, particularly now that Jason's e-mails were coming regularly and the cold weather had made the trek to the library so much less attractive.

She decided to show her appreciation by cooking for them again. They'd demolished the paella last time so maybe she'd do a bouillabaisse. It was finals week and if it was anything like Maribeth remembered, the studying made you famished.

She texted the invitation.

Is the Silver Fox coming? Todd texted back.

She hadn't spoken to Stephen since their lunch last week. To see him now, out of the office, now that they'd kissed, now that she was e-mailing Jason, felt different. He hadn't called her; she sensed he'd left the ball in her court, but she hadn't returned it. Which wasn't to say she didn't want to see him. She did. She suspected that he wanted to see her, too. A dinner party felt like a safe excuse, so she sent him a text: *My kitchen will be smelling good starting tomorrow around five if you'd like to come for dinner. The kids from upstairs are coming, too.*

I'll bring an appropriate amount of wine, he texted back.

He arrived while Maribeth was still scrubbing the clams.

"You're early," she said. "And I'm running late."

"I no longer have a four o'clock patient," he said, smiling. "So I don't know what to do with my afternoons."

"You could try golf. I hear doctors like that. Or scheduling a new patient."

"I'm not really taking on new patients at the moment."

"Why did you take me?"

"To collect the bounty for returning you to Cambridge Springs prison, naturally."

"Naturally."

He came inside. Maribeth was suddenly aware of certain facts: her apartment, empty, the bed in the other room. Her and Stephen. Two kisses. Jason.

354

"What's this?" he picked up the scrapbook holding the twins' letters.

Maribeth grabbed it from him. "Just a scrapbook," she said, shoving the book into a drawer. "Nothing that interesting."

She saw him look around, much the way she'd poked around his house for hints of his life. Through his eyes, she now saw the apartment: its bare walls, its generic Best Western artwork, its lack of any sort of personal effects: diplomas, photos. There were no clues about her life here. Which perhaps was the biggest clue of all. It was less an apartment than a foxhole. But Stephen should get that. He lived in a foxhole, too, albeit one with far nicer furnishings.

"Need help in the kitchen?" he asked.

"How are you with a knife?"

"I'm not a surgeon but I could probably remove an appendix if need be."

"Then you can devein the shrimp."

They worked in companionable silence, breaking open a bottle of cabernet at the respectable hour of six. Right as everything was being laid out on the table, Sunita burst through. "One more semester and I will be out of here." She made a fist pump.

Todd was right behind her. "Rub it in."

"You're only a term behind," she said. "Something smells delicious, M.B."

"Thank you," Maribeth said.

"Can I have some of that wine?" she asked Stephen. "I just crushed my statistics final."

"Because of all that studying you did with Fritz," Todd teased. "He probably didn't even need to take statistics but just did it to be your study buddy."

"Only you can make the term *study buddy* sound lewd," Sunita said.

Todd put his hands under his chin, cocking his head like an angel. He turned to Maribeth and Stephen. "He invited her to a Hanukkah celebration, with his entire family. They've only just met and he wants her to meet the family. I feel it's my duty to report back to Chandra and Nikhil."

"It's not like that. We were talking about Diwali, and how it's a festival of lights, same as Hanukkah, which starts any day now."

"It started two days ago, actually," Maribeth said.

They all looked at her, surprised.

"What? I'm Jewish."

Todd, Sunita, and Stephen exchanged a funny look.

"What?" Maribeth said.

"The Mystery Woman reveals a clue," Todd said in a movie trailer voice.

"Mystery? What's a mystery? My last name is Goldman."

"We wouldn't know," Sunita said. "You don't get any mail."

"And what about your first name, M.B.?" Todd said.

Stephen raised an eyebrow.

"I'm just giving you shit," Todd said, "I think it's cool. Everyone we know over-shares everything all the time. You keep it close to the vest. I appreciate that."

"I'm really not that mysterious."

"We thought you were a drug dealer," Sunita said.

The cockle Maribeth was prying open flew out of her hand. "A drug dealer?"

"Always paying with hundreds. A cheap burner phone you didn't know the number to," Sunita said. "And no computer of your own."

"And you said you were a consultant," Todd said. "What kind of consultant doesn't have a computer?"

"I have a computer, just not with me, and I'm *not* a drug dealer."

"We figured that out," Todd said. "No one ever comes here."

"Also, drug dealers don't e-mail so much," Sunita said.

"That's what young lovers do," Todd joked. "Or older ones."

They all looked at Stephen, who was

coloring slightly. "M.B. communicates with me strictly by text," he said, taking a sip of his wine. "I don't even have her e-mail address."

"Oh?" said Sunita, not getting it.

"Oh," said Todd, getting it.

"Yes," said Stephen, who must have gotten it all along, must have suspected at least, that there was a family out there. And a husband.

"Excuse me," said Maribeth. And with that she ran outside.

Stephen found her out on the stoop. She wasn't wearing a coat so he draped his over her shoulder.

"You should be more careful," she said. "I am an escaped prisoner from Cambridge Hall."

"Cambridge Springs," he corrected.

"Whatever. I'm armed and dangerous."

"I don't know about the armed," he said. "And I'm no shining star."

"You're the shiniest star in the whole sky." She pointed up to show him, but it was cloudy.

"You were a patient. I blurred the lines."

"M. B. Goldman was a patient. That's not really me."

"So who are you?"

"A fuckup. A runaway. A person with terrible judgment," she said.

"Terrible judgment? I'm the doctor who kissed his patient."

"The patient kissed you first."

"And I'm glad she did."

"I'm glad she did, too."

The first time she had kissed him. The second time he had kissed her. The third time, they kissed each other. And this time, it felt wrong. She pulled away.

"I'm sorry," Stephen said.

"No, I'm sorry," Maribeth said. "I guess I'm not good with blurry lines, after all."

"No," he said. "Nor am I."

Back inside Maribeth's apartment, Todd was furious, and taking it out on her dishes.

"Easy there," she said, as he slammed a plate into the sink.

He didn't say anything, just attacked the plate with the sponge.

"Todd," Maribeth touched his arm, but he whipped it away.

"His dad left his mom for his secretary," Sunita said, hunting around the cabinets for Tupperware. "He hasn't got over it."

Todd was now attempting to commit murder with steel wool.

"Here, stop," Maribeth said. "Before you

359

kill that poor pot."

"You shouldn't cheat," he muttered.

She sighed. "Stephen is my doctor."

"Your doctor?" Todd asked. He'd dropped his surly posture and seemed genuinely upset. "Are you sick?"

"No, but I was." She told them then, about her heart attack, her surgery, leaving out the fact that this had all happened in another city, another life.

But then Sunita asked, "If you're all better, why are you still, you know, seeing him?"

The better question was, if she was better, why was she still here?

"And," Todd asked. "If you haven't been e-mailing with him, who have you been e-mailing with?"

That one she could answer.

"My husband," she said.

59

Dear Liv and Oscar,

When I left home, I did not bring very many things with me. Mostly clothes and medicine. I left in a hurry, which is what people do when they are running away.

I did take a photograph of you. Maybe you noticed the empty frame? It was from last summer right around your birthdays, when that man took our picture. Do you remember that day?

The man had been a famous photographer, known for his portraits of celebrities' kids. Elizabeth had thought it would be great to show how he did with "real" families and Maribeth volunteered because Elizabeth said it would only be a small photo in the spread and she'd get a $10,000 family portrait out of the deal.

The photographer had wanted to shoot them in Battery Park, in the afternoon light, on a stool, with the Manhattan skyline behind them. "Nice and easy," he'd said. Famous last words.

Oscar had misunderstood the phrase *shoot a photo* for getting shot with a gun and had been hysterical. Liv had missed her nap and had been tyrannical. In order to get the kids to calm down, Jason had started doing handstands on the grass and Maribeth had attempted her first cartwheel in two decades. Oscar stopped crying. Liv stopped ranting. They'd started doing somersaults. The photographer half-heartedly shot a few frames of their acrobatics before the light died.

"Nothing we can use here," the photo editor had scrawled over the few prints she'd put in Maribeth's inbox. Maribeth got it. The photos were chaotic. Oscar's suit was dirty, Liv's underwear was showing. It was not a *Frap* kind of picture.

I think that picture of you two doing somersaults might be my favorite family photo ever. Which might be a strange thing to say because it's not the whole family, only the two of you. But somehow, it really is the four of us. I can see

362

me and Daddy off to the side, walking on our hands. That's the funny thing about pictures. Sometimes what you see only tells some of the story.

I love you both.

— Mommy

60

At Maribeth's next swimming lesson, Janice made two important announcements. The birth narrative was ready and they might have it by tonight. Monday latest. And with almost equal gravitas, she proclaimed Maribeth ready to graduate from the kickboard. "It's time to put all the pieces together," she said.

At first, it had seemed like another disaster. Maribeth's arms windmilled one way, out of sync with her breath. Her legs went too fast, then too slow, her knees bent. She couldn't get the air fast enough or then she gulped too quickly and wound up hyperventilating. It felt like she was attempting to sew a dress from many different patterns. Nothing fit right, and she was certain she looked ridiculous.

"It's not working," she told Janice.

"Keep trying."

She did. Again and again. It got no better.

The school-aged kids having a lesson were swimming circles around her. She watched them in a sort of awe. Swimming sometimes felt as complicated as landing an airplane in a snowstorm. Not that she had any experience with that.

"I've had enough," Maribeth said.

"Give it five more minutes," Janice said.

It was in those last few minutes that it happened. She didn't know whether it was because she'd stopped working so hard or because she knew her time was almost up. But all of a sudden, she wasn't thinking. She was just listening to the sound of her breath and the gurgle of the water; there was something so womblike about it that she zoned out. And then, she was no longer fighting the water. She was gliding on top of it. There was effort here, exertion, there must've been, but she didn't feel it. It wasn't hard. Not at all.

When she stopped, Janice was watching her, beaming.

"You just swam four lengths," she said.

"Really?" Maribeth replied.

Janice nodded.

Maribeth was elated. The vaunted endorphins flooding her.

"I lost track of it," she said. "I lost track of everything."

Janice nodded, as if Maribeth had discovered a secret.

As they dressed, Maribeth was giddy. She couldn't believe it. She knew it was silly to get this goofy about swimming four lengths, but she'd thought swimming was meant to be hard, harder than running. That was why it was good for you.

Janice laughed when Maribeth told her this. "It's only hard when you do it wrong."

On the way out of the club, the manager intercepted them at the front desk.

"I heard from Dr. Grant," he said, smiling. "He sent over his blessing to use the steam room."

"Did he now?"

The manager was almost obsequious. "I didn't realize you were a friend of the Grants'. Well, I suppose it's just Dr. Grant now."

"Yes. He's my cardiologist."

"Right, of course," the manager said. "We don't see him often these days. His wife was one of our favorite regulars and she is much missed. Tell me, will you be joining us as a member?"

"I don't know," she said. Janice had given Maribeth her five guest passes. They were enough to get through the year. Janice had offered her passes for next year. Stephen said he was going to cancel his membership, though he also said he'd been threatening that for a while.

"Now is an excellent time to join. We have a new member's special. Joining fee is waived. First month is free."

"I really don't know how long I'll be here."

"We have different membership levels. Annual or month to month. If your passes run out next month, say, you could just have a membership for a month or two. What do you think?"

She didn't know. All her life she had been such a planner, a plotter, a plodder. She planned meals the week before so she knew how to shop. She planned vacations a year in advance so they could save on airfare. She planned the feature stories at *Frap* six months in advance. She had the calendar memorized: who was going where, eating what, writing what.

But now? She didn't know what would happen next month. She didn't even know what would happen next week. She didn't know what would happen with Jason. With Stephen. With her children. With her birth mother. A year ago, so much uncertainty would've killed her. Her lists, her plans — they were her parachute, the thing to keep her from total free fall.

She was in free fall now. And it wasn't killing her. In fact, she was beginning to wonder if she might've had it backwards. All that fixating on the fall . . . maybe she should've been paying more attention to the free.

61

Janice called her that afternoon. "I have it! I have the report! It's parent-teacher night so I can't show you now, but first thing tomorrow."

"Can't you just read it to me?"

"No. I won't open it without you. Come over first thing tomorrow."

"Tomorrow?"

"I know. But you've waited this long. You can survive one more day."

Maribeth wasn't sure she could. She knocked on Todd and Sunita's door.

"Please tell me there's a game on," she said. "Something. I need to be occupied."

"Maybe a college game," Sunita said. "We're going to the movies in a while. A double feature. You're welcome to come."

"The genre is action adventure," Todd said. "If your heart can handle it."

At first she thought he was being serious, but then she noted the wicked grin. Some-

where along the line, she had been promoted to Sunita treatment. She found this
thrilling.

"A movie sounds perfect," she said.

"We don't have to leave for an hour," Todd
said, gesturing toward the computer. "If you
need something to do, why don't you go
e-mail your husband?"

From: MBK31270@gmail.com
To: jasbrinx@gmail.com
Subject: You at work?

From: jasbrinx@gmail.com
To: MBK31270@gmail.com
Subject: You at work?

I'm working from home. Want to Gchat?

From: MBK31270@gmail.com
To: jasbrinx@gmail.com
Subject: You at work?

I believe we are officially too old to Gchat.
Our computers will melt if we attempt it.

From: jasbrinx@gmail.com
To: MBK31270@gmail.com
Subject: You at work?

You know I like to live dangerously, Grandma.

A few seconds later, a notice popped up that Jinx would like to chat.
Jinx. That made her smile.

5:40

Jinx: Hi.
Me: Hi.
Jinx: Look at us, Gchatting like kids.
Me: Next thing you know, we'll be Snap-chatting.
Jinx: I don't know what that is.
Me: No. Me, neither.

5:47

Me: So the report is in. About my birth mother. I see it tomorrow.
Jinx: !
Jinx: How do you feel?
Me: Mostly sick.
Me: In a nervous kind of way. Not heart-related.
Me: What if she's dead? What if she died of a heart attack? What if she was a horrible person? What if she was raped? It could be so many dreadful things.
Jinx: Maybe knowing definitively will

ease the fear.

Me: Or increase it.

Jinx: I don't know. There's something about facing your fear head-on. Like when I read your note, it was horrifying but reassuring to see my fears echoed by someone else. It was like proof that I wasn't crazy.

5:52

Jinx: You still there?

Me: Yeah.

Jinx: Thought I scared you off.

Me: No. I was just wondering how to tell you that I don't remember what I wrote in the note, and when you sent it to me, I freaked out and deleted it.

Jinx: Really? Why?

Me: I thought you were throwing it back in my face. That first line . . . It's so hysterical.

Jinx: "I'm scared I'm going to die."

Me: Please don't. I remember that part.

Jinx: But not the rest?

Me: Let's just say I wasn't my best self when I wrote it.

Jinx: I probably wasn't my best self when I sent it back. I was pretty pissed off so I guess I was kind of throwing it back in

your face. You leave, then nothing for a month, then that hail of accusation. But mostly I wanted you to see, in your own words, what you'd asked me to do.
Me: I'm sorry.

5:57

Jinx: That's okay. FWIW, I didn't think you were being hysterical. I thought you were being truthful. And obviously, it was a shared fear. I was also scared you were going to die.

6:01

Me: Jase? Would you send me the note again?
Jinx: Now?
Me: Now. Can you e-mail it to me?
Jinx: I can attach right here if you want. We can read it together.
Me: Really? Okay. Do that.

An attachment popped up right in the chat window. Maribeth clicked on it and read the words she'd written on that worst of days.

I know you think I'm fine but I'm scared I'm going to die.

And it's not the death that scares me. All I can think about is the twins, and them being too young to not have a mother and what would happen to them if I died now.

And then I think of that night when they were newborns and they were sleeping in their carriers on the table. Do you remember that night? I felt so overwhelmed with love for them that I couldn't stop weeping. You laughed and said it was hormones, but it wasn't. It was terror. I felt like my skin had been turned inside out. How could you love someone this much? It made you too vulnerable. That's when I figured out the ugly secret of a mother's love: you protect them, to protect yourself.

But how can I do both? Protect them and me. Protect them from me.

So I have to go away. To take care of me. You take care of them.

I'm sorry. Don't hate me. Let me do this. Leave me be. You said you'd give me a bubble. I need it to be bigger.

— Maribeth

6:09

Jinx: You still there?

Me: Yeah.
Jinx: You okay?
Me: Yeah. Are you?
Jinx: Yeah.
Me: Do you hate me?
Jinx: I've never hated you.
Jinx: Do you hate me?
Me: If I did, I don't anymore.

6:17

Jinx: Maribeth?
Me: Yeah?
Jinx: The kids and I need to hit the road.
Me: Oh.
Jinx: Are you okay?
Me: Yeah.
Jinx: You'll let me now know how tomorrow goes? I'll make sure to check my e-mail.
Me: Yeah.

"Were you Gchatting?" Todd asked, peering over her shoulder. "With your *husband*?"
Maribeth closed the window.
"You little hussy," Todd said.

They left for the movies. Fritz, and the elusive Miles, would be joining them for the second feature.

"I finally get to meet Miles," Maribeth said.

"He works a lot," Todd said. "It's not like I'm keeping him *secret* or anything."

"Really? You sure about that?' "

"Mostly. But if you're nice I might let you talk to him."

"I'm always nice. Maybe I'll even buy the popcorn."

Todd grinned. "Then I might let you sit next to him."

They saw one of the Hobbit movies, which was diverting, if long. When it was over, they met up with Fritz, who, Todd was right, was clearly mooning for Sunita, and Miles, who, Maribeth was surprised to discover, was not so old. Maybe late twenties. And clearly besotted with Todd.

Even though she'd bought the popcorn, Maribeth let the couples sit together, sitting between Sunita and Todd. The second film was the third installment in one of those dystopian franchises. Maribeth had not seen parts one or two so Todd and Sunita whispered in her ear, catching her up as the film played.

"Gale was the one she loved first," Sunita explained. "But now she loves Peeta, too. Classic love triangle."

"I thought those only happened in books," Todd whispered, "until I met you."

"I'm not in a love triangle," Maribeth whispered.

"That's what Katniss said," Todd replied.

62

THE ALLEGHENY CHILDREN'S HOME ADOPTION REFERRAL FORM

Referral:

Mother was referred to Allegheny Children's Home on January 8, 1970, by the Beacon Maternity Home, where she has resided since December 27, 1969. Upon entering the Maternity Home, Mother was in her sixth month of pregnancy and it is both her and her family's wishes that she remain there until the birth of the child.

Mother:

Mother is twenty years old and hails from the ███████████ area of Pittsburgh. She is petite (five foot four, 108 pounds prior to pregnancy) and attractive, with blue eyes, fair skin, brown hair, cut into a modern style. She has a pert nose, some freckling on her cheeks, excellent posture, and straight teeth that did not require braces. She has excellent oral hygiene, and no cavities.

Mother's background is Swedish and English on the paternal side and Polish and German on the maternal side.

Mother is in excellent health. Aside from a childhood bout of rubella, she has had no major illnesses. Before her pregnancy, she was athletic, playing field hockey and ice-skating. Mother is allergic to penicillin and strawberries.

Mother's personality appears to be good natured and intelligent with a keen interest in the arts and world affairs.

In high school, she was an honor roll student, a member of the debate society. Last year she entered ████████████████ College in hopes of transferring to a four-year university to get a degree. It was there that she met the Alleged Father and became pregnant.

Mother was initially shy and reserved at the Maternity Home but after a few weeks, staff say she revealed a sense of humor and a more garrulous nature. While she remained wary of staff and of social workers, she made fast friends with other residents, organizing many events, including a games night and even staging a short comedic play that she wrote and directed.

The pregnancy was a result of an affair between Mother and Alleged Father, a married professor at ███████████████████. While Mother is quite forthcoming about the affair and it being extramarital in nature, she refused to name Alleged Father and offered scant details about the man. It is unclear whether Alleged Father, who Mother says has a family of his own, is aware of the pregnancy.

Mother was resolute in her

decision to relinquish the child. As soon as she became aware of the pregnancy—not until her fifth month, which is not entirely unbelievable given how light she carried—she told her family and immediately was brought to Beacon Maternity Home.

Mother is the only daughter in a family of five children, and since the death of her own mother, she has assumed a care-taking role for her three younger brothers. In describing her family, she seems burdened by this turn of events and bereft by the sudden loss of her mother several years ago.

Mother is Catholic and Protestant by parentage but describes herself as not religious. She has not attended church since the death of her mother.

Family:

Mother's father is fifty-seven years old and in good health. He is the owner of █████████ restaurant in ██████████. He is described as tall, fair, muscular, and athletic.

Mother's mother, whom she described as sharp-witted and sometimes melancholic, is deceased. She collapsed at the age of forty-two, when Mother was sixteen, of a suspected heart attack. Prior to that, she had been in good health.

Siblings: Mother has four siblings, a brother aged twenty-two, brother aged seventeen, and twin brothers aged fourteen. She describes her brothers as energetic, sweet, athletic boys, though lacking intellectual curiosity.

Older brother is currently serving in the army in Vietnam. Seventeen-year-old brother works in the family restaurant. Younger brothers still in school.

Aunt paternal, fifty-one: A spinster aunt lives with the family since the death of the mother. In good health aside from deafness in one ear, a result of childhood meningitis. The aunt's relationship with the Mother appears to be contentious since the death of Mother's mother.

Uncle paternal, fifty-four: A dairy farmer who lives in ███████ ███████████. In good health.

Aunt maternal, forty-seven: In good health, lives in ██████████ ██████.

Grandparents: Maternal grandmother, seventy-two, is in failing health in a nursing home. Maternal grandfather deceased, cause of death unknown. Paternal grandmother, deceased, lung cancer. Paternal grandfather deceased, automobile accident.

Alleged Father: Alleged Father is a professor at ██████████ ████████████ where Mother attended. Mother is reluctant to divulge any further detail, possibly for fear of it leading to professional and personal repercussions because Alleged Father is married.

Evaluation:

Although intelligent, Mother appears to be a naive young woman who entered into an extramarital affair about which she expresses little remorse beyond her disappointment at having to leave community college because of the ensuing pregnancy. While she speaks with pride of being the first member of her family to attain higher education, she seems disconnected from how her own actions have likely derailed her educational aspirations and is therefore unwilling or unable to take full responsibility. She believes that after the pregnancy she will be able to return to college, though Mother's father and aunt say that is unlikely.

Mother makes frequent mention of a desire to escape her household, to escape the family business, and it's not beyond the realm of possibility that she viewed the pregnancy as a means of escape. It is clear that in spite of her age, Mother is by no means ready for motherhood, a fact she readily acknowledges, which suggests at least a modicum of insight and maturity.

Additional Information:

Mother made a particular request that the child not be adopted into a strongly Catholic household.

Birth Information:

Mother gave birth to a healthy baby girl at Shadyside Hospital on 10:55 a.m. on March 12, 1970, three weeks before term. Child's birth weight was a healthy 7 pounds, 4 ounces, which suggests a possible incorrect due date. Mother, who had remained unemotional and removed for much of the pregnancy, became atypically emotional and reflective after the baby's birth. She had previously expressed no desire to name the child but after the birth insisted on giving her a name. Child remained in the hospital for five days before being transferred to nursery at Allegheny Children's Home to await the termination of Mother's parental rights and subsequent adoption.

Court Information:
Relinquishment hearing took place on May 17, 1970. Mother appeared unaccompanied and seemed in good spirits. Birth mother's parental rights were terminated on July 8, 1970.

63

Maribeth read the report in the living room of Janice's tidy brick ranch house. She had to put the paper in her lap. Her hands shook too much to hold it.

"Are you okay, dear?" Janice asked, hovering from a respectful distance.

"I'm fine," Maribeth heard herself say.

"It's lucky that she was at the Beacon." Janice stopped herself. "Maybe lucky is the wrong word. But I can make an appointment to look at the files from the maternity home on Monday. We might be able get more information then. Maybe about that play she put on . . ."

Maribeth wasn't really paying attention. "Okay."

"I'll see to that Monday. I promise."

"Do you think I might use your computer?" Maribeth asked.

"Help yourself," Janice said. "It's in the office."

Maribeth walked down the hall in a daze. Behind her, Janice called, "Can I get you anything? Tea? Whiskey?"

"I'm fine," Maribeth repeated.

She held the form in her still-shaking hand. It told her everything — her grandmother, dead of a heart attack at age forty-two — and yet it told her nothing. The report read almost as if her mother were glad to be rid of her. But then it said she had grown emotional after her birth. What did that mean? Had she loved her at all? Had she wanted to keep her at all? Did she regret abandoning her at all?

She opened her e-mail program. She typed in Jason's address.

I found her, was what she meant to write. Something like that.

But what she wrote was this: *Why did you leave me?*

She stared at the screen, at the question that had been hidden in her heart all this time. And then she started to cry.

She stayed at Janice's all afternoon. They watched reruns of *Bewitched* on TV. They ate microwaved popcorn. When Maribeth wept over a Dove commercial, Janice handed her a tissue and didn't say a thing.

■ ■ ■ ■

She stayed for dinner, the two of them quietly cooking in the kitchen. When they finished and Maribeth was helping with the washing up, she looked around Janice's house. Janice said she'd bought it thirty years ago, but it looked not unlike Maribeth's anonymous furnished apartment, albeit with many more potted plants.

There were no family pictures. No evidence of a husband, children. No framed diplomas or old chipped photo mugs. The pictures on the walls were the yearly class photos of her students at school. And suddenly Maribeth realized she'd gotten Janice wrong. She'd gotten so many things wrong lately.

"You didn't start BurghBirthParents because you were adopted, did you?" Maribeth asked.

"No," Janice said.

"You gave someone up?"

"Little girl, born June 25, 1975."

"No other children?"

" 'Fraid not."

"But weren't you married? I thought you said you and your husband bought this house because of the schools."

"We did." She smiled sadly.

"But you didn't have any?" She corrected herself. "Any others."

"Sadly, no."

"What happened?" Maribeth asked.

"Infertility, if you can believe it," she said. "Not mine. That's pretty clear, though Richard, my ex-husband, insisted it was. I had to undergo so many dreadful tests because, of course, he didn't know. Finally, when I couldn't bear any more tests, or blame, I told him." She held up her palms, then flipped them over, batting away the memory. "He said it was as if I'd cheated on him. Even though it all happened long before we met. He was not a terribly understanding man." She sighed heavily. "Still, I suppose I can understand his point. I probably should have been more honest. I'm not always good at discussing unpleasant things."

"You and me both," Maribeth said. "And your daughter, does she know you're looking?"

Janice nodded. "She knows. She agreed to receive my letters. She just hasn't responded. Yet."

"Yet . . ." Maribeth repeated.

"Yet," Janice said, more emphatically. "Some things take more time."

■ ■ ■ ■

Janice pulled out the couch in the office and made up the bed. She put on fresh sheets that smelled of lavender. She left a glass of water on the nightstand, a box of Kleenex, too.

Maribeth tried but could not sleep. The computer stayed on all night, its hum a gentle reproach.

Maribeth had been caught out again. Only really, she shouldn't have been.

Hadn't it always been there, this knowledge? Behind the locked door in her mind, where she kept the unpleasant things, where she talked herself into thinking chest pains were gas, hadn't she known that she and Jason had not really broken up? There was nothing mutual about it. She loved him. And he had left her. Just like her mother had left her. Like Elizabeth had left her. Like everyone, in the end, would leave her.

She cried, she cried until the sheets were wet. Outside the door she heard Janice pacing, but she never crossed the threshold. It was like she was keeping sentry, allowing Maribeth and her grief this wedding night to get acquainted.

■ ■ ■ ■

Janice had no coffee so the next morning they drove to a Starbucks drive-through and bought a tall latte for Maribeth and a venti caramel macchiato (decaf) for Janice.

They drank their coffee in the car, in the lot, heater blasting. With the windows fogging up, it was cozy.

"I'm sorry I never asked you," Maribeth said. "About your daughter."

"I'm sorry I never told you," Janice replied.

"How long have you been waiting?"

"I sent the first letter ten years ago. The most recent one two years ago. I keep thinking that if only I say the right thing, she will respond. I've been trying to write another letter, but I can't seem to find the words."

"I know," Maribeth replied. "It's hard." She thought for a minute. "Maybe I could help you."

"Aren't you struggling with your own letter?" Janice licked the foam mustache with the tip of her tongue.

Maribeth smiled. "I've always been a much better editor than writer. It's what I did for a living, in fact."

"You're an editor?" Janice asked.

"Well, I was, for more than twenty years."

"Explains why you're such a perfectionist."

"Maybe, but I'm not one anymore."

"Editor or perfectionist?" Janice asked.

Maribeth shrugged. "Maybe both."

When it was time for Maribeth to go home, Janice said, "Come swimming tomorrow." Then she smiled wryly. "In the pool, nobody can see your tears."

Janice swam/cried? The secrets people kept.

"Do you regret it?" Maribeth asked. "Giving her up?"

"Every single day," Janice replied. "And yet, I would still do it again."

"Really?" Maribeth had a hard time believing this. Or maybe she just didn't want to.

But Janice's face was firm, resolute, and peaceful. "It was a not a good situation, where I was. Abusive. Keeping her would've sentenced both of us to that." She turned to look out the window. The parking lot was busy, full of holiday shoppers. Any one of them could've been Janice's daughter. Or Maribeth's mother. "Sometimes leaving someone is the most loving thing you can do."

"Do you honestly believe that?" Maribeth asked.

"I have to."

"I left my children. I left them, too."

Janice squeezed her hand. "Then you have to believe it, too."

64

From: jasbrinx@gmail.com
To: MBK31270@gmail.com
Subject:

Don't ask me why I left.
Ask me why I came back.

From:MBK31270@gmail.com
To: jasbrinx@gmail.com
Subject:

What do you mean?

From: jasbrinx@gmail.com
To: MBK31270@gmail.com
Subject:

Ask me why I came back, Maribeth. Ask
me why I came back to New York.

From: MBK31270@gmail.com

To: jasbrinx@gmail.com
Subject:

I know why you came back. For your job. Your dream job.

From: jasbrinx@gmail.com
To: MBK31270@gmail.com
Subject:

It's not my dream job. It's not why I came back.

From: MBK31270@gmail.com
To: jasbrinx@gmail.com
Subject:

What are you talking about?

From: jasbrinx@gmail.com
To: MBK31270@gmail.com
Subject:

I got a job in New York City so I could come back for you.

From: MBK31270@gmail.com
To: jasbrinx@gmail.com
Subject:

That doesn't make any sense.

From: jasbrinx@gmail.com
To: MBK31270@gmail.com
Subject:

Think about it, Maribeth. And if you don't believe me, ask my dad. I was unhappy in San Francisco, had been for years, wondering how my life had gone so off the rails. And my dad said it was because I'd let you go. He was right. But I knew I couldn't just e-mail you or Facebook you to get you back. I had to undo the damage. I had to come back and win you.

From:MBK31270@gmail.com
To: jasbrinx@gmail.com
Subject:

That doesn't make any sense.

From: jasbrinx@gmail.com
To: MBK31270@gmail.com
Subject:

Think about it. It does.

65

She thought about it.

She thought about so many things.

So many things that had never quite made sense.

For one there was the way Jason had gotten in touch with her, via a Facebook message. A few months before he'd written her, Jason hadn't been on Facebook. Maribeth knew this because she had been an early adopter of the technology and had checked periodically to see if Jason had posted a profile. Three months before he'd contacted her, he hadn't. But then there was this message, something about him being offered his dream job in New York City, "an offer he couldn't refuse," he'd said. So he was relocating. Did she want to meet for a drink?

She'd always assumed he was being relocated for the dream job, that *this* was the offer he couldn't refuse. It was why she'd resented his company for going to all that trouble to bring him to New York City and then not pay him well enough to live here comfortably.

But of course, they hadn't moved him to New York City. Why would they have? Jason worked for a nonprofit, not a huge corporation. And there were probably any number of musicology or MLS grads in New York City who could've filled his position.

And then there was the first meeting. A disaster. The two of them got together for after-work drinks in some dreary midtown bar. It felt less like a date than a wake, mourning people who no longer existed. They spoke vaguely about their lives over the past decade. It was stiff, formal, and an hour later, she was on a subway heading back downtown. Elizabeth was waiting for her on the couch, a bottle of wine already open. "Well, I won't be seeing him again," she'd told Elizabeth, though that was pretty obvious by her early return. Elizabeth, who had emphatically, and uncharacteristically, discouraged Maribeth from going in the first place, didn't try to hide her relief. "Good riddance," Elizabeth said.

But then Jason had called the next day. Maribeth had been shocked when she heard the voicemail message. Not simply because it violated the Rules — that *Rules* book had been very big in Magazineland and years later, in spite of herself, Maribeth had internalized them — but because that first meeting had been so excruciating. But he asked her out again. For Friday night. Which was two days later.

This wasn't what men did. Not attractive eligible men. And let it be said that Jason Brinkley was still attractive, maybe more so; his hairline was a little less robust, and he had the beginnings of etched lines around his eyes, but the eyes themselves still looked like they were in on some delicious joke, and his lips still looked genetically designed for kissing. He'd stopped smoking pot and started running, so his lanky body had become chiseled. No, Jason, by anyone's standards, was a catch.

He'd taken her to see some singer-songwriter she'd never heard of at Joe's Pub. It was otherworldly, a guitar, and string-sounding synthesizers, and as she listened to the music, and to Jason talking about the music, she felt herself thawing. Which was how she understood that, for some time, she'd been frozen.

After the show, they'd gone out to a diner and split a pitcher of beer and platters of comfort food and talked about everything and anything: working in magazines after

9/11, and how she'd thought that things would get smarter, grow deeper, but it seemed to be going in the opposite direction. About how his mother had married some wealthy Southern California real estate developer and bloomed into the person she was meant to be, and how it had sent Jason's father into a deep existential funk, not because he missed Nora but because it was such a confirmation of his failure as her husband. They talked about New York and how it had changed. Of San Francisco and how it had changed. Of where they wanted to live and what they wanted to do and who they wanted to be. They talked about politics and books and plays and music. The conversation was fast, breathless, greedy, as if over the last decade there had been so many things they had stored up to tell each other.

They stayed until the restaurant closed, and then out on the sidewalk of the quieting New York streets, she remembered what he'd said to her, right before he'd kissed her: "Can I still be your Superman, Lois?" And she'd mistaken the comment for a calculating charm, assuming that the yearning she was feeling — god, he was magnet and she was metal — was all her own.

When they'd kissed, it was as if someone

had flipped the breaker in an abandoned house, only to discover that the circuits weren't just still live, but had grown all the more powerful from the disuse.

But again, she'd thought it was her. Because all night long, in spite of her best efforts not to, she'd been remembering what it was like to have sex with Jason: his penchant for kissing nonkissable places, the crooks of elbows, the soles of feet. His delightful unpredictability as a lover, caressing her hair one moment, pinning her hands behind her the next.

The room Jason had sublet in that East Village apartment, she now remembered, was full of unpacked boxes, as if he'd only just arrived, because he *had* only just arrived. The cover on the made bed was turned down slightly, like an invitation, or a prayer.

Once they were in that room, Jason had slammed the door and devoured her with his mouth, his hands, which were everywhere. As if he were ravenous.

And she remembered standing in front of him, her dress a puddle on the floor, and how she'd started to shake, her knees knocking together, like she was a virgin, like this was her first time. Because had she allowed herself to hope, this was what she would've hoped for. And now here it was. And that was terrifying.

Jason had taken her hand and placed it over his bare chest, to his heart, which was pounding wildly, in tandem with hers. She'd thought he was just excited, turned on.

It had not occurred to her that he might be terrified, too.

66

From: MBK31270@gmail.com
To: jasbrinx@gmail.com
Subject: Why . . .

. . . didn't you tell me?

From: jasbrinx@gmail.com
To: MBK31270@gmail.com
Subject: Why . . .

I meant to. But then we just fell back into things and it all was going so well and I got scared that if we touched any of that — what had happened before I'd gone to San Francisco — it would, I don't know, ruin everything. You'd remember what I'd done and then you wouldn't let me stay. Or Elizabeth wouldn't.

From: MBK31270@gmail.com
To: jasbrinx@gmail.com

Subject: Why . . .

Did you think that I'd forget?

From: jasbrinx@gmail.com
To: MBK31270@gmail.com
Subject: Why . . .

No, but I had myself kind of convinced it didn't matter. We got married. We had kids. We'd moved on. But when you left, angry and upset as I was, there was a part of me that was relieved. It was like I'd been expecting it. We were even now. I guess you weren't the only one waiting for the other shoe to drop.

From: MBK31270@gmail.com
To: jasbrinx@gmail.com
Subject: Why . . .

You thought I left for payback?

From: jasbrinx@gmail.com
To: MBK31270@gmail.com
Subject: Why . . .

I thought it was for a lot of reasons, the ones you said, and the ones you didn't.

Because we never talked about any of that.

From: MBK31270@gmail.com
To: jasbrinx@gmail.com
Subject: Why . . .

By any of that, you mean why you left me.

From: jasbrinx@gmail.com
To: MBK31270@gmail.com
Subject: Why . . .

Yeah. Why I left you.

From: MBK31270@gmail.com
To: jasbrinx@gmail.com
Subject: Why . . .

Why'd you leave me, Jason?

From: jasbrinx@gmail.com
To: MBK31270@gmail.com
Subject: Why . . .

It wasn't deliberate. I was twenty-two. My parents were in the middle of their awful divorce. And on one hand, I loved you, and wanted to be with you. But we were so young. What if I was wrong? What if we ended up like them? I didn't want to break up so much as slow down.

From: MBK31270@gmail.com
To: jasbrinx@gmail.com
Subject: Why . . .

That slowed it down all right. Ten years.

From: jasbrinx@gmail.com
To: MBK31270@gmail.com
Subject: Why . . .

Look, I screwed up. I was scared. Then I tried to fix it in an imperfect way. What can I say, Maribeth? I'm not perfect.

From: MBK31270@gmail.com
To: jasbrinx@gmail.com
Subject: Why . . .

Well, neither am I. As I think I've proven beyond a shadow of a doubt.

From: jasbrinx@gmail.com
To: MBK31270@gmail.com
Subject: Why . . .

I don't expect you to be perfect.

From: MBK31270@gmail.com
To: jasbrinx@gmail.com
Subject: Why . . .

I think maybe I expect me to be.

From: jasbrinx@gmail.com
To: MBK31270@gmail.com
Subject: Why . . .

You can't be in our traveling band, Fuck-ups in Training, if you're perfect.
Look, I know you'll probably shoot me for saying this, but when we got back together, ten years later, when we were older and ready for that commitment, I felt like everything had worked out as it was supposed to.

From: MBK31270@gmail.com
To: jasbrinx@gmail.com
Subject: Why . . .

Everything will turn out fine.

From: jasbrinx@gmail.com
To: MBK31270@gmail.com
Subject: Why . . .

In this instance, yeah.

From: MBK31270@gmail.com
To: jasbrinx@gmail.com
Subject: Why . . .

You still believe that?

From: jasbrinx@gmail.com
To: MBK31270@gmail.com
Subject: Why . . .

That depends.

From: MBK31270@gmail.com
To: jasbrinx@gmail.com
Subject: Why . . .

On what?

From: jasbrinx@gmail.com
To: MBK31270@gmail.com
Subject: Why . . .

Whether you do.

67

The day Stephen was due to leave for California, he called Maribeth with an offer. "I know it's last minute but I thought you could use my car while I'm gone," he said. "You could even stay at the house if you like."

Maribeth had no interest in living in his house, no matter how sweet a piece of real estate it might be. As for the car, she wasn't sure. She'd gotten used to the bus. To life without a laptop, a smart phone. It was amazing, really, how little one needed.

"It'll just be sitting there," he added. "And you'll save me the cost of parking at the airport."

"So this is about the parking?"

"No. This is about me wanting to see you before I leave."

"Then see me before you leave."

It was lightly snowing when he picked her

up that afternoon. "Are you okay to drive in this?" he asked.

"I'll be fine," Maribeth said. Then she caught the look of concern on his face. "How about if it gets heavier, we can leave your car at the airport, but I know how to drive in snow."

"You do?"

"I grew up in the suburbs of New York."

"Add another piece to the puzzle."

"Am I really such a puzzle?"

"Yes, but I've always enjoyed puzzles."

They were in the Fort Pitt Tunnel now. Coming back from Janice's yesterday was the first time Maribeth had driven into the city this way.

"I see what the fuss is about," she'd told Janice when they'd emerged onto the dramatic cityscape, the buildings, the slate river, the iron bridges.

"It's a very impressive skyline," Janice had said.

It was. But it was the surprise factor Maribeth had liked best. Coming into the tunnel through rolling Pennsylvania hills, with no hint of what was awaiting you on the other end.

You never knew, did you? Maybe not knowing didn't have to be so terrifying. Maybe it could just be life.

"When do you get back?" Maribeth asked Stephen.

"January 3, though Mallory is angling for me to stay longer."

"How much longer?"

"Why? Are you going to miss me?"

From the tug deep inside her stomach, she knew that she was.

"She's on my case to move there. She says I need a fresh start. Too many ghosts here."

"Ghosts have a way of following you," Maribeth said. She was thinking of her birth mother, the silent ghost who had followed her around her entire life. It had been two days since she'd read the report. Janice had asked her if she wanted to take the next step, to ask the agency to send a letter to her birth mother. But Maribeth wasn't ready for that.

"I suspect you're right," he said. "But it means a lot that Mal wants me to move closer to her. And so I have arranged to meet with a colleague of mine who's now the dean at the UCSF Medical School." He snuck a glance at her. "So how much do you hate San Francisco?"

"It's your basic death-wish loathing."

"That's too bad. Because you know how I bought Mallory tickets for *The Book of Mormon*?"

"For New Year's Eve, right?"

He nodded. "I bought a third ticket." He fiddled with the heater buttons, even though the temperature was fine.

"Oh," she said.

"I know it's a long shot," Stephen said when Maribeth didn't answer. "Given how you feel about the city."

They had arrived at the airport. He headed straight for departures, not the parking garage. "Don't you want me to come in?" she asked.

"You can leave me at the curb," he said. "I'd rather you get back before the snow gets worse."

He pulled over and popped the trunk. Inside was a large suitcase.

"Looks like you might be gone a while."

He shrugged, like he wasn't sure when he'd be back. "Think about New Year's. I'm happy to book you a plane ticket, too. Though that would require you telling me your real name."

"Maribeth," she said. "It's Maribeth." She pulled on his scarf. "Thank you for taking such good care of me, Stephen."

"And you of me, Maribeth."

He closed the trunk. They stared at each other for a moment, and Maribeth knew she could leave it unsaid, Stephen might understand. But this time she wasn't going to do that.

"Find someone to take that third ticket, Stephen. If not now, then soon. It's time. You deserve some happiness. I think Felicity would want that for you."

He blinked a few times, and then he smiled. "That's what Mallory says." He patted his pockets for his wallet and phone before handing her the keys. "You can leave these with Louise when you're done."

She watched as he made his way toward the terminal. He gave one last wave before he went inside.

68

Janice called that night. "You won't believe what I found." Her voice shaking over the phone.

"What?"

"I shouldn't show it to you but I can't help it. Can I come over?"

"I have a car. I can come to you."

She'd expected a smoking gun. Another heart attack, or a testimonial as to why her mother gave her up. But it was just more paperwork. Maribeth didn't see why Janice was so excited.

"Look," Janice said, pointing. "There."

It was a journal entry. In a florid script.

I know I'm having a girl. Everyone says I'm carrying small, and it's a boy, and I come from a family of brothers, but I can tell. I hear my own mother's voice. And she says it's a girl.

I haven't told anyone this because the other girls here are so terribly sentimental about their babies. They all think they will grow up to be president! And they talk about them as if they will know them. "My child will . . ."

She won't be mine. But part of her will. I've decided to name her after myself and after my mother. Even though she's going to a new family and won't ever know her name, it will still be her first name. In that way she'll belong to me. First and forever. She'll be Mary Beth.

"I'm confused. Mary Beth? Is that her? Is that my mother?"

"No, Beth is your mother," Janice replied. "Mary Beth was what she named *you.*"

From: MBK31270@gmail.com
To: jasbrinx@gmail.com
Subject: My birth mother

Was named Beth. Her mother was Mary. She named me Mary Beth. I am Maribeth.

From: jasbrinx@gmail.com
To: MBK31270@gmail.com
Subject: My birth mother

The mystery of your culturally confused name is solved. Did you find out anything else about her?
And how are you?

From: MBK31270@gmail.com
To: jasbrinx@gmail.com
Subject: My birth mother

Mostly confused. My real mother, not Beth but Evelyn, kept the name my birth mother gave me, which was her own name and her mother's name. My entire life, she was so threatened by my birth mother. Like she never believed that I was truly hers.
So why would she do that? Keep the name my birth mother gave me, which was her name, too. Wouldn't this just be a constant reminder that I wasn't really hers?

From: jasbrinx@gmail.com
To: MBK31270@gmail.com
Subject: My birth mother

Or a reminder that you were also someone else's.

From: MBK31270@gmail.com
To: jasbrinx@gmail.com
Subject: My birth mother

I can't believe she did that. And kept it a secret all these years.

From: jasbrinx@gmail.com
To: MBK31270@gmail.com
Subject: My birth mother

Are you going to try to meet her? Beth?

From: MBK31270@gmail.com
To: jasbrinx@gmail.com
Subject: My birth mother

I don't know. Right now, I want to just rest here. For the first time, I am starting to wonder if maybe she loved me, Jase. Maybe she loved me a little bit.

From: jasbrinx@gmail.com
To: MBK31270@gmail.com
Subject: My birth mother

Is that so hard to believe?

69

It was time for another farewell. Sunita was leaving Christmas Eve to spend the winter break in India. The night before, she was having some people over for dinner and invited Maribeth. "This time, I'll do the cooking."

" 'Cooking' is an optimistic term," Todd said. "More like practicing." He turned to Maribeth. "She wants to prove to her mother she can do it so they can advertise her as a good Indian girl when it comes time to marry her off. Fritz will be so heartbroken."

"Shut up!" she said, shoving Todd. To Maribeth: "My parents didn't even have an arranged marriage. They're not marrying anyone off."

"Fritz will be so relieved," Todd said.

"Why are you being such a jerk?" Sunita asked.

"Because you're leaving."

"Oh," Sunita said, softening. "But I'm coming back. Sunny always comes back."

"What if you don't?" Todd asked. "What if you stay there, like your parents?"

Sunita rolled her eyes. "I have to come home and graduate. And get a job."

"What if you get a job over there?"

"Then you'll just have to move to India with me."

This seemed to appease Todd.

"What should I bring to the dinner?" Maribeth asked.

"Wine if you want," Sunita said. "If wine goes with curry. And you can bring Stephen."

"He's in California, but can I bring another friend?"

"You're working *three* guys?" Todd asked.

"Not exactly."

There was a crowd. Fritz. Miles. Two other people from Thanksgiving. Sunita wore a lovely purple *shalwar kameez.* Todd wore a tux.

"I didn't know it was formal," Maribeth said.

"I just came from work," Todd said. "So many functions around the holiday."

"He's just taking on the extra shifts

420

because he's sad Sunita is leaving," Miles said.

"Are you jealous?" Todd asked.

"A little," Miles said. "It's hard to compete."

"My husband used to say the same thing about my best friend," Maribeth said.

"Oh, so now you're marrying me off?" Todd asked.

"Why should I be the only one?" Sunita joked.

Janice arrived. Maribeth introduced her as a friend from the swim club. If Janice called her Maribeth, no one seemed to notice.

They drank the wine. Sunita laid out a tray of *papadum,* crispy lentil crackers. "I didn't make these," she explained. "I bought them. But everything else, I cooked."

The entire apartment was fragrant with spices and the tang of onions. "What did you make?" Janice asked.

"Chicken jalfrezi," she said. "It came out kind of spicy."

"But you didn't burn the onions this time," Todd said. "She really has been practicing all fall."

Sunita snapped off a piece of papadum. "I haven't been to India in more than fifteen years," she said. "It's scary going back."

■ ■ ■ ■

The chicken wasn't kind of spicy; it was lip-burning hot. Maribeth and Todd began to guzzle water. Janice, who had made a valiant effort before abandoning the chicken for the rice and bread, told them that water didn't work. She emptied their wineglasses of the pinot grigio and filled them with milk.

"I feel five years old," Maribeth said.

"Really?" Janice asked. "I drink milk all the time. To ward off osteoporosis." She had poured herself a glass, too, and now wore a tiny milk mustache. Maribeth was beginning to suspect that she gave herself those on purpose.

After they did the dishes, Sunita changed into jeans and a sweater. She, Todd, and the rest of their friends were heading out to a party. As everyone said farewell, Maribeth slipped a card for them on top of the TV. Inside were two tickets for the musical production of *The Wizard of Oz,* which was coming to Pittsburgh in February.

She and Janice watched the young people disappear. Then they went to her apartment. They had business of their own to attend to.

70

My dearest daughter,

This is the third letter from me that you have received. Three letters doesn't seem like much in the ten years since I sent the first one, or the nearly forty years since you were born. I thought I might take this opportunity to tell you about all the letters from me that you have not received.

I wrote you on your first birthday. It was not an actual card; I was still too sad and heartbroken at that point to commemorate your birth in such a concrete way. But I imagined a card I would send. I wrote, "I love you," but I never signed it, because I didn't know what to call myself.

Other birthdays I actually bought you a card. There is one from your Sweet Sixteen. It has a bunch of birthday candles, tied up like a bouquet, and it reads, "Daughter, Sixteen candles. It only gets brighter from here."

I have bought a card or thought a card on every one of your birthdays, the consequential ones like your big 3-0, and the less ballyhooed ones, like twenty-three. Sometimes I feel foolish buying the cards. And other times, proud. Particularly if the salespeople see the card and make small talk as they sometimes do about you, and maybe their own daughters.

I also write you letters; sometimes they are real and sometimes they are imagined. A few months ago, there was a particularly lovely night sky. A big harvest moon, Venus shining brightly, and when I looked up at it, I thought about you looking up from wherever it is you are. It gave me such comfort to think of the same night sky covering us both. So I came home and wrote you about it.

It is not always happy occasions, I must confess. When my mother died — of old age, you will be relieved to know, longevity runs in the family — I thought of you, of the line of women that continues with you. I wondered if you had a daughter.

424

I have written to you before of the difficult circumstances that led to my decision to give you up, so by now I expect you to know, if not to fully understand, the kind of home I grew up in and why I could not raise you in that place, and why I was not remotely equipped to raise you on my own. But I have not really spoken of my own mother, who also endured that home. Maybe that was all she could do. Not fight back against my father, not protect me, but endure. In the end, she outlived him. She outlived that misery. She spent her last years in an old-age home. People think badly of those places but my mother had the best years of her life there. She got to do as she pleased. She got to swim again. She got to read a book if she felt like it. Watch whatever she wanted on the television. No one hit her. No one called her names.

And she began to speak of you, even though when you were born, she had said the most terrible things to me, and over the years acted as if you didn't exist. But now I know that wasn't her talking so much as what she had endured. In the end, she spoke tenderly of you, of all the milestones she'd imagined for you. She called you by the name I gave you. It made me realize that you've been alive in her all those years, too. It made me wonder if, in her own way, she too had been writing you letters in her head. It made me feel like a family.

I will continue to write you letters and to "write" you letters. Maybe one day you will let me share them with you. But even if you don't, it is okay. It is the writing them that matters. And I like to believe that whether you read them or not, they are reaching you just the same.

— Janice Pickering

By the time Janice finished, they were both crying.

"Thank you," Janice said. "Thank you for giving me the idea to write about the letters." She gestured to the scrapbook of notes to the twins Maribeth had shown her. "Will you send those to your children?"

She picked up the scrapbook. The cover was embossed with the word MEMORIES and with all the letters she'd written, it felt heavy, substantial.

Maribeth suspected Janice was right. That it was the writing them that mattered. She liked to think she was right about the love. That it would find its way to them. And that

426

she, too, would find her way to them.
"One day," she said.

71

That night, she woke up suddenly. By the time she'd sat up in bed, her hand had already found its way to her heart.

Shit.

It hurt. Her chest hurt. A corrosive pain that radiated all the way up her torso and down her arm. Her left arm.

If that time at her desk had been subtle, this was as obvious as a punch to the nose.

No! She'd had the heart attack, had her heart tested and dyed and removed from her chest and stopped, operated on, and shocked back to life. She'd gone through all of that to prevent this from happening again.

"A subsequent event . . . fatal . . ." she heard Dr. Sterling say in his stupid hee-haw voice.

Get out of my head, Dr. Sterling. I fired you.

Her heart was beating wildly now, flinging around her chest like a trapped bird.

Calm down, she told herself. *Calm down.*

Take ten deep breaths.

One, two, three.

Breathing hurt. She should go to the hospital. Call someone. Phone? Where was her phone?

She found it, charging next to her bed. She should call 911. But it was Jason's number she dialed. "Hey, it's Jase. You got the dreaded voicemail. Leave me a message."

It was the first she'd heard his voice in months. And it was his fucking voicemail.

"You said you'd pick up on the first ring." She sounded hysterical. "It's me. Maribeth. I think I'm having a heart attack. Call me back. I'm scared."

Ten deep breaths. Where was she at? Three? Four. Keep going. Call 911.

"Nine, one, one, what is your emergency?"

"I think I'm having a cardiac event." Her voice was a whisper.

"Ma'am, can you speak up?"

"Heart attack. I'm having a heart attack. I had one before."

"What is your location, please?"

She recited the address.

"Ma'am, I need you to stay calm. I want you to take some aspirin. Do you have any nearby?"

"Yes."

"Keep me on the phone while you take your aspirin."

As she fumbled for an aspirin, she started to cry.

"Ma'am, are you still with me?"

"I'm all alone," Maribeth cried. "I know we all die alone, but I don't want to be alone."

"Ma'am. You're not dying, and you're not alone. You have me."

"You don't count. I don't mean that. Everybody counts."

"I appreciate that."

"But I don't want to be alone. Can I go get Todd and Sunita? They're my neighbors."

"Go get Todd and Sunita."

"You're nice. What's your name?"

"Kirsten."

"That's a pretty name."

"Keep me on the phone, and go get Todd and Sunita."

She pounded on their door. They could still be out at their party. She had no idea what time it was.

A sleepy-eyed Sunita shuffled to the door in her Steelers night shirt. "M.B., are you okay?"

"I think I'm having a heart attack," Maribeth said.

"What? Todd! Wake up!" she yelled but Todd was already there. "M.B.'s having another heart attack!"

"Call an ambulance," Todd yelled.

"I already did," Maribeth said. She could hear the siren whining in the night. "I think that's for me."

"I'm getting dressed," Sunita said. "I'm coming with you."

"Me, too," said Todd.

Maribeth got back on the phone. "My friends Todd and Sunita are coming with me."

"That's good. They sound like nice friends."

"They are."

Todd met the medics in the hall, and by the time they were entering the apartment, he had filled them in.

"Second heart attack?" the female medic asked, putting the pulse monitor on Maribeth.

Maribeth nodded.

"First one was in October and she had bypass surgery," Todd said.

"Any other symptoms before tonight?" the burly guy medic asked.

Todd looked at Maribeth.

"No. I just woke up with pain in my chest, and my arm. My *left* arm."

"And now, chest pains, anything else? Shortness of breath? Dizziness? Nausea?"

"I don't know. Maybe a little."

"Okay." She spoke into her collar. "Female, forty-four, suspected M.I., vitals good, en route to UPMC."

She was given oxygen and put on a gurney and wheeled toward the door. The ambulance was waiting, lights flashing.

Todd and Sunita rushed after her, their faces encased in worry.

"Can we come with?" Sunita asked. "In the ambulance?"

"Your flight?" Maribeth said.

"Is tomorrow," Sunita said. "Can we come with?"

"And you are?" the medic asked.

"We're her —" Todd began.

"Children!" Maribeth lifted her head off the gurney. "They're my children."

The two medics exchanged an eye roll.

"What? He's bio; I'm adopted," Sunita said.

"We're like the Jolie-Pitts," Todd added.

Neither medic looked convinced, but they let them in the ambulance anyway.

On the ride to the hospital, Todd and Sunita held her hands.

"If I die . . ." Maribeth began.

"You're not going to die!" Todd interrupted.

"But if I do, my name is Maribeth. Maribeth Klein. My husband is Jason Brinkley. In New York."

"Okay, Maribeth Klein," Todd said. "Now you can't die because Sunita and I made a bet over what your real name was and I just won ten bucks and it would be bad taste to collect if you were dead."

"Don't make me laugh," Maribeth said, clutching her chest. "It hurts."

"Then don't die," Todd said.

In the hospital, Todd and Sunita were sent to the waiting room. Maribeth was ushered into triage. She explained her history, her recent bypass.

"Who's your cardiologist?" the intake nurse asked.

She didn't know what to say. Stephen was in California. Dr. Sterling was fired.

"I don't think I have one anymore."

She was used to it now. EKG. Blood work. Waiting.

Todd and Sunita were not permitted in but they kept texting her from the waiting room. *Are you okay?*

Not dead yet, Maribeth texted back.

Still not dead.

Sunita, give Todd $10.

Not until you walk out of here, they wrote back.

"Fine, fine, fine, everything looks fine," the ER cardiologist said. He was tall, tired looking, and had an excessive handlebar mustache that made Maribeth like him immediately. "Your EKG and your blood work, your pulse ox, all look completely normal."

"But that happened last time, too," she said. "It didn't show up right away."

"Which is why we'll monitor you for a few hours. Tell me, is the pain similar to your first heart attack?"

"No. That was more gradual. This I woke up with."

"And how would you describe it? Crushing pain?"

"No. It's more like a burning. But I also felt it in my arm."

"Burning. Okay. Have you eaten anything unusual in the last day or so?"

The chicken jalfrezi. "I had Indian food for dinner."

"Spicy?"

"Very."

"That'll do it," he said. "It could be re-

434

flux. I'm going to give you an antacid to take care of that. It might also be pain related to your heart healing. We'll keep an eye on you for a while, but given you so recently had bypass, and that all your numbers look perfect, I'm not that concerned."

"So I'm not dying of a heart attack."

"Not presently."

"Do you think I could see my friends?" she asked.

"Oh, you mean your 'children' out there?" He smiled. "They've been scratching at the door. Want me to let them in?"

"Please."

"Oh, my god, I feel awful," Sunita said. "My cooking gave you a gas attack!"

"Just don't let it get around Hyderabad," Todd said. "You'll never find a husband. Oh, wait. Fritz can do the cooking. Mmm. Nut loaf."

Maribeth was laughing. She hadn't stopped laughing since they had come back to keep her company. It didn't hurt anymore. Now that she'd taken the antacid, the pain had vanished.

Around six, Sunita started checking her phone. Her flight was at one, but she had to be at the airport by ten.

"You should get going," Maribeth said. "You have your flight. And, Todd, you should get a few hours sleep before you leave for Altoona."

He clutched his chest. "Altoona. You had to remind me."

"You'll be fine," she told Todd. "And so will you," she told Sunita. "And so will I. Everything is going to turn out fine."

She stopped abruptly, shocked that she'd said that. And perhaps even more shocked that she actually believed it.

72

She waited until six-thirty to call Jason. She didn't want to wake him, but she didn't want him to wake up to that voicemail message either. She wanted him to know she was okay, really okay.

She fished her phone out of her bag and saw that there were several missed calls from a 413 area code. Which was a Pittsburgh number, she thought, but not one she recognized. Maybe it was Stephen, though that wasn't his cell number, or Sunita and Todd calling her from a payphone, though that didn't make sense either because several of the calls overlapped with when they'd been with her.

She hit the call back button. When she first heard the voice on the other end, she thought maybe she had had a heart attack, after all, and was now hallucinating. Because the voice calling out — "Maribeth, is that you?" — did not belong to Todd or Sunita.

It belonged to Elizabeth.

"Maribeth, where are you?" Elizabeth was asking. "Jason is going insane."

Elizabeth had called her? Why? And why was she talking to her about Jason?

"Maribeth, say something!" Elizabeth cried.

"Elizabeth?" Maribeth asked, so confused. "Where are you?"

"Where am I? I'm in the country. Where are *you*? Are you okay?"

Maribeth stared at her phone. Pittsburgh's area code was 412, not 413, which she now realized was Elizabeth's area code in the Berkshires. That clarified where Elizabeth was, but only muddled everything else.

"Did you call me?" Maribeth asked.

"No, Jason did. He's been trying to reach you for the last hour."

"Jason's there?" Maribeth asked. "With you?"

"He was. Now he's frantically trying to get cell coverage in case you call him back on his cell. He said you had another heart attack."

"I didn't. They think it's just gas. Where is he?"

"He's headed to Lenox. Or Pittsburgh. I don't know. He's losing his mind, Maribeth. I've never seen him like this. You know how the cell coverage is up here, very dodgy. But it came on enough for him to get your voicemail. And he tried calling back and couldn't get you. He's taken the kids to town to call you. Or e-mail you. Or send a carrier pigeon. I told Tom we should get Wi-Fi here but you know how he likes it rustic."

They were in the country? Jason and the kids? With Elizabeth and Tom?

"Why?" Maribeth asked.

"Christ, I don't know. Because he wants it to be a sanctuary from the stress of daily life."

"No. Why are Jason and the kids up there? With you?"

"Oh. Because tomorrow's Christmas," Elizabeth replied, as if that explained anything.

"But . . . why?" Maribeth repeated.

"They've been coming up a lot, on weekends. And they came for Thanksgiving," she said.

Maribeth let that sink in. Jason and the twins. With Elizabeth. Weekends. Thanksgiving.

Elizabeth continued: "So we thought we'd have a quiet Christmas together, just family, except you're not here, though your mother thinks you are."

"Wait. What? My mother's still in New York?"

"God, no. Jason knew she'd completely freak if she knew what you'd done so he told her you'd come up here on a retreat and she should go back to Florida. She thinks you're still here. That Jason and the twins see you on weekends but that you're not talking to anyone else. I call her with updates. Now she's talking about trying her own retreat. Her friend Herb has done one, apparently."

"You and Jason did that?"

"We colluded." She chuckled softly. "That's been the one fun part in all this."

And with that, Maribeth started to understand. And when she did, she started to cry.

"Oh, darling," Elizabeth said. "Please don't cry. I didn't mean that. It's been great spending time with the twins. And they're doing fine. Really. Jason fired that flakey babysitter and hired this great new lady who they love. And he's with them a lot and Niff comes in the evenings and a bunch of your twins parenting friends have pitched in. And I'm here. I know I should've been here more before, and I'm so sorry that I wasn't. But I'm here now, so you have to believe me when I say that O and L are okay. They have that twins thing where they rely on each other. They miss you. God, do they miss you — we all do — but Jason shows them a nightly video of you and they draw you pictures for when you get back. They know you're coming back. Please don't be sad."

But Maribeth wasn't crying because she was sad. She was remembering the night of her engagement party, when she'd envisioned herself and Elizabeth and Jason as the steady bases of her three-legged stool. Sturdy enough to hold her. To hold, it now seemed, her whole family.

So this was how it was. People entered your life. Some would stay. Some would not. Some would drift but would return to you. Like Elizabeth. Like Jason. And now, like Maribeth, herself, who had left, just as her own mother had, but who would return, as her own mother could not.

And that's when she knew it was time. To return to Jason. To Oscar and Liv. To her life, though she had no idea what that life looked like anymore. Everything about it felt inchoate. Like a scar still healing. Or perhaps like a story still being written.

He must have been back in cell coverage. Because this time Jason picked up on the first ring. And there it was, that voice, the one she'd fallen in love with more than twenty-five years ago, the one she had never stopped loving.

"Jase," she said. "It's me."

"Lois," he managed before the voice broke wide open. And then all she could hear were the shuddering gasps of her husband's silent crying.

"It's okay," she told him. "There was no heart attack. I'm fine."

He still didn't speak. In the background, she heard the boppy sound of the They Might Be Giants CD they played to keep the twins happy on long drives.

"Jason, listen. I'm coming home. Elizabeth's already on her way to pick me up. I'll be back tonight."

"Daddy, why are we stopping?" Oscar's little voice traveled through the line bright and clear. "Who are you talking to?"

And then it was her daughter who she heard. "Mommy?" Liv asked. As if it was the most normal thing in the world for Maribeth to be calling. "Is that Mommy?"

ACKNOWLEDGMENTS

Years ago, when this book first began to percolate, I mentioned my nascent idea to a cardiologist I was seeing for a stress test. He agreed to help. Several years later, when I had written a draft, Dr. Stephen Weiss picked up the phone at his medical practice one night and made good on his promise. I was also lucky enough to meet Dr. Kirsten Healy, a cardiologist and a busy working mother of two young girls, who was able to weigh in on both the medical and the emotional aspects of Maribeth's predicament. Additional thanks to Dr. Lucy N. Painter and Dr. Mukesh Prasad for technical assistance and generosity.

Kristin Thompson of the Children's Home of Pittsburgh graciously, and patiently, walked me through the specifics of Pittsburgh and Pennsylvania adoption law and the particulars of birth-parent searches. She also provided essential notes as a native

Pittsburgher. As did Siobhan Vivian, who took time out of her busy writing and parenting schedule to school me in the multitudinous wonders of the city and take me on a tour.

Stephen Melzer informed me exactly what would happen if a tax return went unfiled (no immediate handcuffs!) and how a person might withdraw huge sums of money from her savings account (rather easily). Joe Dalton made sure I got the specifics of archiving correct (data migration!). Sarah Patzwahl may be about forty years younger than Janice, but she nevertheless employed the kickboard just as frequently when teaching me to swim and, in doing so, inspired not just a character but an obsession. Thank you also to Courtney Sheinmel for early encouragement. To Eshani Agrawal for reading so quickly and astutely. To Karen Forman for the eagle-eyed proofing. To Stephanie Perkins for weighing in with her as-always fantastic notes. To Robin Wasserman for title suggestions. To Deb Shapiro for strategic brilliance. To Emily Mahon for the beautiful jacket. To Courtney Stevens for sharing a bit of her own blue-whale size heart. And to Tori Hill for, once again, being the elf in the night.

My three-legged stool has so many bases

it works better as metaphor than furniture. When I run away, or as we call it, "take a work trip" (no, really), I rely on many people to fill in the gaps, including the amazing Beth Ann Kurahara and our neighborhood compound (in geographical, not alphabetical, order): the Wilsons, the Clarkes, the Iannicellis, and the Brost-Wangs.

I also rely daily on the intelligence, humor, and honesty of my dearest friends: Tamara Glenny, Marjorie Ingall, Kathy Kline, Isabel Kyriacou, E. Lockhart, and Tamar Schamhart. And bonus points to my beloved Libba Bray, who listened to me read about half this book out loud, out of order. Bless her heart.

Speaking of people on whose intelligence, humor, and honesty I rely: Michael Bourret encourages me to be vulnerable on the page and bold off of it. Thank you also to Lauren Abramo, Erin Young, and the whole team at Dystel & Goderich, as well to Caspian Dennis and Dana Spector.

It is cliché to claim a publisher feels like family, but in the case of Algonquin Books, it feels true — not my family, perhaps, but a family business that I'm a part of. Thank you Jackie Burke, Steve Godwin, Brunson Hoole, Debra Linn, Annie Mazes, Michael

McKenzie, Lauren Moseley, Craig Popelars, Kendra Poster, Elisabeth Scharlatt, Ina Stern, and Anne Winslow for welcoming me to the table. And thank you to Amy Gash, an editor whose bionic memory for detail, deep insight for character, and sleeves-up love of process is matched only by her sense of humor. As my gift, Amy, please note the absence of italics in these acknowledgments.

And finally, on to family. A warm blanket thank-you to all the Forman/Tucker/Schamharts, with a special callout to Ruth Forman. My mother had her first bypass surgery at forty-eight, and though this book is dedicated to my daughters, it was inspired by her.

As for my daughters, Willa and Denbele, and their father, Nick, my husband and partner for so many years now: You are the people I run toward.

ABOUT THE AUTHOR

Gayle Forman is a bestselling, award-winning author of young adult novels. *Leave Me* is her first novel for adults. Her novel *If I Stay* won the 2009 NAIBA Book of the Year Award and was a 2010 Indie Choice Honor Award winner. The film adaptation of *If I Stay* was released in 2014. Forman is also a journalist whose articles have appeared in numerous publications, including *Seventeen*, *Cosmopolitan*, and *Elle*. She has visited more than forty countries and wrote a nonfiction book about her travels titled *You Can't Get There from Here: A Year on the Fringes of a Shrinking World*. Forman lives in Brooklyn, New York, with her husband and two daughters.